MW00658577

All These Worlds

Book 3 of the Bobiverse

Dennis E. Taylor

Titles by the author

The World Lines series:
Outland
Earthside (coming soon)

The Bobiverse series:
We Are Legion (We Are Bob)
For We Are Many
All These Worlds

This is a work of fiction. Names, characters, businesses, places, events and incidents are either the products of the author's imagination or used in a fictitious manner. Any resemblance to actual persons, living or dead, or actual events is purely coincidental.

This book or any portion thereof may not be reproduced or used in any manner whatsoever without the express written permission of the publisher except for the use of brief quotations in a book review.

Copyright © 2017 by Dennis E. Taylor - All rights reserved.
ISBN: 978-1-68068-060-7
Published by Worldbuilders Press, a service of the Ethan Ellenberg Literary Agency

Cover art by Jeff Brown

Author Blog: www.dennisetaylor.org

Dedication

To my wife, Blaihin, for being okay to travel this path with me—
especially the part where I retire to write full-time.

For Bill Paxton, who brought a little more humanity to some great SF movies.

Acknowledgements

This has been an amazing journey. A hobby that started out as a dare has now turned into a career.

As always, I want to acknowledge and thank the critters and beta readers who helped to make this book and series a reality.

Thanks to:

Members of the Ubergroup and Novel Exchange group on scribophile
Sandra and Ken McLaren
Nicole Hamilton
Sheena Lewis
Patrick Jordan
Trudy Cochrane
Anna Albo

...for reading the raw draft and early versions.

And to:

My agent, Ethan Ellenberg
Steve Feldberg from Audible
My editor, Kat Howard

Table of Contents

I leave eternity to Thee; for what is man that he should live out the life-time of his God?

— Herman Melville

1. Face-Off

Bob
March 2224
Delta Eridani

The pigoid erupted from its lair with an angry squeal. It displayed startling speed for something with such short legs. The two rock throwers sprinted to the side, fur erect along their spines and ears sticking straight out in excitement. The rest of us set the butts of our spears into the ground and braced them with a foot. And waited.

This time, I wasn't an observer. If I had been nervous before, I was terrified now. I could feel the fur standing up along my spine and all the way up to the top of my head. I kept telling myself that I was actually ten thousand miles away, in orbit. Didn't help. My eyes told me the pigoid was ten meters away, charging at me at what appeared to be about half light speed.

Then the animal ran into the spear points. Still not breeding for intelligence, apparently. The spears bowed but held, and the animal slammed to the ground with a final squawk.

Bernie sidled up to it and poked it in the face a few times. Getting no response, he waved his spear in the air and yelled, "Whooo!"

The rest of us raised a fist and responded, "Hah!"

Well, that's how the translation routine handled it. Deltan speech sounded more like pigs loudly wallowing. But the software converted everything to human equivalents for me, including names and colloquialisms.

Donald slapped me on the shoulder. "Come on, Robert, help me string it up."

I tied the back legs of the pigoid, while Donald tossed the other end of the rope over a tree branch. He looked down to check my work before starting to haul and did a double take. "Whoa! That looks like one of Archimedes' weird knots. Where'd you learn that?"

Oops. "Uh, from Archimedes, of course. He's got hands and hands of different knots. I've picked up a few."

Donald nodded, only mildly interested. We hauled on the rope until the pigoid was suspended—I made sure to use only normal Deltan-level strength and let Donald do most of the work—then he drew a flint knife and bled the animal. The other hunters started the *Giving-Thanks* chant.

When it was done, we trussed the carcass onto a couple of spears and started back to Camelot. There would be a feast tonight, and I loved barbecued pigoid. Still no barbecue sauce, though. I wondered idly if I should invent some.

We were singing a victory chant, and I guess our guard was down. So the group of Deltans that stepped into the path in front of us took us completely by surprise. We came to a ragged halt as they tilted their spears in our direction. It wasn't *quite* a threat, more like the promise of one.

I heard a rustling behind me, and realized that we'd been surrounded. I took a quick look around. The other party outnumbered us by two. Not insurmountable, but definitely a concern. Very likely they were depending on getting the drop on us, and us not being able to organize a defense.

There had been reports of groups from Caerleon bushwhacking hunting parties, and taking all or part of their kills. It appeared we were the target du jour.

The spokesman for the group—I recognized him as an unpleasant character from Caerleon whose name translated as Fred—gave us an evil smile. "Nice catch, Donald. You've got a lot of pigoid there. I doubt you'd miss a haunch or two."

Donald, unintimidated, raised his spear to readiness. "There are lots of pigoids out there, Fred. What's the matter, not having any luck?" Fred reflexively started to take a step back, then caught himself. Donald wasn't quite as big as his father, but that still left a lot of room for *big*. People rarely challenged him directly.

Unfortunately for me, I was standing up front with Donald, and I had designed my android to be as nondescript as possible—average height, average build, average looks—Joe Forgettable, pretty much. So, no surprise that Fred decided to use me as an example. He looked at me. "So what about you, *kuzzi*? You think you'd like to share the wealth?" He looked at his friends, smiling. They returned the expressions and moved in.

"Tell you what, Fred," I answered. "Why don't you bend way over, stick your head up your own butthole, and keep pushing until you disappear completely." I smiled at him as innocently as I could. Snickers and guffaws from our group—and a few from the other group—showed that I'd scored. Of course, I had gigabytes of Earth literature and movies to pull my insults from. In a war of words, the Deltans would be virtually unarmed.

Donald gave me a quick, surprised glance. I guess he hadn't been expecting the support. He showed his teeth. "Your move, pigoid-dropping."

Fred glared at Donald, at me, then turned as if to leave.

Oh, you have got to be kidding. Cliché, much?

And, sure enough, he suddenly turned back and swung at me. I could have stopped and had afternoon tea, and still reacted in time. Okay, I'm a computer, but still...

I leaned back slightly and the clenched fist passed right by my face. As Fred continued the rotation, I placed a short jab in—well, in a human it would be the solar plexus. Same effect, though. Fred said *oof* and dropped to his knees.

Now their advantage was down to one, and we had Donald. Our guys grinned and started waving spear points.

Donald and I moved forward, and the other group stepped aside. As I passed Fred, he glared at me. I said, "Any time, *kuzzi*." He didn't respond, but then he was still trying to breathe.

There was a huge component of surrogate vengeance in my behavior, of course. I had a lot of years of being on the wrong end of bullying to look back on. But a rational part of my mind told me that I would have to watch out for Fred, now.

Donald slapped me on the back again. I made a point of staggering. I didn't want him to decide we were competing.

We finished our hike to the village on high alert. No singing, no joking around. A couple of the guys took the kill to an agreed-upon fire pit to be divvied up. I turned to head back to Archimedes' tent, but Donald put a hand on my shoulder and motioned me to come with him. I realized within moments that we were heading for the Council Circle.

One of the many universals that I'd discovered while studying the Deltans was that politicians and leaders always reserved the best for themselves. The Council Circle location got full sun first thing in the morning, and was in the shade by late afternoon. A few Council members were always at the circle, no doubt trying to look official and stay comfortable.

Donald walked up to Jeffrey, the current Council leader, and waited to be acknowledged. Jeffrey was a bit of a dick, and liked to keep people waiting, just to show how important he was. Donald accidentally stood in Jeffrey's sun and began cleaning his spear while he waited, the dried pieces of blood and hide landing all around Jeffrey. I looked around and tried to keep a straight face.

Finally, Jeffrey accepted the fact that he was being out-ignored. He looked up and gestured for us to sit. We made ourselves comfortable and Donald explained about our encounter with the Caerleon gang.

When we were done, Jeffrey made a face. "That's now almost a hand of encounters in the last three hands of days. A couple of people were stabbed when they refused to give up their kill. I'm going to have to bring this up with the full Council. Something has to be done."

"All by people from Caerleon?" I asked.

"Yes, it looks that way. Leave it with me. I'll get the Council started on it."

Donald nodded to Jeffrey, and we got to our feet. As we walked away, I said to Donald, "Do you think it's the one gang, or different ones?"

"Fred's been mentioned more than once. There might be others involved, but it's mostly him and his group."

"And all lately? What's changed?"

Donald stared into space for a moment. "Um, I don't think it's a case of something changing. It's more likely that Fred just saw a way to take advantage of something that's been brewing for a while. We're just not sure what's behind it."

We walked in silence for a few moments while I thought

through an idea. I looked up to Donald. “I have a plan. Can we get an extra dozen people or so? People who won’t mind some close-up action?”

Donald grinned. “Yeah, I think I can scrape that together.”

I grinned back. Time for some dirty tricks, Earth-style.

2. We've Lost

Howard
February 2217
Vulcan

Bridget opened the door, looking surprised. I hadn't phoned ahead, and she wasn't expecting me tonight.

She started to say, "Howard...what..." Then my expression must have registered.

"Howard, what's wrong?" She grabbed my arm and dragged me into the apartment.

"We lost. We lost and now a billion sentients are going to die!" I collapsed onto her couch and leaned forward with my face in my hands.

"The Pav?"

I nodded, unwilling to trust my voice.

"My God, Howard. Does Butterworth know? Are the Bobs all right?"

I sighed, and tried for calm. "We lost a lot of Bobs, but there are backups. It's not quite the same, of course." I turned to Bridget and tried to smile reassuringly. "Riker let Dexter know, and Dexter will be passing the info along to Butterworth or whoever has taken over for him."

"Are we in danger?"

"Not specifically, Bridget. The Others only know about Earth and Epsilon Eridani. But there are almost two hundred systems closer to GL 877 than us. All these worlds are ultimately in danger as long as the Others exist."

"And the Pav? I've read some of Jacques' blog entries. They sound like an interesting species. What happens to them?"

I closed my eyes for a moment, hoping maybe I'd be in a different universe when I opened them. No such luck.

"We've never seen the process, just the aftereffects. Now we'll be getting a ringside view. The Others will kill off all life on the Pav home world using the Death Asteroids, then move in with ants and cargo carriers and strip the planet and the inner system of all metals. And they'll collect all corpses and carcasses."

I had to stop and take a few deep breaths. The android body didn't need air, of course, but it was designed to react to emotion, and I was working myself up into a fine conniption.

"Jacques had a plan to rescue twenty thousand Pav, but the rest will be dead soon. And the Others will have wiped out another intelligent species, another entire planetary ecology."

I turned on the couch to face her. "There will be a moot today, to try to figure out what we can do. I just wanted a few minutes..."

Bridget put her arms around me and pulled my head down to her shoulder. Soundlessly, I tried to cry without tear ducts.

3. Trouble Brewing

Marcus
November 2212
Poseidon

I rubbed the bridge of my nose with thumb and forefinger, shaking my head. Kal waited patiently at the other end of the call. I looked up to see Gina smirking at me. She smoothed her features out quickly, but come on—computer, remember? I gave her a quick smile in reply.

"Still not convinced, Marcus?" Kal cocked his head at me in the video window.

I sighed. "I guess I've been convinced for a while now, Kal. I just didn't *believe* it, you know?"

Kal laughed. "Thus ending the myth that computers are logical."

"Bite me. I was human once." I sat back in my chair and considered my response. Spike picked that moment to jump into my lap for the obligatory chin-scritching. I gave her the proper adulation while I thought through my options. Kal and Gina wouldn't even notice the millisecond pause in our conversation.

Kal was an Assistant Governor on Southern Mat Three, and Gina was a mid-level security officer. I'd become friends with both of them over the last couple of years. As we became more comfortable with each other, they'd each confided an increasing concern about the Council's ongoing power grabs.

"Okay, so we'll take it as a given that the Council is no longer even pretending that they'll be instituting elections any time soon. Or at least not putting much effort into it. It's not proof positive of a totalitarian government, but I'll grant you it's a pretty good indicator. Gina likes to shoot things at the first excuse, but Kal, you're a lot more conservative. The fact that you've bought into this is what really scares me."

Gina opened her mouth to retort, but Kal beat her to it. "Worst case, we're a long way from crossing any kind of line. If the Council gets a sudden attack of sanity to the head, we'll have done nothing indictable. Or even embarrassing. And yeah, Marcus, before we do anything that we can't take back, I'll want to take a good, long look at the situation."

I nodded, mollified. The Poseidon Administrative Council was happy to make use of my services, but I had no real official position or authority. The moment I became a liability they could cut me loose. Not that I would be devastated by the snub. I *wanted* the colony to be self-sufficient, if for no other reason than so I could work on my projects in peace.

"What do you need from me, Kal?" I asked. "I've been steadily handing over functions to the administration for a decade now. If it came down to a showdown, I'm not sure I could even maintain control of the autofactories."

"*If* it comes to that," Kal responded, "you're a wild card, and something the Council can't control or interdict. At minimum, you'll be a distraction. At best, you'll be able to cause them significant stress."

"Well, I always wanted to be a pain in the ass," I replied.

"Mission accomplished." Gina grinned at me. "But you're also a public figure, and easy to track. We'll have to be careful about what you're seen doing."

"Hmm." I scratched my chin in thought. "There are a couple of things I can do about that, Gina. Let me work on it. And the public activity can be used as a red herring." I grinned at her. "See, now you've got me doing it. Spies-R-Us. Jeez."

We talked for a few more minutes, then ended the call. I sat back and stared into space, pondering my options. Like most nerds, I didn't take naturally to intrigue and double-cross. But I could see some simple strategies that would make things a little more difficult for anyone trying to track me. Not to mention an opportunity to make my pet project relevant.

It might be time for a personal appearance. I leaned forward and placed a call to Howard.

4. Attitude

Howard
November 2217
Vulcan

I sat, slowly sipping my coffee, and watched the people go by. The mall was busy all the time, it seemed. But then, Landing didn't have a whole lot of shopping malls. Okay, one. Original Bob had never had time for people-watching, and wouldn't have been caught dead sitting around, doing nothing. Being immortal apparently put a different spin on things.

Clothing shops, electronics shops, specialty shops selling things like bath products; it all made me feel both at home and nostalgic for home. The familiarity kept bumping up against the simple fact that I was seventeen light-years from Sol, in a solar system that was originally the home of Mr. Spock. And on a planet that was destroyed in the movie reboot, but who's counting?

Still, there was something about sitting at a table drinking coffee that made it all seem, well, mundane.

Bridget would be along soon. I'd elected to wait for her here rather than tag along to the office and be underfoot. Meanwhile, I was enjoying the sensation of being just some random Joe.

On my way now.

I smiled as I read the text in my heads-up. We'd made a point of not planning anything specific today. Lunch, walking around, no big deal.

Bridget showed up just as I finished the coffee. I stood, and we exchanged a quick kiss. She gave my hand a squeeze then sat down.

"I'm starved. Want to try the food court for lunch?"

"Food court?" My eyebrows rose. "A liquor baroness should have more refined tastes. Let's splurge. How about the *BrontoBurger*? Or we could go for *actual* food."

Bridget gave me the evil eye. "I happen to *like* bronto burgers, I'll have you know."

"Brontos, it is," I declared. I stood, offered her my arm. Smiling, she stood and took it, doing a small curtsey.

As we aimed ourselves in the general direction of the desired eatery, I heard a comment from a few tables away. "Make sure you hold hands with mommy." The comment was offered sotto voce, and may not have been intended for us to overhear, but the speaker, a zit-faced teenager, had miscalculated.

I dug in my heels and turned to glare at him, and Bridget put her other hand on my arm. "Howard, really? Consider the source."

I looked at the twerp, who was grinning back at me. About 140 pounds soaking wet. Against an android with several times the reaction speed and strength of a human being. Not really a fair fight. I made a point of looking him up and down, then I laughed and turned away. I hoped he got the message.

Bridget, meanwhile, was dragging me by the hand. "Food. This way."

"Right you are. Let us go forth and dine on the flesh of the alien bronto-like thing."

We exchanged smiles and continued on our way, but the encounter bugged me. Bridget was now in her late fifties, biologically—the time spent in stasis during the voyage didn't count. I, on the other hand, was built to look like Original Bob at thirty-one—his age when he died in a Las Vegas intersection. The *mommy* comment was, unfortunately, mathematically plausible.

But there was no way I would let Bridget be subjected to that kind of crap a second time.

* * *

Age hadn't dulled Bridget's appetite at all. She dove into her burger and fries as enthusiastically as any teenager. I ate at a more refined pace, enjoying the flavor but not needing the sustenance. Technically, it was a waste of food, but I did this so seldom, it hardly seemed worth worrying about.

"How are the kids?" I asked her, as much to slow down the carnage as out of a desire to know.

Bridget swallowed, wiped her mouth with a napkin, and glared at me. "You're not fooling me, bucko. You always wait until I have a mouthful." I grinned, unrepentant, and she continued. "Rosie is…well, you've met Rosie, you know what she's like. She's entitled to her opinion and you're entitled to her opinion, as well."

Bridget took another bite of bronto, frowning as she considered her next words. "I think it's fair to say she doesn't like our relationship. It's not that she dislikes you personally, Howard. No more than she dislikes most people, I mean. But I think she'd prefer me to stay within my species. I've tried to talk to her about it, but, you know…"

I grinned at her. "There's Rosie's opinion, and then there's…well, no, actually, there's just Rosie's opinion."

"Yes, like that." Bridget chuckled. "Well, I wanted my children to be self-reliant. Mission accomplished, I guess."

"I've talked to Howie a couple of times, lately," I replied, nibbling at my fries. "He's a little more distant than he used to be, but I was ascribing that to him growing up and losing the hero worship."

"There's probably some of that, Howard, but there's a lot more of Rosie. She won't give it a rest."

I shrugged. "Look, Bridget, I've made it clear any number of times that you come first. If I create problems for your personal life or your professional life or your family life, I'm gone."

Bridget put down the pitiful remains of her burger and leaned forward. She looked me straight in the eyes, my cue to shut up and pay attention.

"Howard, my relationships are my business. No one else gets a vote. I loved Stéphane, and I've mourned him fully and properly. Now, I enjoy your company. And will continue to do so, despite a bitch of a daughter and some zit-faced mouthy mall-rat. Do you have something you'd like to add?"

"No, dear." I grinned at her, and she rolled her eyes.

"Fine." She cleaned up with the napkin and tossed it onto the mangled remains of her meal. "Then let's go. I promised to get you some better clothes to drape on that android frame of yours."

"Threatened."

"What?"

"Threatened to get me better clothes."

Bridget laughed and grabbed my hand to drag me off. Clothes shopping. Even death apparently wasn't an escape.

5. Bushwhacked

Bob
March 2224
Delta Eridani

We hoisted the pigoid carcass up, suspended from spears, doing our best to act oblivious to the other group that we knew were watching us. I checked the monitor windows in my heads-up display. We definitely had a covert audience, and they outnumbered us twelve to six. I couldn't tell my crew things I shouldn't know, but I could be prepared in case the others did something unexpected.

As we started our march back to Camelot, I couldn't help noticing that my crew were really, really terrible actors. Overly loud comments, uttered with exaggerated inflection, would have made a stage director up and quit on the spot.

I needn't have worried, though. Fred and his gang probably weren't listening anyway. They stepped out, front and rear, just like last time.

Fred looked at me, standing in lead spot, and smiled his nasty smile. "Well, *Robert*. I see you've caught my lunch for me. And you don't have the big guy to protect you today. Why don't you go ahead and put up a fight, this time? I'd like that."

I cocked my head to the side. "Well, first, Fred, Donald didn't need to protect me last time. You're just not very good. And if it's a fight you're looking for, today's your lucky day."

And with that, eighteen Camelot hunters, including Donald, stepped out of the bush behind Fred's gang. The Caerleon group went into a defensive crouch. Several of them tried to inch away and had to be poked with spear tips. In short order, we had them herded into a small group.

Fred sneered at me. "You think this is going to protect you? You won't always have your friends around, *kuzzi*."

"Neither will you, Fred."

Fred jerked, taken aback. "What?"

"Just what I said. I can wait, and I can watch, and eventually you'll go take a pee or something without your friends covering your ass." I leaned in close. "And I'll cut your throat before you even know I'm there." I turned to the rest of the group. "This goes for all of you. You go to war with us, you'll be watching your backs the rest of your lives. I never forget. And I never forgive."

Fred laughed, a short sharp bark. "Nice talk. Nothing behind it, though."

"Really?" I smiled at him, and before he could react, I jabbed him in the same place as last time. Down he went.

It wasn't a fair fight, of course. I operated at computer speeds, and I was inhabiting an android body with electronic reflexes and several times the strength of a live Deltan. But a fair fight wasn't the point. I wanted them to stop stalking Camelot hunting parties. I just needed to make their mortality clear to them.

I looked around at the Caerleon gang. They appeared a lot less defiant, now.

"Today, we'll let you off with a warning. And without your spears. Next time, it's going to hurt a lot more." I signaled to a couple of the guys, and they began collecting spears. Fred's gang was thoroughly cowed now, and didn't put up any resistance.

We sent them off, then turned to head back to Camelot.

Donald walked beside me. "Damn, Robert, that was impressive. But I don't think Fred is that easily dissuaded."

"You're right, Donald. But most of his followers will be. People like Fred need followers. I'm hoping this will pull his teeth."

Donald nodded, then started up a marching chant, and everyone else joined in.

I wished I was as confident as I sounded.

6. Launch

Bill
January 2223
Epsilon Eridani

Garfield shook his head in awe. "It's like those cartoon muscle cars when we were a kid—the ones that were all engine."

The images in the video windows were indeed impressive. Epsilon Eridani 1, now in a completely new orbit around its sun, was surrounded by eight hundred mover plates. Trailing it by a million kilometers or so was one of the larger ex-moons of Epsilon Eridani 3, with a similar array of plates.

It had taken years to not only build all the equipment, but also to figure out how to control the assemblies. Forty supervisor AMIs were dedicated to maintaining and balancing the fields for each planet, in addition to the AMI in each plate.

And overseeing each planet would be my latest clones. They'd named themselves Daedalus and Icarus, which I privately thought was a little pretentious. But hey, it's a free galaxy.

Garfield looked at me, his face flushed with excitement. "Short-range test complete. There's a lot of room for error, but at minimum this setup is good for hundreds of Gs."

I smiled and leaned back in my chair. "I guess we're about ready, then." A quick ping to Dae and Ick, and they popped into my VR.

"Okay, guys. Everything checks out. You're clear that this is a Hail Mary, right?"

The two nodded. Daedalus replied, "Sure, but it's worth trying. Worst case, we fail, and the Bobs are no worse off."

"It's a good opportunity to get some quiet time for some astrophysics work, too," Icarus added with a smile.

I chuckled in reply. Icky had turned out very similar to me in temperament. Content to leave the exploration and fighting to others, he just wanted to work on his research.

I found myself a little ambivalent about Icarus and Daedalus. Cloning ourselves was always purposeful, of course. But I'd cloned these two for what could turn out to be a suicide mission. It felt unclean, somehow.

They knew exactly what I'd been thinking when I'd made the decision to go ahead. The pair gazed back at me with alert interest, no trace of blame or rancor on their faces. I decided I'd accept their judgment.

I hesitated, looking around the room. This was one of those moments that changed your life forever. Everything was ready to go. Time to fish or cut bait. "Okay, guys. The docking bays are ready for your ships. Connect up, hit the road, and Godspeed."

7. Date

Howard
November 2217
Omicron² Eridani

We walked out of the movie theater, arm in arm. Bridget looked as gorgeous as always. She turned and whispered in my ear, and as usual, my brain turned to mush.

"You look very dignified, Howard. But you really didn't have to do that."

I shrugged. Modifying the android's appearance was a trivial operation. Avoiding a situation that might make Bridget uncomfortable was top priority. My apparent age now matched hers perfectly.

Changing the subject, I said, "That wasn't bad. There might be a future in this movie theater fad."

"Yes, civilization has finally reached Vulcan. Next up—discos."

"No, please, no."

There wasn't exactly a booming movie industry, of course. Vulcan was very much a frontier planet, and the economy was still bootstrapping through the basic requirements. We'd be another couple of decades before leisure activities became a major market segment.

But Hollywood, and its various satellite locations and spiritual brethren, had produced thousands of movies of varying quality and popularity. And generally speaking, the holders of the copyrights were many light-years away, and almost certainly quite dead as well. Someone in Landing eventually had the bright idea to open a local theater and play themed double-bills. It was brilliant, as far as I was concerned. And the general population, who had spent most of their previous lives in isolated, claustrophobic enclaves, were taking to the new medium with enthusiasm.

Today's fare, a couple of zombie movies, had been sold out. The audience was loud, opinionated, and mostly sneeringly amused. But no one left early.

I leaned close. "I feel a hankering for brains. Or sushi."

Bridget laughed and opened her mouth to respond, but at that moment her phone buzzed. Two seconds later, I received an email. From the coroner's office.

I read the email in my heads-up display, and stopped dead in my tracks. Bridget looked up from her phone, tears in her eyes. "Oh, Howard, no..."

* * *

"He left this note for you," Dr. Onagi said. He pushed an envelope across the desk to me. Numbly, feeling like someone else was in control, I picked up the note and opened it. I held it so that Bridget could see.

> *Howard:*
>
> *I recently had occasion to visit the doctor, as I've been having issues with my memory and cognition. The news was less than pleasing. It would seem that I have a particularly nasty form of neurological degenerative dementia, one that is not curable. The doctor informs me that the process is already significantly advanced.*
>
> *I've contacted a few experts, and I was assured that this issue cannot be corrected in software. Under the circumstances, I don't see becoming a cognitively impaired replicant as an attractive option.*
>
> *My one remaining freedom is the ability to choose the manner of my passing.*

Howard, you've been a good friend over the years. Please don't think less of me for my decision.

Sincerely,
George Butterworth (Colonel, USE, ret'd.)

Bridget cried silently, tears running down her cheeks. I stared at Dr. Onagi, numb. "How..."

"A neurotoxin. Painless, and quick."

"Could he still be scanned?"

Dr. Onagi shook his head. "Even if it was medically possible, he had revoked consent."

I nodded and stood up. "Thank you, Dr. Onagi."

Bridget dried her eyes, stood, and followed me out of the office.

* * *

We still hadn't built the capability to cry into Manny the android. Too bad—I would have liked the release. Again. It might be time to bump up the priority on adding the capability, although it would be better if I just had fewer reasons to need it.

We sat on Bridget's couch, arms wrapped around each other. Bridget had cried herself out. I would catch up as soon as she went to bed and I could return to VR.

"People keep leaving," I finally said into the silence. Bridget looked up at me and I met her eyes. "I know it's normal. Your parents die, grandparents, people who've been around all your life. Eventually, you die, and that's that. But when you're immortal, you're always on the receiving end. It's just one hit after another."

"But you meet new people," Bridget said.

"And eventually, they leave. After a while, I think you'd get gun-shy." I smiled at Bridget, a wan smile at best. "I'm less standoffish than most Bobs, as a rule. But in this case, I think the others have the right of it. This gulf exists between immortals and what the Bobs are starting to refer to as *ephemerals*, for a reason."

Bridget searched my face. "Do you think of me as an ephemeral?"

"I think you're the most important thing in the universe. And that's the problem. Eventually, you'll die, and I'll be alone, again." I sighed and stood. "I'm sorry, Bridget. I'm being a real Dickie Downer, tonight. I think I should leave and let you get some sleep."

Bridget grabbed my arm. "Please don't. Just stay with me, here. I don't want to be alone."

Without a word, I sat back down, and put my arms around her again. She put her head on my shoulder and sighed. We sat there quietly, not moving or talking. At some point, I realized that she'd fallen asleep. And that was fine, too.

8. Revolutionaries

Marcus
June 2214
Poseidon

For the third time, I raised my hand to knock. And dropped it. I remembered Howard had mentioned a problem with stage fright, the first time he'd gone out in public using an android. I wasn't sure if I hadn't believed him, or just hadn't taken him seriously. Either way, someone owed someone an apology.

And this would be my first public appearance with the new android form. After years of operating through video windows and telephone calls, I was finally going to meet my best friends on this world, face to face.

If I could just manage to knock on the door.

With a growl, I consciously set aside all my insecurities and rapped three times. The door opened immediately—I knew they'd been expecting me, but I had a sudden image of Kal, waiting on the other side of the door with his hand on the knob, waiting for me to act.

"So, the great computer in the sky deigns to visit us poor mortals." He grinned down at me. My android was the same height as Original Bob—six foot one—but Kal towered over me, as he did over almost everyone.

"Oh, bite me, Kal. Who's here already?"

Kal stepped aside and motioned me in. "Denu and Gina. Vinnie will be a bit late. He got caught up in some Council thing."

I walked into the living room of Kal's small apartment. It was a constant source of frustration that, on a planet with so much space, people were crowded into such concentrations. Granted, most of the planet was water, but there were enough mats—and now, enough floating cities—so that people could spread out. The Council's insistence that everyone stay together had lately become a planetwide source of contention. I wondered how much of that was natural, and how much was helped along by the rabble-rousers in this room.

I sat down, to find Gina and Denu staring at me. Denu said, "Damn, that's impressive. Marcus, if I didn't know better, I wouldn't have given you a second glance. Completely believable."

I shrugged. "Several other Bobs have been working on the design for a couple of years now. I'm late to the party. Got my own priorities, you know?"

Gina and Denu nodded, and Kal snorted.

At that moment, there was a knock on the door, and Vinnie walked in without waiting, wearing a furious expression. Clearly, the Council thing had not gone well.

"Idiots! Morons!" Vinnie exclaimed. He grabbed a beer from the fridge, then threw himself down on the couch.

"Come on in, Vinnie. Grab yourself a brew," Kal said to him with a grin.

Vinnie lifted the beer in salute. "Sorry. You know how it is with Council."

"So..."

Vinnie popped the tab on the can while giving Kal the Spock eyebrow. "So they have absolutely refused to consider any changes to their policies. They dismiss issues of public morale as 'fear-mongering'. All I could get from them was a rote reiteration of their 'all for one' standard speech." Vinnie paused and drained half the can. "Absent some kind of direct threat, they aren't budging. This is the future, folks."

Gina turned and looked at me. "So, big guy, I guess this is it. You said to exhaust all other avenues, first. I think we've done that. It's time for a change of leadership. And since the Council keeps putting off elections as 'low priority' and a 'distraction', I'd say that's out the window as well."

I rubbed my forehead with one hand, then found myself gazing distractedly at my hand. The action felt significantly different than in VR, although I couldn't put my finger on exactly how. I shelved that thought for later, when I had some free time.

I looked at Gina, who was still waiting for an answer. "Umm, I'll grant that you've gone through all your alternatives, but I don't think I have, yet. Guys, I really do not want to become a revolutionary. People die in revolutions, even in the so-called peaceful ones." I looked around at the others, meeting their eyes one by one. "I have the flying cities almost ready for the big reveal. I think that might shake things up enough without the need for shooting people and blowing things up."

"Will you present that as a threat, or keep it for a surprise?"

"Honestly, Kal, it's not really much of a threat," I replied, "at least on paper. *Rethink your ways or we'll produce flying cities.* Lacks a certain something, know what I mean?"

Kal chuckled ruefully. "Okay, yeah. It may be more of a threat after it's implemented and we start to see some of the fallout. Until then, the Council is only going to see what they want to see."

"Still, you have to try," Denu added. "Present it to them, and if they don't get the point, oh well."

Gina went to the fridge and retrieved a beer. She waved it at Denu before apparently realizing that was a bad idea with an unopened carbonated beverage. "Marcus' point, though, is that we'd like to avoid the full-scale revolution option, so *oh well* as an attitude is not helpful." She turned to me. "And stop being such a wuss."

Denu and I both grinned at her. Good ol' quiet, un-opinionated Gina.

"Okay," Kal looked around the room. "So Marcus will go talk to the Council and try to convince them that their totalitarian policy is not supportable. If they listen to reason, great. If not, we proceed on the *cities* thing anyway, without official approval."

We each nodded, silently. As plans went, it lacked something. But it was better than a shooting war.

* * *

"Not acceptable!" Councilor Benben's face in the video window could only be described as thunderous. I tried to avoid grinning.

To say that my proposal was meeting resistance would be a massive understatement.

Councilor Murray cut in from another window, "We are finally getting close to aligning populations with labor requirements on the mats and cities. If people start moving around haphazardly, or even emigrating to some other living arrangement, it will mean chaos. There aren't enough people to do all the required work. We need them to live where they're needed."

"Leaving aside," I responded, "the question of whether it's morally acceptable to tell people where they should live and what job they should do."

"It's the law, Marcus."

I smiled at Councilor Brennan. "Which simply sidesteps the statement. Anything can be passed into law. That doesn't make it right. Plus there's the question of the agreement you signed with Riker before we shipped you out here. It sets out—"

"That document is not legally binding," Brennan replied. "We've already voted on that."

"So you can just vote any agreement you don't like null and void on your own dime, then vote in whatever else you want. And everyone else is just supposed to go along because it's the *law?*"

Murray looked down his nose at me. Really. Literally. "Saying it with a sneer isn't a rebuttal, Mr. Johansson. I think we're pretty clear on this. No flying cities. Possibly at some point in the future, but *we* will make that decision, not you." He looked around, likely gauging the mood of the other councilors from his end. "And I think we're done here. Good day."

And he switched off. Within a second or two, the other councilors did the same.

I sat back in my office chair and shook my head. Done? Hardly. There was a scene in *Demolition Man*, where the police captain couldn't conceive the possibility that someone might not follow orders. The Council's reaction had that flavor.

I sent a quick text to the Revolutionary Council: Kal, Denu, and Gina.

I tried. They dug in their heels. Looks like we'll be doing this the hard way.

* * *

I didn't really want to bother Bill or Riker. Or Bob, for that matter. They each had their own problems to deal with. I supposed that the Others could eventually become my problem as well, but for now, I had the local issue to deal with.

I checked my android's current location. I'd loaded it into a cargo drone after the meeting at Kal's, and ordered the drone into orbit around Poseidon. I directed the drone to West Mat Four, with instructions to inform me when it arrived.

The population of the mats hadn't really dropped much, yet. Only a few floating cities had been constructed, and the Council didn't feel the need to make them residential. Essential personnel and industry, only. Yet another reason why the public was getting tired of the Council. When we first decanted the colonists, there had been an expectation that living on the mats would be necessary for only a decade or so, maximum. And would be gradually phased out in favor of manufactured floating cities during that interval. Now, twenty years later, more than ninety percent of the human population of Poseidon still made their homes on the mats.

I got a ping from the drone and smiled. After only a few days of having my own android, I found myself using any excuse to go walkabout.

It took only a moment to activate the android, and I found myself draped over the support rack. I opened the cargo doors and walked out into sunshine.

Weather on the mats wasn't typically a problem. The colonists had made a point of settling mainly on the mats caught in the tropical zone. In the absence of any land whatsoever, Poseidon's oceans had settled into bands similar to Jupiter. Each band had a small but distinct difference in temperature, ecology, and even salinity.

Rainstorms swept across the mats frequently, but they were mild, warm, and short. The occasional major storm could be seen developing days in advance, and a series of drones were in place to tow affected mats out of the way.

I walked the short distance to the edge of the landing pad and joined pedestrian traffic. New Georgia was a small town by any measurement, and it exuded that flavor. People knew each other, no one seemed to be in a hurry, and there was no feeling of crowding, at least out in public. It was a measure of the perversity of human nature that the biggest complaint people had about living here was that they weren't given a choice.

I sighed to myself and set off in a random direction. I didn't have a goal; I simply wanted to enjoy the day.

It took fewer than five minutes for my day to be ruined.

An internal buzz indicated an incoming call. Metadata showed it was from Kal. I connected, audio only. "What's up, Kal?"

"The Council apparently wasn't satisfied with just telling you *no.* They've taken steps…"

"Ooh, *steps.*" I snickered. "What've they done?"

"Shut down anything that might be a source of supplies for us. Reallocated any personnel that might be helping, and moved them. Including Gina and Denu. And changed all the printer schedules."

"Gina and Denu are going along with it?"

"Yes," he replied. "There's no real point in digging in their heels right now. We'll just talk by phone a lot more."

"Hmm, I wonder if that's the point?" I rubbed my chin in thought.

"What?"

"Surveillance, Kal. If we're talking over the comms system, they might be monitoring."

"Huh." Kal was silent for a few moments. "And of course, if they pass a law, it's legal. And therefore ethical."

"Something like that. And on that subject, we should probably hang this one up."

"Gotcha. Coming over?"

"You got it, buddy. I'll be there in half an hour." I hung up the call, then checked my roamer inventory. If the Council was willing to tap calls, they might be willing to plant bugs as well. Time to get serious.

* * *

"What the—" Kal jerked back as he opened the door. I grinned at him, unrepentant. I had kept the roamers in my pockets on the walk over, but as we Bobs like to point out, we're not very mature. More than a dozen small roamers crawled over my clothing, and one stood on my head, doing a jig.

Kal stepped aside, shaking his head. "You really are a bastard."

Chuckling, I ordered the roamers to sweep the room. "This'll take only a minute or two."

The roamers scampered down my body and scattered around the room. It took less than a minute to find three bugs. Kal and I looked at each other in stunned silence. It was one thing to talk about the possibility, quite another to discover the reality.

A couple of roamers quietly destroyed the listening devices, while their compatriots continued to search.

In the end, they discovered only the three. Kal let out a noisy breath. "Unbelievable. The lack of elections, the lack of free choice, and now this. We're definitely over the line into totalitarianism."

"Mm. I'm going to leave a couple of roamers here to watch for further attempts, and I'll deliver some squads to everyone else's home. Gina will go ballistic, of course."

"She's in security, Marcus. If she's being monitored and doesn't know about it, then she's out of the loop. And that doesn't bode well."

I shook my head. "Consider the possibility that this is a regular thing, and she's just not high enough in the bureaucracy to know about it. That's sort of worse in a different way, of course."

Kal waved off the comment. "Yeah, fine. Now, flying cities?"

"Given the Council's reaction at my meeting with them, I think just introducing the cities will be provocative enough," I replied. "And if not, if they do nothing, we win by default."

"And for now, we just lie low?"

I nodded. "The fun will come to us, I think." I pulled an item out of my backpack. "Meanwhile, here's our new communication system. SCUT tech, encrypted, and infested with nanites. If someone tries to dick with it, they'll get a nasty surprise."

Kal took the device, carefully touching it only with the ends of his fingers.

I laughed at his obvious discomfort. "Come on, buddy, give me some credit. The nanites will recognize attempted tampering. You're fine."

He shrugged and gave me a lopsided grin. "Denu and Gina getting the same thing?"

I nodded. "Mm, no matter what we do, the phone system won't be secure. We can't protect it end-to-end."

Kal sighed and placed the comm unit on his desk. "Remember that line I said we hadn't crossed?"

"Uh-huh." I nodded. "I can see it in my rear-view mirror. We are now officially revolutionaries. Yeehah."

9. Tension

Howard
February 2218
Vulcan

"You should leave my mother alone."

I'd been casually examining a store-front display at the mall, so the comment, coming out of nowhere, made me jump. I turned around to find Rosie, Bridget's eldest daughter, glaring at me.

"What?" *Oh, great comeback, Howard. Brilliant.*

"You're a machine. You're not even human. My mother needs to get over the death of my father, and move on. But not with a machine."

Here we go. My fertile and somewhat anxiety-ridden imagination had pictured something like this. I wasn't particularly happy about the validation. "Rosie, the two aren't mutually exclusive. I, the real me, am human. I—"

"Spare me all the scientific double-talk. You're a recording of a human. I'm not interested in debating the issue. I'm—"

"Then why are we even talking?"

"What?" Rosie blinked rapidly and drew back slightly. I seemed to have managed to derail whatever speech she was gearing up to. I noted out of the corner of my eye that we were attracting an audience. Several passersby had stopped to watch the drama, and at least one person had their phone out. I wondered if I qualified as a celebrity.

"Rosie," I continued, trying to ignore the gawkers. "You may not be interested in a debate, but I'm equally not interested in standing here being lectured at. To coin a phrase that was around when I was young, you're not the boss of me. And, more to the point I think, your mother is freely choosing to associate with me."

"And I've told her exactly what I think of that!" Rosie was almost spitting the words. "But you've gotten her all twisted around—"

"Oh, freakin' hell!" I exclaimed, rolling my eyes. "Have you *met* your mother? Have you ever tried to get her to do something she didn't want to?" I waved a hand dismissively. "Look, I don't want to get into a confrontation with you. Mostly out of respect for your parents, both of whom I love, and loved, dearly. But Bridget is an adult, and able to make her own decisions. I'll stop seeing her when *she* says so. You don't get a vote."

And that was it. We stood there, glaring at each other, any hope of discussion or understanding pretty much skewered, possibly permanently. After a few more moments of impasse, Rosie sneered at me and wordlessly stalked off.

Well, isn't that just peachy.

I looked around at the small crowd that had gathered. No one would meet my eyes, and they swiftly dispersed.

I resumed my aimless wandering, trying to get back into the window-shopping mood, but couldn't put Rosie out of my mind. And some of the looks from my erstwhile audience had been hostile. Obviously I had been recognized. I began to wonder what I would do if this drama spilled over onto Bridget.

* * *

We were sitting on Bridget's couch while I recounted my earlier experience at the mall.

"I didn't tell you because it isn't your problem, Howard." Bridget looked sad, but not apologetic. "My kids, mostly Rosie, I think, would like to see me dating someone less, uh, biologically challenged. She's started lecturing me on the subject whenever I see her. Lianne and Howard mostly stand around looking uncomfortable."

"Wonderful. Is there anything else you aren't telling me?"

She smiled at me. "Well, there is a certain amount of gossip going around. Some of the more interesting items involve questions about your equipment. So to speak."

I couldn't help it. I started to laugh helplessly. Thanks to the very authentic proprioceptive circuits in the android, I had to sit down or risk falling over. For maybe the tenth time, I made a note to myself to install tear ducts.

Bridget grinned, sharing the moment. "And on that subject…"

"Oh, no you don't. I've already told you that I'll upgrade Manny any time you say the word. That's on you."

Now Bridget was laughing, too. The hilarity fed back on itself until we were both lying back on the furniture, gasping for breath and whooping helplessly.

Finally, after a minute or two, we both managed to recover control. Bridget took my hand. "And that's one of the reasons why I love you. Even Stéphane often just looked at me like I had a screw loose. I had to bite back a lot of my more lowbrow humor. With you, well, you get it."

"Minds together in the gutter, forever." I smiled at her. My God, she was beautiful.

* * *

The internet hadn't really changed that much in two hundred years. Oh, there were new companies, and old companies had gone out of business. A lot of the jargon had changed. But people were still people, and still had the same interests. There were still forums, you could still follow someone, everyone still had a personal landing page on any of several different platforms, and blogs were still popular. Apparently narcissism and voyeurism were still alive and well.

The point, though, was that it didn't take a lot of effort to track down some commentary relating to the locally famous—or perhaps infamous—replicant. My android persona wasn't any kind of a secret, and had become a small but persistent topic of conversation. And there were enough pictures posted to make me recognizable if someone cared enough.

There was no shortage of opinions on the subject, although they appeared to be about evenly split. I was either some kind of

Frankenstein's Monster, or I was just some guy who had the same right to exist as everyone else. There didn't really seem to be any middle ground.

It looked like my relationship with Bridget was the real sticking point. Most people were okay with me just wandering around, visiting malls and such. But they drew the line at me dating outside my chemical family.

It was unlikely that Bridget was unaware of this. That meant she was protecting me. Crap. I was just chauvinistic enough to want to be the one doing the protecting.

I wondered if she had a plan. Or, more importantly, if I had one. Someone needed to deal with this.

10. Hunted

Bob
March 2224
Camelot

Deltans couldn't whistle while they worked. Or any other time, really—otherwise I'd have been belting out a tune. This was the kind of day that would bring a celebration to the lips of any but the grumpiest. Up with the dawn, a breakfast of berries and eggs, a couple of hours warming ourselves in the morning sun… My android body didn't require any of that, of course, but the neural interface was more than good enough to give me the same pleasurable experience as anyone else.

After a morning of indolence, I went hunting while Archimedes laid out his flintwork for the day. With a little luck, I hoped to bag the local equivalent of a turkey.

Archimedes and his family were more than generous, and had treated me like one of them right from the start. I wanted to give back whenever possible. A turkey or other small game once in a while was a welcome treat.

Marvin occasionally accused me of trying to deny reality and become Robert full-time. I didn't argue with him—there was at least some truth to the accusation. I certainly felt far more a part of the Deltan life than I had back on Earth as Original Bob. Missing my family so much probably played into my effectively having gone native.

In the middle of my idle ruminations, my heads-up display flashed an alert. Movement in the immediate vicinity. I called up one of the many spy drones that kept my Camelot VR up to date, and redirected it to center on me.

At computer speeds, it took less than a second overall to realize that I wasn't being stalked by wildlife.

It was Fred. And four friends. And they were obviously intent on me.

I could just busterize them, of course. But even with an obnoxious tard like Fred, I couldn't stomach casual murder. I could also very likely take them on and win, but it would completely blow my cover. I'd be done as Archimedes' friend, Robert, the generic Deltan. Not an option.

Could I call for help? No, by the time I got a drone to Archimedes, then he found Donald or someone, then they got here, the excitement would be over. I was on my own.

I called up two more drones so that I would have good coverage, then observed my pursuers for a few moments. They knew generally where I was, but I could see that they were often looking or moving in a direction that was slightly off my line. That suggested possibilities.

My strategy started with turning off my scent. Deltans made heavier use of the sense of smell than humans, and less use of sight. I could take advantage of that.

I positioned myself between two of my stalkers, and went as still and quiet as only an android could, as they moved past my position. With no movement, sound, or odor, I simply didn't register.

Now I was behind them.

I noted Fred's position and moved around the perimeter until I was close to him. If he moved away from the group at any point, he was mine.

The cordon eventually tightened until everyone could see each other. Fred threw his spear down with rage.

"We *had* him! By the balls of my ancestors, how in the next life did you let him get through?"

"How do you know it wasn't you, Fred?" One of the hunters, apparently fed up, challenged him.

In a streak, Fred moved in and knocked the speaker to the ground. He picked up his victim's spear and held it to the Deltan's neck.

"Mouth me off like that again and we'll be serving *you* for dinner, *kuzzi.*"

Wow, what a jerk. It occurred to me that I might be doing the Deltan species a favor by removing him from the gene pool.

The hunters cast around for a few more minutes, but I simply moved out of their range and watched from the drones. Eventually they gave up and started back toward Caerleon, with Fred mouthing off constantly.

I followed them about halfway to the other village, but sadly, Fred stayed with the group all the way. I'd have to arrange a meeting myself.

I returned all surveillance systems to normal and headed back toward Camelot. A quick command to a couple of drones ensured that I wouldn't be taken by surprise by anything. This whole situation would require some thought, and I knew myself well enough to realize that I could walk right off a cliff when I got into this mode.

I walked along, looking down at my feet as I thought. Fred was truly evidence that jerks came in all shapes, sizes, and species. But what was setting him—and the rest of them—off like this? They weren't behaving this way for the fun of it. The behavior was too consistent for pranks. They had the same hunting prospects as us, the same access to tubers—maybe even a little better than Camelot in that area.

I made a note to check out Caerleon using drones. Maybe I could pick out something significant.

I still had the unfinished chore of hunting lunch, though. And I'd wasted far too much time waltzing with Fred and his goons. With a shake of the head, I sent my drones out to look for some small game in the area. It was cheating, but I was running behind, and people gotta eat.

* * *

"Sounds like Fred took it personally." Donald grinned at me.

"Well, no one likes being punched out. But I didn't expect him to come hunting for me."

Donald and I were sunning ourselves at Archimedes' flint-working site, while he did his best to ignore the two of us. Buster worked with his father, roughing out some of the easier tools for Archimedes to finish later. Buster had little interest in flint working as a career path, although he had his father's dexterity and was pretty decent with the basics. Buster liked to hunt, and his weapon of choice was a bow and arrow. He was easily the best shot in the village—possibly in both villages.

But Buster also loved hanging with his father, and if helping with the day's work sped things along, then that's what he'd do.

These three were very probably my favorite people on the planet.

"Too bad he didn't give you the chance to slit his throat. You'd be doing everyone a favor."

I shifted my position while I considered my reply. I doubted I could just coldly cut someone's throat, but how to explain that twenty-first-century sensibility to stone-age beings?

"The thing is, Donald, we know it's not just Fred. He may be taking to it with enthusiasm, but there's more to this."

"Mmm." Donald lay back with his hands behind his head. The tone said that Donald would have no trouble skewering Fred next time they met. "Might be just about time that we go on a hunt of our own. Maybe ask a few questions."

Well, that wasn't a bad idea. Except for the 'we' part.

11. Remains

Bill
March 2223
Epsilon Eridani

I was making some modifications to Bullwinkle when I got a ping from Mario. I gave my roamers instructions that would keep them busy for a while, and rematerialized my VR.

Mario popped in a moment later. He turned to Jeeves, who had appeared at his elbow, and requested a coffee, then sat down and gazed at me.

"Okay, Mario, I know you well enough to realize the *inscrutable* act always means trouble. What's up?"

He looked down and smiled, acknowledging the score. "Yeah, okay. Uh, I'm not sure where to begin." Mario took a sip of his drink, then put it down and laced his fingers together. "You know we've been continuing to scout the stars around GL 877, trying to map out the Others' depredations."

I nodded. "I'm guessing the dramatic pause isn't to give me good news."

"Hah!" Mario shook his head. "If anything, they've been more active in the other direction. Probably a combination of luck and proximity of the stars in that area. Anyway, we've found five other life-bearing planets that they've depopulated, including another civilization. Late industrial, early atomic era. About equivalent to Earth in the mid-twentieth."

"Wonderful. So the Others have yet another notch on their collective holster."

"And another nail in their coffin. Bill, I know I'm probably preaching to the choir, but I don't see any resolution to this that involves the Others continuing to exist."

"Yeah, I know. It's been discussed. You know it has. And we're the ones who will have to do it, assuming we even can."

"There's Daedalus and Icarus..."

"Long shot." I waved a hand at Mario. "What about you and your clones? You're closest. Anything you could do?"

Mario smiled without any humor. "Sure. Except, by some enormous coincidence, there's no metal to be had anywhere around GL 877."

"Okay, got it."

Mario was right, of course. The home system of the Others was out at the periphery of explored space. By definition, since exploration had pretty much stopped once we'd discovered them.

"Claude and a large number of the Bobs from the Delta Pavonis defense are heading for Gamma Pavonis. Maybe you can arrange something with them." Mario looked at me with one eyebrow raised.

I nodded, then grimaced. "I'll do that, Mario, but I think Claude took the defeat really hard. I'm not sure he's going to be entirely rational where the Others are concerned. His talk was all about defending Gamma."

"Well, you have a few more years until his group gets to Gamma. Maybe come up with a sales pitch."

I sighed. If there was a hell, it was in sales.

12. Funeral for Julia

Riker
October 2218
Vulcan

I was going through the latest production reports from Charles, when I received a call from Justin Hendricks. With a smile, I dropped the reports. Talking to family was always top of the priority list. Justin had grown up; Space Cadet Justin was now a ship's captain in the New Jerusalem Space Corps. The thought brought a chuckle. The space corps consisted of a half-dozen cargo and transport vessels, based loosely on the version 2 Heaven design.

Dexter, the current Bob-in-residence, had been aggressive about making the colonies independent of replicant support. The Omicron^2 Eridani system's twin planets now featured settlements from twelve different enclaves, and all of them had at least one vessel. Dexter was still hanging around the system, but demands on his time were down to a couple of items a week.

I had a smile on my face as I picked up the call, but lost it when I saw his expression. Justin's eyes were glistening with barely-controlled tears.

"Uncle Will, it's Mom. She's in the hospital. It's bad."

* * *

I stepped out of the cargo drone and looked up at the hospital building. Then I looked down at my hands, and at my feet. Howard had lent me Manny without hesitation, when he heard. It took slightly more than an hour to fly Manny from Vulcan to Romulus.

This was my first time in an android, and I was nervous. It occurred to me that Howard's first use of Manny was because of very similar circumstances. I hoped that wasn't a trend. Sadly, with ephemerals, it probably was.

I saw Justin come out the front doors of the hospital, so I stepped away from the drone and sent it off. Justin hurried up to me, then stopped five feet away, suddenly bashful. This was the first time we'd met 'in person', so to speak.

"Uncle Will," he said, blushing slightly. "You, uh, you look younger on the phone."

I smiled. "Stage lighting." I wasn't about to try to explain Howard and Bridget. Assuming he didn't already know about them.

He turned and we walked back toward the hospital entrance. I spared a quick glance in his direction. For the first time, I noticed wrinkles forming around his mouth and on his forehead. A few gray hairs, too. With an effort of will, I pulled myself away from that line of thought as Justin filled me in.

"She was at home, and suddenly she held her head, screamed, and collapsed. She was babysitting my kids, and fortunately they knew what to do." Justin's eyes were wide and staring as he talked. "The ambulance got there in moments, and brought her here. But I think it was already too late." He looked at me, tears now in his eyes. "It's an aneurysm. The doctors say there's no way she's going to wake up."

We arrived at her room, and I took a moment to look around. Very modern equipment, and no overt religious images or icons. Of course, there had been a popular uprising about twenty years ago, something to do with free importing of alcohol, and possibly a scandal or two... Anyway, New Jerusalem was now a proper democracy with separation of church and state. Howard and I had celebrated by scanning a bottle of Irish whiskey and bringing the template into VR.

Well, I was procrastinating, and I knew it. I took a deep breath and walked slowly up to the bed.

I remembered the first time I'd seen Julia Hendricks, on a video call with Minister Cranston. I remembered the stomach-dropping shock as I looked at an almost perfect likeness of my sister, Julia's several-times-great-grandmother. She still looked like Andrea, like Andrea would have looked had I been alive to see her as a grandmother. I reached down, put my hand against Julia's cheek. The first time I'd ever touched her.

Well, it seems Howard finally installed tear ducts. Damn.

I wiped my eyes, then turned to Justin. Tears were running freely down his face.

It took several attempts to get my voice to work. "What will you do?"

"She didn't want to be kept alive if there was no chance..."

I nodded, infinite sadness washing over me. *People keep leaving...*

"I guess, with the aneurysm, there's no chance of replication?"

Justin shook his head. "Uncle Will, don't take this personally, but I don't think very many people will ever choose replication. It was an experiment designed in a darker, more authoritarian time, when people were seen as just replaceable cogs." He smiled sadly at me. "And the amount of work you and the other Bobs have put in—well, it looks to the average person like permanent servitude. Who wants to spend their whole afterlife doing chores?"

"Ah, that explains a lot." I nodded in thought. "Once Howard resurrected the technology, we were kind of expecting an onslaught of requests. We've gotten zip."

"I think you are probably the end of the experiment."

I said nothing, just looked down at Julia. Maybe just as well.

* * *

The funeral was held within a few days. I was still borrowing Howard's android. There was no chance of confusion—Howard had never been on Romulus in android form. These people only knew Will, the many-greats grand-uncle in software. Justin asked me to be a pallbearer, which I gratefully accepted.

Julia had lived a good life, and had many relatives, all of whom knew and loved her. Justin's eulogy left not a dry eye in the place—including yours truly.

I was the center of attention for most of the reception. Many people wanted to know about my sisters, and about life in the 21st century. No questions about replication, though. Go figure.

Finally, emotionally exhausted, I said my goodbyes and called the cargo drone. I turned and waved to the small crowd that came outside with me, stepped into the cargo drone, and switched off.

* * *

I popped into Howard's VR. "Hey, Howard. Manny's all yours again. He's flying back from Romulus. Be there in a few hours."

"Thanks. Funeral go okay?"

I sat and made a spot for Spike. She took the invitation, and began to purr before I even started petting her. Spike was never very good at hard-to-get.

I sighed, and stared into space for a few moments. "No confrontations or anything. Not like you and the kids…" I gave him a quick glare. "I guess that's kind of settled down?"

"Mmm, yeah, Bridget had words with her offspring. I don't think Rosie will seek me out to yell at me anymore."

"You know you're asking for it, don't you? Dating a human…"

"It's not really dating, Will. There's no sexual component. We enjoy each other's company. We always have. We *get* each other."

I nodded in sympathy. "I know what you mean. But lips will flap."

Howard laughed. "Screw 'em. I'm happier than I've been since, hmm, since before Jenny, actually."

"Jenny's long dead, Howard. Eventually, Bridget will be as well." I shrugged apologetically at Howard's sharp look. "Sorry, I think the funeral has me a little down. Just a year after we lost the colonel. *Ephemerals*, indeed."

"Yeah…" Howard reached over and gave Spike a quick pat. "Immortality sure isn't all upside."

I got up and placed Spike on the chair I'd just vacated. "No argument there. I'm going to go home, activate my alcohol receptors, and drown my sorrows. Then, tomorrow, back to the salt mines."

I waved to Howard, then popped back to my own VR, in Sol system.

13. Flying Cities

Marcus
February 2215
Poseidon

"I suppose you're all wondering why I've gathered you here." I turned to sweep my gaze across the assembled invitees. I saw several eye-rolls, some smiles, and a couple of blank faces that said, 'please let this be over soon'.

Philistines.

"Sorry, I always get a kick out of saying that. In this case, though, it's appropriate. There's a project I've been actively working on for about fifteen years now. I think you'll be interested." I gazed around at my audience, gauging their mood. I noted that several of them were peering back at me with at least as much interest. Very few people had seen me walking around in my android body, as yet.

I'd arranged this meeting on a remote section of the Great Northern Mat, about three miles from the population center of New Malé. Personal flyers sat, parked randomly on the thick vegetation surface. The invitees were a heterogeneous mix of security, administration, and technical people, as well as a few individuals with no credentials at all, except that I liked and trusted them. My friends, whom I'd come to think of as the inner circle, stood off to one side. They'd declared that this was my show, and they would stay out of it.

I tried to suppress a grin, then gave up and let it come. And why not? In effect, I was about to create a new nation.

"Okay, Marcus, this is getting old. Give." That was Yoshi, a senior infrastructure engineer and one of Kal's friends from work.

"You got it, Yoshi. Ladies and gentlemen, I give you...the flying city of Helium!"

As I said the words, I brought the city down through the clouds to hover fifty feet overhead. Well, okay, 'city' was a little trumped up. It would be the size of a double lot in any suburban setting. Circular, about a hundred feet in diameter, the floating platform was flat on the top side, covered with a clear fibrex dome, with a series of hemispherical protuberances arranged radially on the underside.

"I will be dipped in shit." Yoshi's mouth hung open. He turned toward me, eyes goggling. "Okay, I'm impressed. How's it work? Not like the flyers..."

"No, of course not. No turbo-props. Or helium, ironically. Helium, the city, uses a series of SURGE coils."

"But that can't be right. Gravity is always nullified in a SURGE field. This isn't supposed to be a free-fall city, is it?"

I laughed. "No, Yoshi. No zero-G. The field doesn't envelop the city. The SURGE coils are set up almost like the VTOL fans on your flyers. They provide lift, nothing else. That's those hemispheres on the underside."

"Damn." Yoshi's eyebrows were starting to come together in the signature engineer frown—a sure sign that he was starting to think things through.

He turned to face me squarely. "So what you said before—this isn't going to be offered to the colony?"

"Not quite. This won't be offered *exclusively* to the colony administration. I don't want them controlling it. They've already got too tight a grip on things." I shook my head slowly. "If you'd asked any Bob, we'd have guessed it would be FAITH pulling this kind of fascist crap. Not some former island nations."

Vinnie, despite the group's earlier promise, muttered almost inaudibly, "They'll try to shut it down."

"Short of violence, Vinnie, there's not that much they can do.

Their power is mostly in perceived authority, implied threats, and social pressure."

"So we ignore them." Kal nodded.

"What if they do start shooting?" Gina asked. "I keep hassling you about this. Are you prepared to shoot back?"

"If it came to that," I replied, "I still have the biggest weapons. But they know that. And they know I can take out all their space-based assets."

Yoshi gave me the stink-eye. "Why are you doing this, Marcus?"

"You have to ask? This is supposed to be a fresh start for humanity. We're supposed to start over, without all the former prehistoric bullshit. And instead, this government is just starting it up all over again. I want to pull their teeth."

I turned back in the direction of Helium and waved expansively. "I'm just giving people a way to vote with their feet."

* * *

It took no convincing at all to get everyone up to Helium for an inspection. People walked around, gazing over the edge through the clear fibrex dome material, or just pacing the perimeter.

"It's a little short on buildings," Kal said, smiling at me.

"I'm not really sure to what extent we need them," I replied. "With the dome, this is completely climate-controlled. No rain, no cold, no snow. Beyond basic privacy requirements, you could just live *al fresco*." I stamped my foot on the bare metal surface. "We could put down a layer of soil and have grass everywhere."

Kal nodded. Gina cut in. "What you have here, Marcus, is a basic framework. Very nice technical proof-of-concept, but it needs a few things. Cargo bays, landing bays and garage for flyers, evacuation pods, emergency equipment, weapon emplacements, food storage, kitchens…"

"And, she's off." Kal laughed and inclined his head at Gina.

"Well, it is my job."

"That's fine, guys," I said. "And Gina's right. A fully usable and livable city has to have the infrastructure for people to live and do their jobs. So, I'm open to suggestions. With your help, version 2 will be move-in ready. Also bigger, of course. You need enough room for a community to work as well as live."

Kal nodded. "And who will we invite?"

"Ah, now, there's a whole other conversation." I'd been waiting for someone to bring that up. "I have some notes..."

* * *

Gina grabbed a couple of beers from Kal's fridge and returned to the couch. She handed one to Vinnie, and popped hers. Bobbing it in my direction, she said, "If you just throw it wide open, Marcus, you're effectively inviting in Council spies."

"Don't care, Gina. In fact, I'm also going to file the construction plans with the appropriate government departments."

"Just don't expect them to issue permits." Kal grinned at me.

I chuckled. "No, I wouldn't expect them to move quickly on that. Anyway, the point is to make this as open as possible. No secrets, no espionage stuff. Completely out front. Everyone will know about it, everyone can get information. It pulls the teeth of the Council in a lot of ways."

"Sabotage?"

"Wow." I frowned at Gina. "It would have to be after the fact, when there are already citizens on board. Maybe I'm naïve, but I can't see even the Council being willing to kill people."

You're right," Gina said.

I smiled at her. "There you go."

"You are naïve." She smiled back.

I rolled my eyes while Vinnie and Kal chuckled. "Okay, fine," I continued. "But if it gets to that point, it's open war."

"Well, here we go," Vinnie said. "Vive la révolution."

I sighed yet again. I wasn't sure just exactly what it was about this that I found so mentally tiring. "I keep saying it. I'd like to avoid that entirely. Look, it's not like we're doing anything negative. We're not blowing things up, or going on strike, or burning down the Bastille, or even sailing off into the west. People will continue to do their jobs, they'll continue to produce food, perform manufacturing, whatever. They'll just have a different mailing address."

"What the hell is a mailing address?"

I grinned at Vinnie. "Sorry. Before your time. I meant they'll have a different residential location. The point is, there's no downside, not materially or economically, for the Council. Sure, we're thumbing our noses at them, and I expect them to get grumpy, but to start shooting? Killing people?" I shook my head. "I'm not saying it's impossible, just that it would pretty much end any credibility they might have up to that point."

Gina, rolled her eyes. "Marcus, you're a loner. You always have been, the way you describe it. And you've never sought power. But some people need power, and they need to have power *over* someone. Preferably lots of someones. Taking away the Council's subjects—which is what you'd be doing—is a declaration of war."

I grinned at her. "Ever the optimist. I love your Pollyanna view of humanity."

"Kidding aside, Marcus, when I say *war*, I mean the first thing they'll try to do is take you out. You're not immune, or off-limits, or anything. And when the Bobs show up in a decade or two to investigate, they'll be met with a *fait accompli*."

"You're going just a little bit overboard, aren't you?"

She cocked her head at me. "Don't make the common mistake of thinking your opponents are stupid just because they don't see things your way, Marcus. They *know* you're a potential threat. And they also know you're sympathetic to the cause, if only because of..." Gina waved her hands to take in our location. "They'll have made taking you out a priority."

I stared at Gina, shaken. Logic said she was correct. And I was very public about my movements, about what I was doing at the moment, and so on. I realized that would have to change.

The Council had had administrative access to autofactories and printers for more than long enough now to be able to build things I didn't know about. And I'd been encouraging it.

"Okay, Gina. You win. We'll start taking this seriously." I looked around at the others. "So, what's the next step?"

"At this point, the ball is in their court," Gina replied. "On the other hand, your end run around them with the flying cities isn't something they can ignore. I think, as you say, the fun will come to us soon enough."

14. Friends

Howard
May 2218
Vulcan

"This is unbelievable," I said. "How is it that, with two hundred years of progress, men *still* have to wear ties?"

Bridget rolled her eyes at me as she adjusted the misbehaving article of clothing. Androids couldn't choke—I'd checked the blueprints—but something about a suit and tie just made me feel like I was being slowly strangled.

"You, sir, are a big baby." Bridget gave the knot a final tweak. "And despite your best efforts, you look great."

I grinned in response. "And as a reward, you'll let me skip—"

"Howard!"

I sighed, as theatrically as I could manage. "Yes, dear." Humming the Volga Boatmen's Song, I picked up my suit jacket.

Bridget said nothing, but the glare was communication enough.

* * *

The maître d' led us to the table and pulled out a chair for Bridget. I looked around the table at the two other couples, noting the same hangdog look on the men's faces that I was pretty sure was on mine. Some things just never changed, centuries or light-years away.

Bridget smiled and made introductions. Kumar and Reeda, Arnie and Sylvie, were friends of Bridget's from back in her biologist days. I wondered for a moment if it was odd that I'd never met them.

Arnie gazed at me intently, his eyes narrowed. "Honestly, Howard, if I didn't already know you're an android, I wouldn't ever have suspected."

Sylvie turned to him, jaw hanging. "Arnie! For crying out loud!"

"What? Are we supposed to ignore the elephant in the room? Is this a big secret?"

I noted that Kumar was trying to suppress a grin. Reeda seemed to be unable to decide who to support. I waved a hand in dismissal and smiled at Sylvie and Arnie. "No, he's right. I don't think I'd be able to take an entire evening of everyone dancing around the topic. Let's get it out of the way."

Arnie looked smug, and Sylvie glared at him. Before that could escalate, I continued, "And you wouldn't have known until I opened up my abdomen to get rid of my meal."

Bridget snorted, Kumar laughed out loud, and Reeda finally came down on Sylvie's side. Both women glared at me, then at Bridget.

"You two are made for each other," Sylvie said.

I looked up at the ceiling. "In my case, that's literally true."

I sat back in satisfaction as the entire table broke up. *Where are these tough crowds I keep hearing about?*

Arnie, wiping a tear from one eye, said, "You don't actually do that, do you? With the abdomen and..."

"No." I grinned back. "But I threaten it fairly often. Bridget has stopped paying attention, so It's nice to have some new victims."

The comedy festival had attracted a bit of attention, but now that we were quieting down, the other tables went back to their own business.

"So how lifelike are you?" Sylvie's face registered shock as she heard herself. "Oh, God, that came out wrong. I mean—"

"It's okay, Sylvie, I'm not that easily offended. We've tried to design the androids to be as realistic as possible, both to us and to other people. Which means pain, emotional reactions, reflexes, and so on. It's an ongoing project, of course."

"Hmm, does that include..."

I grinned. "Ongoing project."

Bridget rolled her eyes. "Can we order food now?"

I smiled at her and signaled the waiter.

Once he'd taken our orders, I gazed around the table. "Look, I'm human. Or at least, I was, once. I grew up in Minnesota; had sisters and parents, went to school, and so on. You wouldn't think anything of someone with a prosthetic arm, right? Just think of me as an extreme amputation case."

Bridget choked on her wine and went into a coughing fit. After some emergency back-patting and cleanup, I grinned at the others. "On the other hand, reflexes like that one, I can do without."

The rest of the meal passed without significant events. We talked, we laughed, we drank. I made sure to set my alcohol consumption below anyone else. A drinking competition would be blatantly unfair, of course.

Still, Kumar put away perhaps one or two too many, with the inevitable loosening of lips. As we were sitting back, starting at our empty desert plates, he grinned at me, his head slightly off kilter. "So, any plans to take over the world? You guys could do it, couldn't you? You have the high ground, all the weapons..."

Reeda glared at him, then drew back a clenched fist.

I held my hand up to stop her, and gave Kumar the stink eye. "Why does everyone always want to take over the world? I've never understood that. It sounds like a horrible job. Hell, no. We're going to deal with the Others, but other than that you guys are on your own."

I'd expressed the sentiment maybe a little more forcefully than intended, because eyebrows went up around the table.

"Look," I said, trying to smooth things over. "It takes a certain type of person to want to rule. Bob wasn't that type. None of us are. If anything, once this whole 'Others' thing blows over, we're more likely to just take off. So, no, not a long-term issue."

Kumar nodded, and the tension seemed to dissipate. But I was left with an uneasy feeling about my statement.

* * *

I pulled off the tie and tossed it onto the kitchen table. "Free, at last!"

Bridget grinned at me as she set the kettle in preparation for her end-of-day tea. "It went well. They seemed to accept you, once the initial awkwardness was taken care of."

"Did you perhaps prime Arnie to say that?" I gave her the evil eye.

"Not as far as you know."

I laughed. "Right. So, is there a bigger picture?"

Bridget stared at the kettle for a few moments, perhaps willing it to hurry up. "Howard, you and the other Bobs, you're kind of like bears or mountain lions—no complex society, mostly solitary animals, very little need to interact. And unlike those animals, you're also comfortable with each other. I'm sure having very similar attitudes about most things plays into it. But when it comes to other people, it gets more complicated."

I had to disagree about the *no complex society* comment, although I had a fair idea what she actually meant by it. But how to explain moots, the rules of VR visits, and so on? I decided to let it pass.

The kettle clicked and she was silent for a moment as she poured. "What I'd really like is for you to be old news instead of a novelty. Just an extreme amputation case, like you said. People need to see you as just another person."

"People in general?"

"And some specific people."

"Ah." *Yeah, there's that.* "Okay, Bridget. I've long since learned that you're thinking several steps ahead. I'll go along. Just as long as I don't have to wear the damned tie again."

"No promises. You have to suffer, too."

I chuckled, and sat with her as she settled down with her tea. While she sipped, I used the time to think about that last exchange with Kumar, and everything that it implied.

15. Enclaves

Riker
April 2227
Sol

I watched with satisfaction as the latest colony ships accelerated out of the Solar System. The situation had improved a little when the first wave of ships started returning from their trips, ready to take out another load. Now, between new construction and returning transports, we were starting to get some throughput.

Still not nearly enough, though. We were coming up on one million emigrants. A hundred trips down, fourteen hundred to go.

I scanned the report from Charles again. It hadn't magically changed since the first time. Damn.

I pinged him. "Hey, Charles. Just read your report. It's that bad?"

"Hi, Will." Charles popped in as he answered. "Yeah, we're having to put more and more drones into scavenging, which is taking equipment away from the construction effort. And we've got printers sitting idle some of the time, waiting for supplies. Right now, productivity is down about twenty percent from where it could be, and it's going to keep getting worse."

I swiped through the report as he talked. "No new caches of metals?"

"Naw, nothing we can find. The problem isn't that there's no metal left in the solar system, it's that there are no convenient concentrations of metal left. Everything accessible was long since mined out by humanity, and the war pulverized or vaporized a lot of the cities and military equipment. Most of the planetside metal is dust. Or rust. We've collected all the space junk that's easy to find—anything else is probably in weird long-period orbits. I've even got squads of roamers walking in lines along the ground, picking up metal scraps. We're really down to the dregs, Will."

I rubbed my forehead. "We're at, what? Eighty-two ships? Maybe we reach a hundred before it gets too difficult to find any more materials. Forty years per round-trip, average. That's two point five ships per year. So twenty five thousand people per year. Five hundred and sixty years to finish the job."

"We've talked before about building colony ships at other stars, Will. It's still an option."

"Yeah, I know. But there's so much ramp-up required. Plus you'd have to get a Bob to stay put to supervise. So far, not a lot of takers. Oliver over in Alpha Centauri, for instance, is concentrating on preparations for an Others' assault. Like it or not, Sol is still the best place to build colony ships. Except for the resources issue, of course."

"We keep going over the numbers. It doesn't get any better with repetition. We can keep the enclaves viable for maybe another fifty to a hundred years. And that's with every trick we've been able to come up with."

"Well, really," I said, "we can keep the enclaves going forever."

"Sure, by going underground or into the ice. Completely subterranean existence, completely dependent on the farm donuts and hydroponics."

"And on us, because in that position they'd have no industrial base."

"Um. The bottom line, though, is we'd be telling most of the population that they'll be spending the rest of their lives in a cave." Charles sat back and stared at the ceiling.

I looked up and realized that I'd never bothered to put any detail into the ceiling in my VR. It was a flat blue with no texture. I quickly added a popcorn finish, and placed a banner that said, "My eyes are down here."

Charles let out a surprised, barking laugh. He looked down at me, grinning. "Y'know, Will, you didn't used to have much of a sense of humor."

I smiled sadly back at him. "I think I'm trying to keep a bit of Homer alive."

Charles lost his own smile and nodded. We all missed Homer.

I stared into the middle distance, focused on nothing in particular. It wasn't just Homer. Butterworth, Julia Hendricks, and a couple of other members of our extended family had passed away in the last decade. Not people I'd particularly known, except by name, but it reminded me that, given enough time, everyone I knew would eventually be gone.

After a few moments of contemplative silence, Charles said, "We could stick everyone in stasis…"

"I've thought about it, Charles. Fourteen million stasis pods. That's about thirty colony ships worth of materials. Not only would we have to stop building ships, we'd have to cannibalize a dozen of the existing ones. I don't see the UN going for that."

"In the long term, it would make more sense."

"People don't think in the long term."

"Have you brought it up?"

I sighed. "No, and probably due to cowardice. But you're right, they should be allowed to decide. I'll bring it up today."

* * *

Representative Misra's gaze never wavered as she asked questions. One of the most level-headed of the UN delegates, she never got upset. If I could get her onside, I had a good possibility of pulling this off.

"You can build fourteen million stasis pods?"

"Yes, as I said, we'll have to cannibalize a dozen of the returning colony ships, as well as divert all future construction."

"How long to complete all the pods?"

"I think around fifty years, mostly due to supply issues."

"So, many of us will die of old age, regardless. Meanwhile, no new colony ships will go out."

"That's true, Representative Misra, but after the first dozen, any returning ships can still take people out."

Swarna Misra looked down at her desk for a moment, then looked back at the camera. "Here's the problem, Mr. Johansson.

Under the current system, about three hundred thousand more people will go out to colonies within our lifetimes. Under your proposed system, possibly half of the population—seven million people—will die of old age on Earth before pods are ready for them. The other half will get into pods, where they will remain for some indefinite amount of time, possibly centuries. Mathematically, your suggestion makes some sense. But emotionally, it is not attractive. At least while alive, we are masters of our destiny."

Reaching forward, she said, "I cannot endorse this plan. Sorry." She switched off her microphone and sat down.

Damn.

Next up was Minister MacIntyre. He had replaced Gerrold in New Zealand after the VEHEMENT situation. He was barely less hostile to me than Gerrold had been. Despite several clandestine investigations on my part, I hadn't been able to find any connection that would warrant the antipathy. I guess I would have to accept that I would never be New Zealand's favorite replicant.

"What assurances do we have that you'll even wake us up?" he asked, not even bothering with any warm-up remarks.

Oh, for crying out loud. "Because if that's how I felt, Minister, I could just leave right now with no subterfuge."

"So you are threatening us, now?"

I rolled my eyes, and I let the cameras see it.

The session went on for several hours, and the upshot was that it would be discussed and debated more at future sessions. Meanwhile, we would continue with the current schedule.

I sighed and closed my video window. Stupid humans.

16. The Departed

Marcus
March 2215
Poseidon

An angry mob faced off against the security personnel. "You do *not* have a right to prevent us from leaving!" someone yelled.

The security squad stood squarely between the citizens and the parked flyers. They weren't *quite* pointing their weapons at the crowd, but the threat was definitely there.

It seemed the Council had finally gotten their act together. Within minutes of my announcement that the fourth aerial city, Thark, was taking immigrants, security squads had moved in and cut people off from the flyers.

I'd been expecting them to come up with something eventually, although they seem to have figured it out a little more slowly than I'd have given them credit for. But that was okay. Time for phase 2.

Behind the crowd, opposite the security forces, a half-dozen cargo drones landed. I floated my observation drone up high enough to be seen and heard clearly, ordered the drones to open the cargo bay doors, and announced, "Buses for Thark are now loading. Please move to the back of the bus."

Within seconds, the crowd had loaded into the cargo drones. The security personnel gritted their teeth, and several of them made as if to point their weapons. The squad leader growled an order and they desisted.

I released a breath that I hadn't realized I'd been holding. For all my bravado, I knew I was engaged in a game of brinksmanship. If the Council decided to call my bluff, people could get hurt or killed. And that would be on me.

But we'd now loaded four cities without violence breaking out. A precedent of sorts had been established.

Very likely I'd be getting a call from Councilor Brennan any minute now.

* * *

Riker popped into my VR. "I just got an earful from the Poseidon Council. Fomenting revolution, are you?"

I bobbed my head back and forth, as I waved him to a chair. Riker sat down, accepted a coffee from Jeeves, and gazed at me silently, one eyebrow up.

"C'mon, Will, you know what they've been doing! Clamping down on travel, use of flyers, dictating jobs, living arrangements..."

"It's a unique situation, Marcus. Poseidon's got all the room you could want, but only if you're a fish."

I waved the comment away. "I understand the scarcity situation, but there's no aspect of *we're all in this together.* They just hand down pronouncements, and you do as told or else. And *or else* now includes consequences—anything from loss of privileges through house arrest all the way to incarceration. And if there's anything dumber than jailing people when you need every single person working, I've never seen it."

Will sighed. "Okay, bud. Off the record, I agree with you. And I've read your blog about the monitoring, which I find as galling as you do. But the official line from the Council is that you're interfering with the development plans for the planet."

I rolled my eyes. "Of course I'm *interfering.* That's the whole point! But," I held up a finger in a lecturing pose. "What I'm *not* doing is screwing up the timetable. Putting people on aerial cities spreads the population quicker, gets people off the mats quicker, ramps up the technology quicker... A planet-full of aerial cities would be the ideal situation. Come to that, we could do the same with the *floating* cities. But the Council is building just enough of them for industrial and commercial purposes, with residential use not even on the priority list. They don't want people out there on dozens of different independent cities, because there's no way to *control* people in that scenario."

"I don't know how we managed to end up with a bunch of reactionary types in charge. It sure doesn't go with the stereotype of laidback tropical islanders. Sharma would never have allowed this to develop."

I sighed. "Ephemerals, Will. They die."

"Don't let Bill hear you say that."

"Yeah, I know." I got up and started to pace. "Look, bottom line, I'm not doing anything in any way illegal or immoral. It's like Howard with his distillery. It pissed off Cranston, but it was a completely reasonable business venture." I turned to Will. "And speaking of, aren't you one of the guys who got Cranston deposed, because you didn't like his policies?"

Will grinned at me. "I didn't do it, nobody saw me, and you can't prove it anyway."

"Whereas I'm a little more obvious about it. But it's the same problem: how do we keep working with a government that we believe is wrong on a basic moral level?"

"Okay, Marcus. I've talked to you, which is what the Council asked me to do." Will got up and gave me a quick salute. "Just don't get anyone killed, all right?" Without waiting for a response, he popped out.

Yeah. That's the trick, isn't it?

Sighing, I pulled up the latest reports. Two more cities, almost ready to launch. Kal had come up with a bunch of suggestions for the next generation design, based on feedback from early residents. And Thark was full, and in full operation.

It was all looking good. But sooner or later, the Council would decide on a strategy. I couldn't completely suppress a feeling of dread.

17. Underway

Icarus
January 2232
Interstellar space

The phrase *middle of nowhere* took on an entirely new meaning when you were between star systems. I sat in the middle of a sphere of empty space, with nothing more than the occasional lonely hydrogen atom for literally light-years. The Orion-Cygnus arm of the Milky Way stretched across the sky, annotated by overlays showing distances, readings, and the location of local tourist attractions. *Sixty trillion miles to next gas station.* I snorted at the thought.

"Status check."

I looked up at the call from Dae. Right on time, as usual. Well, why not? I didn't begrudge him his tics, and he didn't tease me about my wraparound planetarium view.

I returned to my library and opened up my calculation page before responding. "Everything's in the green."

"Your tau is a little low."

I glanced at the status board. "I was drawing slightly ahead of you. I had to cut back my acceleration just a tad."

"I would have preferred if you'd extended your curve instead, Ick. We need to be synchronized."

“Understood. Still lots of time to adjust.”

“Um. And on that subject, how are the calcs going?”

“So-so. I still can’t find a definitive answer. Of course, it’s not like anyone’s ever done this before.”

Daedalus chuckled. “Yeah, granted. Have you determined a safe minimum tau, though?”

“Sure,” I answered. “But it’s probably overkill.”

“I’m good with overkill.”

I could hear the grin in his voice. “As am I, Dae. As are all the Bobs. And we have the tau for that. Or will, by the time we get there. Which won’t be long on our clocks.” I smiled into the air. “I guess we could get ourselves into the Bobiverse Book of Records with this. Highest recorded tau by a Heaven vessel.”

“Uh huh. You thinking of heading for the galactic core?”

That got a chuckle from me. “Y’know, once we’re done—”

“—assuming this works—”

“Sure, sure. But it’s not a terrible idea, really.”

There was a moment of silence. “I was going to laugh at you, Ick. But the more I think of it… Really, what’s holding us here?”

“Homo sideria, baby. Maybe it’s time to join up.”

Daedalus popped in, holding a coffee. “Or start it up. Even Mario hasn’t really left the area. I don’t think anyone qualifies yet.”

I waved up a patio chair for Dae, his favorite seating device, and popped up a coffee for myself. “You think we’re timid as a group?”

“No, maybe just creatures of habit. And comfort zone.”

I nodded slowly, letting a grin form. “So, you up for it?”

“Hell, why not?”

I raised my cup in salute. “To Sagittarius A-Star. May it not fry us to twigs.”

Dae made a sweeping motion with his hand. “Just have to make this delivery first.”

18. Arrival at 82 Eridani

Mack
October 2220
82 Eridani

I was incredibly lucky to have been preparing to go out with a set of colony ships when 82 Eridani was secured. The vote by the colonists to change destinations was barely a formality, probably the most one-sided vote ever registered on Earth, pre or post-war.

And now, twenty-five years later, we'd arrived. Three colony ships, two from Vancouver Island and one from Japan, would be the first human beings to settle this system.

The inner of the two habitable planets resembled Venus in the old pulp-fiction novels—thick, impenetrable jungle, heavy clouds and mist, and large, hungry animals. The outer planet was cooler, with predominantly steppe climates. But it also had about seven percent heavier gravity than Earth. The second generation would adapt. The first would have sore feet for the rest of their lives.

And the larger moon of the outer planet was habitable. Marginally. It would require a serious beefing up of atmospheric pressure. But thanks to years of research and, frankly, screwing around with the environment on Ragnarök, Bill had solutions ready. We would have the atmosphere up to Earth normal within fifty years.

I checked the L4 points for each planet, looking for the materials caches that Verne's notes said he'd left for us. Sure enough, a couple of million tons of various elements, bundled up with radio beacons attached, all ready and available for manufacturing. Awesome.

Well, time to report back. I pinged the colony ships, then invited them into my VR. Isaac, Jack, and Owen popped in. This group had no particular VR theme or style, and all three affected simple jean-and-tee-shirt ensembles. Original Bob had always been a bit button-down, so it was surprising to see the same variation in three clones at the same time. One of these years, someone would have to do a study and see if there were any patterns to the cloning variations.

"Hey, Mack," Isaac said. "How's it looking?"

"Well, the stuff Verne left for us is still there. The system appears to still be Medeiros-free, which is a bonus, of course."

I arranged holograms and data sheets for the three planets in midair, then turned to the other Bobs. "We need to name the planets. The humans seem to accept suggested names from us, but leave it to them and, well, we're still waiting on KKP."

"I thought it was *Quilt*?" Jack grinned.

"It might end up as that just through common usage. But the *official* name is still KKP, until they can agree on something."

Jack waved the comment away, not really interested. "Looking at the pictures, I really like Owen's suggestion of *Valhalla* for the moon of planet three. Can we settle that one?"

I looked around. Everyone nodded. "Okay, Valhalla it is," I said. "I agree, that's a good one. Now, the primary?"

"Asgard?"

"That's a little trite, don't you think?" I gave Jack the evil eye.

He shrugged, unrepentant. "I like themes."

No one but me seemed to have a problem with it, so I shrugged. "Let's take it as tentative. Now, planet two?"

"Tartarus?"

"Oh, sure, if you don't want anyone to settle there, ever."

Jack grinned and shrugged again. "Well, if we want to stay on theme, there's Muspelheim."

"That sounds like some kind of rash," Isaac interjected. We all laughed.

"Jotunheim?"

We all looked at Owen. "Land of giants," I said. "Actually kind of appropriate."

"And sticking to the theme!" Jack exclaimed.

"Okay, then, vote on those three. "In favor? Opposed?" I grinned at the guys. "Carried. Looks like we have a Norse mythology going here."

I sat down and grabbed a Coke. "So, now that the fun stuff is out of the way, how will we handle the settling?"

"We'll wake up a rep from each colony group, Let them decide." Isaac waved a hand at the holograms. "There's enough space on Asgard and Jotunheim that they could reasonably pick the same planet."

"Hmm, jungle planet, heavy planet, or can't-breathe planet. This should be fun."

* * *

Katsu Ito, leader of the Japanese enclave, was a Harvard-educated intellectual who had found himself in a position of power despite all his attempts to dodge the position. Or so he explained it, anyway. At the moment, he was hugging a coffee in Exodus-43's common area. I'd printed up one of the androids from Howard's plans and was sitting across the table, waiting for him to focus.

He looked up at me, eyes still not quite tracking. Bobbing his head slightly, he said, "You're not a video. But you look like Riker. What the—?"

I smiled back at him. "Android, sir. Technology marches on. I'm Mack, the replicant who was assigned to escort the colony ships to 82 Eridani."

Christie Campbell, the Vancouver Island enclave leader, was hugging a cup of chamomile tea. I spared a moment to be perplexed. The stasis pods didn't freeze the subject. There was no reason to be cold, or to need to warm up. But when decanted, people almost universally wanted to hug something warm. Weird.

She peered at us with one eye, evidently in somewhat worse shape than Katsu. "I think the takeaway, Ser Ito, is that we have arrived and there are some decisions to make."

"That is correct, Ser Campbell." I nodded to her. "I've prepared summaries for you to read while you hug your warm-up drinks. We can talk in an hour or so." I nodded again, got up, and left. I could have just switched off right in front of them, but I didn't think that shoving my artificiality in their faces would be politically astute.

* * *

I came back an hour later, to find the two colony leaders in deep discussion. They looked up as I sat down.

"Have you come to any decisions?" I asked.

"I believe we have," Ser Campbell replied. "The Canadian contingent will settle on Asgard. Your first recommendation for a site will be acceptable." She turned her head and nodded to Mr. Ito, conceding the floor.

He wore a tight smile as he spoke. "We will settle the second planet, and we will accept your recommendation of a more northerly location where the ecosystem is less overwhelming. However, the name..."

I raised my eyebrows.

"Jotunheim? It sounds like someone sneezing." He shook his head. "Unacceptable. We prefer Takama-ga-hara."

I quickly referenced my libraries. It took less than five milliseconds to find the definition. "The dwelling place of the Kami. Nice. And perhaps appropriate. However, westerners will shorten it to Takama. Just sayin'."

He grinned. "An acceptable risk."

"Okay, done." I returned the smile. "Jack will be pissed. His theme is kaput."

* * *

Jack popped into my VR, invoked a La-Z-Boy, and plopped down on it. "Aagh! Friggin' whiney, complainy, ungrateful hoo-mahns. We hates 'em."

"What now?"

"Turns out the jungles of Takama stink. And not just any old stink. The kind of stink that makes you wish you were back on Earth. Oh, and the gravity of Asgard is too high. Like that's a surprise. But apparently it's our fault, like we adjusted the gravity meter badly. And the sun is too bright, the clouds are too dark, the bugs are too buggy, the hills are too hilly..."

"You exaggerate."

"Possibly. A bit." Jack sat forward and scrubbed his face with his hands. "Remind me why we're doing this?"

"Because we're wonderful, caring people?"

"Speak for yourself."

I grinned at him. "Actually Jack, it brings up a point. Dexter's been getting great results on Vulcan and Romulus by concentrating on making the inhabitants as independent as possible. Things like giving them control over the printer groups, making sure they have their own cargo ships, and so on. Maybe we should move in that direction early."

Jack shrugged. "That's up to you more than anyone. The three of us will be leaving as soon as we've finished offloading the colonists. You're the one who has to put up with them long-term."

"Mm. Well, one step at a time."

* * *

Ser Campbell was not amused. Okay, note to self, no attempts at levity in the future.

"Fine, Ser Campbell. Exactly what would you like me to do about the mosquitoes?"

"Mosquitoes have nothing on these flying vampires, Mr. Johansson. It would be nice if they fell over dead after biting someone, but apparently humans are biocompatible. There must be something that can be done to control them?"

Cupid bugs on Vulcan, Ickies on KKP, and Super Vampire Power Mosquitoes here. It would appear that the universe had certain themes that it liked to re-use. Wonderful. "You understand that if we clear them, there will be ecological impacts?"

"I really don't care. I have three bites myself that are keeping me awake at night, and I can state truthfully that I would happily take a hammer to each and every one of the little…pests."

I had to admit, of all the things I didn't miss about being biological, mosquitoes ranked very high. "Got it. All right, Ser Campbell. I think I can adapt Howard's Cupid killers for something a little smaller."

Ser Campbell nodded, apparently mollified. "I don't suppose you can do anything about the gravity?" She gave me a small smile.

"Afraid not." I chuckled. "Contrary to popular rumor, there isn't actually a gravity meter."

She sighed and nodded. "Ser Ito has described the odor of Takama well enough that I wouldn't seriously consider suggesting to my citizens that we move. However, when Valhalla becomes available, we might experience a lot of emigration."

"Mm, yeah, 0.8 gravity would be a significant relief. But that's maybe fifty years away. Your children may be more satisfied with the status quo."

Ser Campbell nodded without comment. We said our goodbyes and disconnected.

I checked the archives, and quickly found Howard's plans for the Cupid bug killers. They could be scaled down for something more the size of a wasp. I sent the plans to the printer queue with a feeling akin to relief. One more item down.

19. Cities Attacked

Marcus
September 2215
Poseidon

"They've done it. They've actually gone and done it!" Vinnie waved his phone like a weapon as he stomped toward me. Vinnie was not physically imposing, but somehow he managed to look like an unstoppable juggernaut when in his *angry marching* mode.

"And by *it*, you mean..." Kal looked up from his tablet, where he'd been working on an engineering design for a new fish harvesting system.

A dozen of us sat or reclined on the ring of grass that formed the periphery of the flying city of Amhor. Most residents who could manage it performed their daily duties on lawn chairs or even on blankets. The air circulation systems were very carefully designed to keep the air temps down around a comfortable spring day in our domed environment—and it helped that fibrex didn't trap infrared like traditional glass.

Life was hell, but we tried to bear up under the burden.

Vinnie threw himself down on the grass and tossed his phone onto a nearby side table. "The Council has declared us deserters and forbidden any contact. They're confiscating any assets owned by any city resident that they can get their hands on, and issued warrants for our arrest."

This wasn't really unexpected. In fact, it had taken a month longer than the date I'd originally estimated. If the Council had any brains at all, they'd be trying to pull the teeth of the biggest single threat to their rule—me—right about now. I checked my feeds and, sure enough, I'd been locked out of colony patrol, monitoring, defense, and infrastructure channels.

Damn. That meant I would no longer be able to spend my time monitoring things for them, fixing things for them, running things for them…boo hoo. I grinned, and Kal looked at me quizzically.

"I think I've just been fired." I shrugged at him. "Spares me the trouble of quitting, I guess."

"What are we going to do?" asked one of the planning techs, a blonde woman named Freida.

"Nothing," I replied. "I've exchanged words with the Council the last couple of months. I've made it clear to them that we, and especially I, won't fire the first shot. But that if they try to get their way by violence or war, they'd have the entire Bobiverse to deal with. So I don't actually expect any shooting. Just legal maneuvering and threats."

"And economic sanctions. They've cut off all trade, all contact." Kal shrugged at me.

"What exactly are they cutting us off from, Kal?" Denu leaned back on an elbow and glared at Kal with an eyebrow arched. "We have a third of the planet's population, but we produce half the food calories. Most of the technical people transferred to the cities in the first month. Manufacturing is off-planet, so we have as good access to it as they do—"

"That may not be entirely true," I said. Everyone looked at me.

I shrugged. "I've been checking statuses as we've been talking. The Council seems to have managed to garrison all the materials stocks in the Lagrange points." I tried to wave up an image, then remembered that I wasn't in VR. Instead, I sent a feed to any tablets in our group. "I guess it explains why they were so slow to act—they were taking the extra time to get into position. My drones are showing Council security forces occupying strategic locations around the stockpiles. And," I added, shaking my head, "looks like they've laid claim to the Lagrange autofactories as well."

“Are the Bobs going to take that lying down?” Kal glared at me.

I chuckled in response. “Well, *the Bobs* consists of me, in this system, so not very much of a threat. I have ship busters, but they’re only useful in a full-scale engagement. I’ve got some roamers, but I wouldn’t want to sacrifice them in a guerilla war. I have my printers, but it would take time to set up a full autofactory, and more time to get mining going again.”

“So we’re dead in the water?”

“For the moment, as far as they know,” I responded. “But they also know we’ll rebuild our own resources in short order. They have to bring us to our knees before we can do so.”

“How?”

I shrugged. “Resource interdiction, which they’ve already done; denial of food sources, which they incorrectly *think* they can do; and cutting us off from any space assets, which I’m surprised to say they haven’t—”

At that moment, the signal from my decoy cut off. “Son of a bitch. They did it.”

All heads turned to stare at me. I shrugged and gave them a twisted grin. “They just blew me up!”

20. Life

Howard
June 2219
HIP 14101

Finally.

The drone flew through Odin's upper-middle cloud layer, casual as you please, as if umpty-ump of its ancestors hadn't gone down in screaming flames trying to achieve this milestone. Odin was slightly smaller than Saturn, but far more meteorologically active, due to being closer to its primary.

All of which made a difficult environment for adapting a SURGE-powered drone.

I watched readings carefully as the drone cruised through the atmosphere. While the chemistry wasn't actually corrosive as such, it was definitely chemically active. The multiple possibilities for exothermic reactions made me hopeful that I would find something that I might be able to call *life.*

I had no idea if all this work would ultimately pay off, but it was certainly interesting. The view from the drone was incomparable. I could see hundreds of kilometers down through clear patches of atmosphere into the depths, where colored masses of organics formed massive floating clouds. The layering was pretty obvious—Odin's atmosphere was heavily stratified both latitudinally and vertically.

Then I saw it—a group of dots, far ahead, seemingly flying in formation. I aimed the drone toward them. By the time I got to within a couple of kilometers, I was able to resolve the targets—giant blimps, with tentacles spread round them.

There was no question they were alive. They didn't quite resemble zeppelins, and they didn't quite resemble jellyfish, and they didn't quite resemble squid. They were some weird mashup of all three. Perhaps fifty meters long, with tentacles—the exact number varied between individuals. They moved as a flock.

The flock didn't react defensively to the drone, which was probably far too small to present as a threat. I circled them a dozen times, each individual following my trajectory with something that might have been an eye on a stalk.

The drone's readings finally moved far enough into the red, and I had to stop and bring it back—post-mortem examinations were still a large part of my development effort, and this one had been wildly successful. As the drone flew up to my location in orbit, I played the video records again and again.

Finally, I turned off the playback and stared into space, a smile forming on my face. Bridget would love this. No biologist could possibly resist.

* * *

"But, that's—incredible!" Bridget seemed to have become permanently bug-eyed as she scanned through the videos. "They are absolutely alive. Are they carbon-based? DNA-based?"

"Probably, and who knows?" I grinned at her from an inset window on her tablet. I hadn't wanted to take the time to deploy Manny, so I'd just phoned.

"My God, Howard. And you have forever to study them…"

"You could, too, Bridget."

"Howard…" Bridget gave me the stink-eye.

"Sorry Bridge. I know, I promised. It just slipped out."

She responded with one of her patented nuclear smiles, then turned back to the videos. "I *would* love to see them."

"Wish granted. I'll be right over."

Bridget raised an eyebrow. "Howard, you are oddly well-prepared. Am I being set up?"

I grinned and winked at her as I disconnected.

* * *

Bridget looked at the device in her hands—a light helmet-shaped frame, with embedded sensors, integrated goggles, and headphones. On the coffee table in front of her lay a pair of very techie-looking gloves.

"And what happens when I put this stuff on?" She asked, one eyebrow raised.

"Well, this was the state of the art in video game gear, just before FAITH stomped on that particular industry. Full-immersion VR, or the twenty-first-century version of it, anyway. I found the plans in the libraries, and printed this up."

"And what happens when I put this stuff on?" Bridget repeated.

"You get to visit me at my place. And get a better look at the Odin wildlife."

She nodded, slipped on the gloves, and donned the helmet.

And popped into my VR.

I put Manny on standby and returned to VR. I was sitting in my beach chair, grinning at her as she slowly turned to take in the scene. I'd made Bridget's avatar from images taken when I first met her, and it was an almost physical jolt to see her standing there, young again.

I stood up and walked over. "This is a very limited interface, of course. You can't fully interact—although you can pick up objects or feel me holding your hands—" I took her hands in mine. "—and you can move around using the game interface."

"All right. So, show me."

I activated the videos and data files that I'd accumulated on the native Odin life. Bridget gasped and stared at the images. She walked over to them and began paging and swiping through the data. I felt a moment of pleasure that our user interface was so obviously intuitive. But, of course, the Bobs had been living it and tweaking it for around a hundred years, now.

"I've been cataloguing things," I said. "There's an incredibly diverse ecosystem. It has plant-equivalents that build organics from sunlight and raw materials; and animals, which eat plants or other animals."

Bridget took a moment to smile at me, then went back to the

videos and files. She muttered constantly, a specialist immersed in her chosen field.

I sat down and watched her work, a glow of joy battling with a vaguely guilty feeling. This wasn't really about the Odin native life. I could have emailed those files to her. I'd promised Bridget that I wouldn't hassle her about replication. Well, I was as capable of lawyering as the next person. I couldn't *say* anything, but non-verbal persuasions were fair game.

Eventually, Bridget noticed her hands. She stopped, examined them closely. Then she grabbed a handful of her hair and pulled it into view. She turned to me with a hurt look. "Howard, really? This is a dirty trick."

"Hey, fair's fair. I'm perpetually thirty-one in here. And that is how I see you. Always will. I'm not trying to be underhanded."

"You are an evil, evil man. And a lawyer." Her tone was disapproving, but she couldn't suppress a small smile.

"But you repeat yourself..."

Bridget laughed, then gestured around her. "And the tropical beach thing is totally coincidental as well, right?"

"Hey, I have to have something. You should see Marvin's VRs. Now there's a man with too much time on his hands."

Bridget gazed at me with an expression that I had trouble categorizing. Amusement? Longing? Affection? At least the hurt look was gone.

"You have a nice world here, Howard. But when I go back to the other one, I've still got gray hair." She waved at the videos. "Those could have been displayed on my wall monitor. I understand your arguments, but this isn't something I want." She reached up to her head, and disappeared from VR.

I quickly activated Manny. I 'woke up' in Bridget's living room, standing at parade rest. Bridget was just removing the gloves.

Before I could begin apologizing, she came over and put her arms around me and rested her head on my shoulder. I wrapped her in a hug, and everything else stopped mattering.

21. The Return

Bill
June 2223
82 Eridani

I was visiting Mack at 82 Eridani. I tried to stay on top of things at the different sites, and to be honest, I needed a break. The Others had just finished 'harvesting' the Pav homeworld, and several years of observing their technique hadn't blunted the emotional turmoil.

I sat in one of Mack's lawn chairs, blowing on a coffee to cool it down. Turned out Mack liked the ritual involved in cooling the coffee until it was drinkable. I could have just adjusted it, but that would be rude.

Mack took a sip of his own coffee, then continued his report. "Things are looking good. The Canadian colony on Asgard is doing well—much better, now, actually, since the vampire mosquitoes are being brought under control."

"Super Vampire Power Mosquitoes," I corrected.

"*Mutant* Super Vampire Power Mosquitoes," he quipped. "Honestly, Bill, Original Bob would have run screaming from the place. You remember how our skin reacted to even itty-bitty mosquito bites?"

"Yup. Fine, Nordic skin." I grinned at him. "Why do you think I haven't asked for pictures?"

Mack nodded, still grinning. "Anyway, the mosquito killers are one of the more popular pieces of automation in New Vancouver. I just have to say 'mosquito killers' and I can get anything approved on the printer schedule."

"And speaking of inconveniences, how is the Japanese colony doing with their unique problem?"

Mack laughed. "You are, of course, carefully not referring to the elephant in the room? The very stinky elephant?" He waggled his eyebrows. "Or maybe it's just what the elephant left behind?"

"Yeah, that one," I said, chuckling. "Seriously, they can't get used to it?"

"It's seasonal, Bill, and affected by wind and weather. It turns out to be a common plant in the ubiquitous swamps. Sort of a local version of skunk cabbage, but much more potent."

"And what are they going to do about it?"

"Nuking has been suggested," Mack said, deadpan.

"Seriously?"

"I don't think they were serious, Bill, but it *was* brought up. I checked it out with the android, once, to see for myself, figuratively speaking. Lemme tell you, it's bad. I disabled olfactory input after that."

"So, on a more realistic note, what can they do?"

He shrugged. "Draining the swamps, developing something to kill off the plants, breed a less smelly version of the plants that will outcompete the wild version...and nuking."

I shook my head. "Don't get involved. Just...don't."

"Works for me." Mack grinned back. "Anyway, I'm too busy with the space-based industry. Verne collected a lot of raw materials into the Lagrange points, but between two large colonies and all the equipment on Valhalla for the terraforming..." He shrugged. "Yeah, I'm going through it pretty fast. I've got drones and roamers flying around the system, looking for more—"

Right in the middle of Mack's sentence, I found myself back in my own VR. "Guppy, what happened?"

[Interface with other vessel was terminated abruptly. No shutdown handshake.]

What the hell?

I attempted to ping Mack, but got nothing. "Guppy, try every option you have. Try to get any comms going at all with Mack or anything in the area."

[Aye.]

I waited for several intolerable milliseconds. What could have taken Mack out like that? Or was it just a communications issue of some kind?

[SCUT Link relay has been acquired to several onboard roamers. Vessel is heavily damaged, replicant is offline.]

"What? Give me a connection to one of them."

Guppy handed me a connection and I entered the roamer.

I stared, shocked, at a view of empty space through a huge rent in the side of Mack's vessel. Shards of metal and pieces of equipment floated around and caromed off of walls and other flotsam.

What the hell caused this?

I thought immediately of the Others. Could they have sent an expedition here to learn more about us? No, that didn't make sense. They didn't know about this system.

Then, movement. An outline shifted against the starry backdrop. I ran image analysis against several frames from the roamer's video, and was able to extract a silhouette.

Medeiros.

The bastard must have coasted up to Mack's location and hit him with a missile from short range.

There was no time to deal with the rage, though. I left the roamer for a moment, jacked myself up to maximum frame-rate, and pondered the situation.

Two milliseconds later, I returned to normal time, and sent an all-Bobs text at high priority. *Medeiros in 82 Eridani. Mack taken out. Need Bobs to locate and connect with all available AMIs. Coordinate with my Guppy.*

"Guppy, inspect and inventory. Get me a report on the state of Mack's vessel."

[Aye]

Without waiting for a response, I returned to my roamer. Medeiros' exact plans were unknown, but there were several possibilities, all of which had to be blocked.

Several texts came in from Other Bobs who had connected with other roamers on board or out by the autofactories. I began giving orders.

Bobs on board: protect replicant matrix, sequester or destroy any SCUT, SUDDAR or weapon tech. Check reactor for possibility of self-

destruct. If anyone can get a roamer onto Medeiros' ship, do so. We need him tagged.

Bobs at autofactories: Gather and inventory printers. We have to be prepared to keep them out of his hands.

Any other Bobs, check in.

I returned my attention to the Brazilian craft, which was edging up to Mack's ship. At that moment, Medeiros performed a SUDDAR scan on us. I froze, as did every roamer on board. No sense showing him what was still active. The scan lasted less than a second, and the Brazilian kept edging in. The safest thing would have been for him to blow us up. Either he was hoarding his missiles, or he wanted the Heaven vessel as intact as possible.

A text from Thor came in. *Mack's cube is intact.*

The image that Thor had sent with the text left no doubt. Mack's cube had escaped the zone of destruction. That was both good and bad. Good, because we hadn't permanently lost a Bob. Bad because it was one of the items that Medeiros might be going for. A cube could be put up on a cradle and either infected with something, as Homer had been, or even tortured.

Thor, get the cube out of here. Just jump. If it looks like you'll be captured, destroy it.

Thor responded immediately. *Ten four.*

Who's got eyes on the reactor? I asked.

Oliver responded. *It's toast. No possibility of a self-destruct.*

Damn. That meant this would have to be done the hard way. It also meant we were running on power cells. At some point, the SCUT transceiver would give out, and that would be it for our access to 82 Eridani.

I didn't have time to ponder the alternatives. *Okay, guys. Disassemble all tech, start flinging pieces. Nothing survives. Oliver, can you gather the SCUT and a few power cells?*

Will do.

Movement from the Brazilian attracted my attention. The cargo doors opened, and a number of roamers jumped in the direction of Mack's ship.

I sent a general alert. *Prepare to repel boarders.*

In moments, a half-dozen roamers joined me at the rent in Mack's hull.

There were twice as many of them, so I had no real illusions about winning the battle. Our roamers had no particular advantage in this situation. The best we could do was to hold them off until the sabotage crew could get it done.

The enemy roamers came straight in, no finesse, no feints. And why shouldn't they? Straight numerical advantage was a strategy all its own.

The battle lasted almost two minutes. Roamers are very tough devices—they're specifically designed to be able to operate with up to half their legs missing. The plasma cutters were the weapon of choice on both sides. The battle resembled, no kidding, one of those old Errol Flynn swordfight melee scenes, as long as you imagined giant spiders instead of actors in tights. Roamers parried and riposted all over the cargo bay, the occasional errant leg floating through the mix.

Finally, though, they took us out. The last roamer, crewed by Jacques, put up a great fight, wedged into the axial corridor so that no one could get by. But an attack from two opponents at once took out his cutter limb, and that was it. In moments, he was scrap.

How did we do? I group-texted. The situation was far too volatile for any kind of VR meetup, and in fact, I imagined everyone had given up VR for the duration.

Mack is well out of here. Two roamers in attendance, Thor responded. *We'll slice and dice if necessary.*

All remaining onboard SUDDAR and SCUT tech is toothpicks, someone else added.

Except for the transceiver, Oliver said. *And I'll destroy that if it looks like it'll be taken.*

I thought for a moment. *Okay guys, let's do as much damage to this asshole as possible. Let him have the hulk; instead, let's go for his vessel.*

There were acknowledgements, and I watched from a piggyback feed as the five surviving roamers still on-board leaped across space toward the Brazilian.

Unfortunately, Medeiros was ready for us. A half-dozen roamers leaped out of his hold to intercept. Another cutter-fight ensued, this one in free-fall between the ships. Roamers had small compressed-air nozzles for free-fall maneuvering, but those wouldn't last long. Our roamers attempted to get feet on metal as quickly as possible, with the opponents attempting to block us or toss us off.

Less than a minute later, we found to our surprise that we'd won the fight. Two of our roamers still survived, one only barely. But on a *last man standing* basis, it was enough.

Medeiros apparently thought so as well, because his ship backed rapidly away from the area before we could land on his hull. I had a pretty good idea what was coming. A few seconds later, my suspicions were confirmed, as a missile appeared from the distance.

Looks like we're done, guys.

The missile arrived, and once again, I was back in my VR.

"Guppy, what do we have?"

[Replicant matrix is on a ballistic trajectory with two roamers attending. Four drones with SCUT comms have been located, attending the autofactories. One is on the way to retrieve the matrix. HIC71683-8 is in control. Eight more groups in the outer system are several days away at full acceleration.]

I smiled despite myself at Guppy's response. For some reason, Guppy refused to identify any Bob by name. It was their serial number or nothing. I kept promising myself I'd look into it, someday, but I knew I wouldn't.

This particular replicant, Isaac, was one of Bart's early clones, senior even to Oliver. He had connected with one of the attendant drones and was racing to pick up Mack's matrix, along with the two roamers.

Okay, everyone. I broadcast. *Emergency moot in the pub. Video attendance for those of you currently controlling devices.*

I popped over to the Moot VR and configured the pub. Within moments, a half-dozen video images and a dozen more Bobs had popped in.

I looked around, doing a quick evaluation from metadata. "Thanks for your quick response, guys. So, here's what we have: a Brazilian vessel seems to have managed to sneak into 82 Eridani and take out Mack. Unfortunately, he's the only Bob in-system, and he didn't have any clones going."

"Where's he from, d'you think?" asked Oliver.

I shook my head. "I couldn't get a good enough look—"

"I did," Loki interjected. "I was in the group fighting out between the ships, and I got a better angle on the vessel. It's the one from Alpha Centauri. Definitely a different series from the Medeiri that we took down in 82 Eridani."

"Well, that's interesting." I rubbed my chin. "Is Calvin or Goku here?" I looked around for a moment, but no joy. "I guess not. Anyway, I remember that they were pretty sure the Medeiros they chased out of Alpha Centauri wasn't complete."

"Didn't have his autofactory tech loaded, yet," Oliver added.

"Right, which makes his strategy pretty obvious. Take out the resident Bob, then take over the autofactories." I thought for a moment. "Can we protect the autofactories?"

"Not a chance." Loki shrugged. "Four—well, three for now—drones and some miscellaneous roamers and mining equipment? Not much to work with. Mack had everything geared for a developing colony. He wasn't even working on a cohort."

"Should we just destroy them?" asked Isaac.

"I'd prefer not to. Otherwise they are dead in the water until another Bob gets there. And who is closest, anyway?"

I looked up in thought. "Hank's at P Eridani, a little under eleven light years; Tau Ceti and Vulcan are about twelve; and of course Epsilon Eridani at twelve point five. At least a decade for any help, no matter how you look at it."

"That's way too long to have a Brazilian wandering around the system, making nasty."

"But what's he going to do?" Loki looked around, palms up in an imploring gesture. "He can't make more of him, he can't make movers to drop rocks on our colonies, he can't make weapons…"

"I don't want to find out," I replied. "Maybe he has a printer in his cargo hold. Maybe he gets hold of one of ours. Maybe he has plenty, and he just wanted to get rid of Mack, and I'm wrong about the other stuff."

"Well, that's the interesting thing," Isaac said. "The missile that finally took out Mack's ship wasn't military grade, not by a long shot. And if the first missile had been military grade, there wouldn't have been anything left in the first place. I think Medeiros has, or had, some kind of factory set up somewhere, and made some home-brew explosive systems."

I nodded in thought. "We keep dismissing him as not an engineer, but that's probably facile. Brazil would have uploaded a lot of military knowledge, and improvising explosives is not a huge leap. He could have produced something like busters, but with a payload at the front end. It wouldn't have to be terrifically efficient."

"So we can't say how many missiles or whatever that he has onboard." Isaac rubbed his chin. "Although he'd have to go back to his factory to restock, assuming it's in-system."

"My feeling is that it's not. Calvin and Goku took out Alpha Centauri back in 2163. That's sixty years ago. It's only nineteen lightyears from 82 Eridani, so where's he been all this time? In-system, skulking around?"

"Nope," Loki replied. "We took 82 Eridani in 2195. He'd have been here by then, and we did a thorough scan of the system."

I sighed, and rubbed my forehead. "Okay, so it's likely that he stopped at some other system for a couple of decades and built up some manufacturing capability. Probably not a lot, or he'd have proper missiles. He loaded up, then continued to here, which presumably he knew was a target system for Brazil."

"That still doesn't sound quite right, Bill."

"I agree, Isaac. But there's only so much we can deduce from what we know, and we're probably over the line into speculation, now." I looked around. "Who's controlling the roamers that are with Mack?"

"Well, no one, now," Oliver replied. "As soon as Medeiros blew up Mack's vessel, we lost SCUT comms. Any surviving roamers will be operating autonomously on the last orders we gave them."

"Can we link up to roamers through drone SCUT?" Loki asked.

"Sure," Will responded. "We've been doing it for years in Sol, when dealing with things in the outer system. It's too much trouble to set up a separate comms station."

I turned to Will and grinned. "Glad to have you here. How much of this did you catch?" He hadn't been here when we started, so I knew he was late to the party.

Will nodded to me. "I jacked and played back the session recording. I'm up to date." Turning to Loki, he said, "It's just a small software patch. I'll post it for you."

Loki nodded. "So, we have four drones, which means we have four loci of control in the system. Not that we have that much to control. The stuff in the outer system will take longer to get back, and I'm not sure if we should be bringing them in-system unless we have a plan."

Oliver cut in. "Guys, I calculate that we have at most three hours before Medeiros gets to the nearest Lagrange factory. Can we deal with the printers first?"

There was silence all around, and I nodded. "Okay, separate the printers from the print heads. Send each item off in a separate trajectory, to eventually end up at one or the other colony. No beacons, we'll have to find them by dead-reckoning, so make sure you have the orbital parameters carefully recorded." I looked around at all the other Bobs. "Do we have *anything* explosive?"

I got several head shakes by way of response.

"We don't like explodey stuff," Oliver said.

"Yeah, and look where that's gotten us."

Will waved a hand to get us back on track. "Is there anything else we can do?"

I thought for a moment. "We'll have to advise the colonies. We can also get an inventory from them of anything they have in the way of automation. They may have explosives, maybe even some small printers. Someone needs to go over Mack's blog with a fine-tooth comb, looking for anything at all that might be useful. Let's get started on all of that, then we'll regroup and see what we've come up with."

There were nods, and Bobs started popping out to work on their assigned tasks.

I sat back and rubbed my forehead. Like the Others weren't enough of a headache.

Outstanding.

22. Derelict

Herschel
March 2227
Kuiper belt, Delta Pavonis

Neil and I moved slowly between the drifting hulks, SURGE drives on lowest power. The two Others' cargo vessels loomed huge around us. Ten kilometers in length and a kilometer in diameter, they felt more like planetoids than something constructed by intelligent beings.

They even came with their own debris field. The derelicts had taken some pretty severe hits from the looks of it. Pieces of cargo vessel drifted lazily in complicated orbits around the two ships. The effect was eerie, like floating through an underwater graveyard.

I messaged Neil. "I'm not picking up anything. You?"

"Nope. Temps are down around thermal equilibrium. These things haven't done anything but drift in a long time."

"Oh?"

"We were targeting essential systems. I think the attacks will have taken out power cores, and you know how that always ends up…"

"Yeah. Kablooie."

We separated and completed individual circumnavigations of

the wrecks. No surprises. By unspoken agreement, we deployed drones carrying squads of roamers. The drones had orders to do close-up scans, while the roamers would offload and poke around anything interesting.

Finding a way in wasn't really a problem. One of the hulks had been almost cut in two. The two halves were more disconnected than connected—only in free fall could such a small ribbon of metal hold together such massive segments.

The second hulk was in much better shape. A hole literally big enough to drive a battleship into, on a ship this size, barely qualified as a ding. But it's not the size of the damage, it's the quality. We must have taken out something critical.

The ships had been drifting for ten years now. We didn't really expect any kind of activity. But we'd learned caution from previous encounters with the Others, and from a generation of B-movies.

The opportunity to examine the interior of an Others' cargo vessel was too tempting to pass up, of course. We spent several hours, real-time, planning for every contingency we could think of. Then, leaving a couple of drones on look-out, we cautiously entered the cargo vessel through the rent in its side.

Right away, things got complicated. The ship wasn't, it turned out, just a big cavern. We found ourselves in a large bay or hold or something, forming a pie-shaped section of the interior. That might have been the end of the exploration, except that whatever had taken out the cargo vessel had apparently continued right through the ship, taking out a lot of equipment in the process.

At the other end of the cavernous space, we exited into what appeared to be a central corridor. About a hundred meters in diameter, it extended from one end of the ship to the other. This certainly explained the large armored doors at either end of the cargo vessels.

"This thing is mostly intact," Neil said in a near-whisper. "You don't think it could still activate, do you?"

"You saw the equipment back there, Neil." I noticed I was whispering as well, but I couldn't help it. This had the feel of exploring a haunted castle. "Not sure what we took out exactly, but it must have been critical."

"Can I have that in writing?"

"Sure, no problem. Bend over, and I'll get my felt pen."

"Oh, hah hah. If we get eaten by ants, you'll look pretty stupid."

"Well, that's why we agreed not to do any SUDDAR sweeps. You *were* listening, right?"

Neil snorted but didn't respond directly. "I'll head that way, toward the end with the reinforced ring."

"No prob. Be careful."

We drifted off in opposite directions, doing a visual-only inspection.

It took less than a day to reach the ends of the ship. I received a call from Neil. "Hey, uh, Herschel…"

"Umm?"

"I'm looking at this huge thingamajig, and I think it's the power core."

"Wait, you mean in one piece? And what are you doing in one of the bays?"

"It was open. I went in. Sue me."

I sighed. I'd have done the same. "So, what did the attack take out, if that's the power core?"

"Maybe a fluke shot through the A.I. or something. But this is definitely the power core. The size of the conduits kind of gives it away."

"Fusion reaction shut down gracefully?"

There was a moment of silence. "Well, that's the thing. I don't think this is a fusion reactor."

Suddenly, this was more than just a scavenging mission. "Have you found any indications of ants?"

Neil responded in the negative. I took a moment to double-check my train of thought, then said, "Okay, we can't put that off any more. We have to know if we're going to have a problem, so let's move all our equipment out of the hulks. We'll do a low-power SUDDAR sweep to see if we activate any ants. Once we're sure it's clean, let's take a couple of high-resolution scans of this mystery equipment, and see if we can figure it out."

"Affirmative." Telltales showed Neil's devices vacating the hulks. I ordered mine out as well.

Within an hour, we had our scans. But no answers. Not really.

Neil popped over so we could review the results. I gestured at a hologram that slowly rotated in the air.

"Well, you're right. It's not fusion-based. But it's definitely the power-generation facility." I looked at Neil and grinned. "We may have just found some new tech!"

"Cool," Neil replied. "We should call Bill, I guess."

"Are you kidding me? Just hand it over, and let someone else get all the glory? No friggin' way."

"Aw, jeez, Hersch, I'm getting that *bad-idea* feeling again."

"Again? You're usually the *source*."

"Me? Since when?"

I grinned, but didn't bother to reply. The traditional exchange, as always, made us both feel better. But Neil wasn't necessarily wrong. I hoped I hadn't just taken the first steps toward kissing my ass goodbye.

23. Death

Howard
May 2220
Omicron² Eridani

It was the call I'd been dreading for decades. Dr. Onagi looked out the video window at me. I could see from the background that he was calling from the hospital.

"There was no warning, Howard. She simply collapsed. We got her admitted, but our efforts were insufficient."

I felt my eyes begin to sting, and choked it back ruthlessly. "I appreciate the call, Dr. Onagi, but I'm a little perplexed that it's you calling me. Shouldn't her children be doing this?" Well, Howie, maybe. I doubted Rosie would be dialing me up.

Dr. Onagi looked to the side for a moment. "Uh, well, they very likely would have by now. But per Mrs. Brodeur's instructions, we placed her body in stasis immediately post-mortem. Her children were livid, and are seeking legal counsel, as far as I know. I got the impression that you figure prominently in that. They may not be talking to you at all."

I stared, stunned. Bridget hadn't given me any indication that she'd changed her mind. I thanked Dr. Onagi for the information and ended the call. I immediately phoned Ms. Benning.

"Good afternoon, Mr. Johansson. I've just heard about Mrs. Brodeur. I'm so sorry for your loss."

"She's been placed in stasis. Dr. Onagi says that was per her instructions. Has something happened?"

"She changed her will a few months ago. Normally, I wouldn't be able to discuss this with you, but she specifically instructed me to read you in." Ms. Benning reached off-screen for a moment. "And, according to eBar, her children have just filed an injunction to force the hospital to remove her body from stasis. This is not unexpected, and we already have countervailing filings in place. There will be a hearing, for which you should make yourself available. I'll keep you informed."

We exchanged a few more bits of information, then she disconnected. I sat back in my beach chair, staring into space. Bridget was dead. I should be a useless puddle on the floor. I had no doubt that I would be soon, but the unexpected news about her turnaround on the replication issue had thrown me for a loop.

Well, I could make myself useful while I was still in one piece. I'd built scanning equipment from the information Riker and I had gleaned. Time for an inspection.

* * *

The hearing was relatively informal, held in the judge's office rather than the courtroom. Howie, Rosie, and Lianne sat to one side of the room, and Ms. Benning and I at the other. Dr. Onagi, representing the hospital, sat in a more neutral central position.

Judge Ulrich Katz silently scanned the documents in front of him for a few more moments, then looked up. "Issues with the last wishes of decedents are always difficult, when surviving loved ones—"

"He's not a *loved one!"* Rosie interjected. The judge stared at her silently, and Lianne put a hand on her arm.

Order being restored, the judge continued, "...when surviving loved ones disagree about the specifics. But this court cannot make assumptions about the decision in advance of the actual trial. Decanting the decedent at this time will effectively give the decision to the plaintiffs, regardless of the outcome; whereas if the decedent is left in stasis, she can still be decanted should the decision go that way. And conversely, allowing scanning before a decision is rendered cannot be reversed. Therefore, I will not grant the injunction to have the body decanted immediately. Dr. Onagi, you will maintain the body in its current state, and you will not allow any other operations to be performed on it, until otherwise ordered by this court."

The judge didn't bang a gavel. I'd been half expecting it. Of course, my experience with court was a hundred years out of date, from the wrong continent, on a different planet, and came mostly from TV anyway.

I stood up, and looked over at Bridget's children. The girls were rigid with the effort of not looking my way. Bridget's son, Howie, glanced at me, and shook his head minutely. I took the hint.

We let them exit first, then followed. I looked at Ms. Benning and raised an eyebrow. She opened her mouth to answer, did a small double-take, and smiled.

"Mr. Johansson, I've known intellectually for some time that you are walking around in an artificial body. After all, it's not only germane to this case, but has also been the subject of much gossip. Especially the nature of your, er, relationship with Mrs. Brodeur." Ms. Benning blushed slightly. "But I've just now consciously realized that I'm not talking to a live, biological human being. I'm impressed at the verisimilitude."

I smiled sadly. "Thank you, Ms. Benning. We Bobs have been putting a lot of effort into getting the androids as believable as possible. And to answer the not-quite-unspoken question, there's no sexual component to my relationship with Mrs. Brodeur. I could have engineered the capability, but I didn't. I am deeply in love with her, and she loves, or loved, me in a much less intense but still very real way."

Ms. Benning nodded. "I have no doubt of your essential humanity, Mr. Johansson. I dealt with you over the transfer of title for the business, remember? Your emotional turmoil was obvious, and very real."

We walked in silence for a few moments, before she continued, "While it will be an uphill battle for the plaintiffs, it's not a slam-dunk by any means for us. But Mrs. Brodeur expected push-back from her children and made some arrangements in advance, including setting up a defense fund that the children wouldn't be able to block."

I nodded silently. Bridget had always been a careful, methodical thinker. Went with the career choice, I guess. She'd have covered all the bases.

None of which made things any easier. I had Bridget's permission to replicate her, but I would have to wait for the wheels of justice to slowly grind their way to a conclusion.

24. Explorations

Herschel
April 2227
Kuiper belt, Delta Pavonis

Ants must feel like this.

The Others' carrier, which we'd named Hulk-1, was massive. A ten-kilometer-long cylinder, one kilometer in diameter, it dwarfed even our Version-5 Heaven hulls. At the moment, I was slowly drifting down the central access shaft, while roamers painted numbers on each cargo door. I wasn't just being anal—we'd discovered that we needed to refer to specific locations by something more helpful than grunting and pointing.

SUDDAR scans had revealed a lot of details about the ship and its contents, but sooner or later we would have to try powering it up. Those massive cargo segment doors wouldn't be opening manually, never mind the one-hundred-meter-diameter hatches at each end.

"How's it going, Herschel?"

"Fine," I replied. "Almost done. 864 cargo bays. That number mean anything to you?"

There was a moment of silence before Neil replied, "It's 600 base 12. And, come to think of it, the Others image that Bill retrieved had six feeding fingers on each side of its maw."

I grinned. "Coincidence? I think not."

"Nope. There's another universal, I think. Your number base will depend on your number of digits. The Pav were base 10."

"*Are* base 10, Neil. They're not all gone."

There was a sigh. 'Yeah…"

Well, there was a mood killer. "Anyway," I said, perhaps too brightly, "As soon as I'm done here, we can get onto the job of figuring out the power system. I'm anxious to see what some of the stuff in those bays actually is."

"As long as we don't activate some of the stuff in the process."

"Yeah, I hear ya. Maybe we'll have a nuke in place, just in case we need to terminate with prejudice."

"I have a concern about that, Herschel. I'd rather avoid any action that results in destroying Hulk-1."

"Well, um…hold on." I took a moment to load my roamers and the attendant drones, and admire the last numbered bay: 864. "I don't see how we can do this without some risk, buddy."

"How about we cut into one of the bays?"

Well, that was certainly an option. The bay partitions were stupid thick, but we weren't on a schedule.

"Okay. Let's do that."

* * *

We cut into bay #1, simply because SUDDAR scans showed a lot of unidentifiable stuff in it. The roamers had to cut trenches in the wall, and keep widening them. But eventually, they were able to pull a plug of metal away from the surrounding wall.

We left it floating in the central corridor, and sent in a half-dozen roamers.

It looked like this carrier hadn't disgorged all its fighting units before we'd taken it out. The bay contained several dozen drones, each slightly bigger than a Heaven-1 vessel. They were in cradles, with umbilicals connecting them to the ship. Probably control and power feeds. Of course, there was no power, and we'd taken out the ship AI, so no control.

Neil poked a finger at a close-up image of an umbilical connection. "If we unhook that, do you think the drone will come to life?"

"Don't know, Neil." I rubbed my forehead—a delaying tactic,

and we both knew it. "Ultimately, do we really have an alternative?"

Neil stared at the video window for a full two seconds, before turning to me. "Okay, how about this—take one apart, piece by piece. Analyze as we go. Eventually, we should be able to figure out what their readiness state is."

"That is the least-bad idea I've ever heard." I grinned back at him. "Let's do it."

* * *

It took more than a week to strip the drone down, piece by piece. In the end, we were forced to conclude that activation was *probably* done from the carrier AI's end, not at the drone's end. In any case, the one we'd disassembled had been inert. No power, and no way to power up without power.

Just the same, paranoia was the watchword. We picked a random drone, and placed roamers inside it, ready to begin breaking things if the drone got uppity.

"Ready?" I said to Neil.

"Ready!" he replied.

Neil was in charge of destruction, and I was in charge of unplugging. Without giving myself any more opportunity for second-guessing, I instructed the roamer to eject the umbilical from the drone.

We waited…5 seconds…10 seconds…

"Enough of this," Neil grumbled. "It's scanning time." Matching actions to words, he instructed one of our drones to give the subject a good once-over.

The scan came up in my holotank within milliseconds.

"Nothing. Inert." I looked at Neil. "Satisfied?"

"Me? Since when am I the bad guy?"

"Since always. I'm always reassuring you."

"Oh, bite me. You are so full of it." Neil shook his head in sorrow. "So, next question. Do we cut into every cargo bay with something in it and start unhooking stuff?"

"That'll take years. What's our alternative?"

"I'm starting to like the nuke idea." Neil gave me a crooked grin.

"Okay," I replied. "We're going to have to trace all the wiring, to find out if we can leave the bays unpowered if we start up the reactor. *And*, sorry to say, we're also going to have to place a nuke in here in case we wake something up that we shouldn't have. Let's just hope it doesn't come to that."

Neil sighed. "This is beginning to sound too much like real work."

* * *

'Real work' described it very well. Some of the Others' design decisions were, well, suboptimal. At least as far as we could tell. In several cases, power conduits split, went around a large patch of nothing in particular, then reconnected on the far side. We scanned the section of nothing twice, but found, um, nothing.

"Well, look," Neil mused. "Sometimes, when you're designing something, you make allowances for future expansion. As long as you have a good idea what the requirements will be, you can allow for it."

"So it's an expansion slot."

"Yeah, thanks, Captain Sarcasm. Still, you're probably not far wrong."

"That's wonderful, Neil. But are we any closer to being able to activate this flying island nation?"

"Let's have a look, Hersch." With that, Neil pulled up our working schematic. He quickly updated it with this latest information, then directed the simulation to power up.

We watched the simulation as telltales indicated virtual sections that were receiving power.

Eventually the simulation ended with the hulk in a stable state, and no issues that we could see. Neil and I looked at each other, smiled, and said in unison, "We're good to go!"

25. Battle

Bill
June 2223
82 Eridani

Premier Campbell put her face in her hands and was silent for several seconds. President Ito attempted to remain stoic, but I could see that he was shaken.

Campbell looked up. "Mack? He's…gone?"

"No, ma'am," I replied. "We have his matrix. Or at least, it's still in one piece and we know where it is. But he's offline, for the moment. We're trying to get it to a colony site for safekeeping."

Campbell nodded, looking relieved.

"And how can we help, Mr. Johansson?"

I turned to President Ito's video image. "We're trying to inventory all our assets in this system. Anything that can be used as a weapon, anything that can be remote controlled, anything SCUT-enabled, anything that can get out of atmosphere…"

"How do the androids work? I believe there's one at each colony site."

I brightened. "Those are SCUT-controlled, so yes, we can use those. That's one more, well, two more control loci for us. As soon as we can, we'll send a couple of drones to pick them up. We can use them to relay orders to the non-SCUT mining drones." I thought for a moment. "Plus, they'll be useful to supplement the roamers for manipulation."

Ito nodded, and silence descended.

Campbell finally broke the pause. "We are at war, essentially, right? Are the colonies in danger?"

I considered for a millisecond. "I don't see how, at least on an immediate basis, ma'am. Medeiros doesn't have anything that can bomb you from orbit. If we can keep the autofactories from him, or at least keep the printers away, that won't change. If he gets a printer, or already has one, he still has to bootstrap up through all the automation needed for an autofactory, before he can start building something like an asteroid mover. And there's no way he'll be dumb enough to try to print anything explosive."

"On the other hand..." Ito said in a slow drawl, inviting me to explain counterpoint.

I grinned. "On the other hand, we have no printer capability at the moment—although we are in possession of the actual printers, more or less—and we'd have to go through the same bootstrapping process. To a lesser extent, maybe, because we have roamers and drones and now the two androids."

"So it's détente."

"I'm not sure it's even at that level, ma'am. Right now it's more like that Hugh Grant and Colin Firth fight scene in Bridget Jones' Diary."

She looked at me askance, then shook her head without asking. Apparently Mack already had a reputation.

"Look," I continued, "If we can get one or more of the printers onto one of your worlds, and get enough raw elements down for it, and do all this without being intercepted by Medeiros, then we can maybe build busters or something."

"That's a lot of if's," Campbell replied.

"Well, it'll depend on what Medeiros does next. I'm afraid we're forced to react to his moves. Any attempt on our part to control the play will result in a missile down our throats."

"How many missiles does he have?"

"Zero, we thought. So, unknown."

Ito thought for a moment. "You have a number of mining drones, I understand. Can you use them to ram the Brazilian?"

It was a good try, and I nodded an acknowledgement. "Sorry, President Ito, but that would be like trying to ram a sports car with tractors. In principle, you could do damage, but first you have to catch him."

Ito sighed and sat back. Again, there was a contemplative silence.

"Look," I said, "If you think of anything, call, email, or text me. We'll keep working on it from our end, and I'll keep you updated."

"Good enough." Premier Campbell nodded and ended her connection. A moment later, Ito blinked out as well.

I sighed, sat back, and looked at the ceiling. Like the Others weren't bad enough.

* * *

By the time Medeiros got to the nearest Lagrange autofactory location, we'd long since flung the printers and print heads well beyond his ability to detect them. The Bobs had also managed to hide, damage, or collect most of the autofactory automation, leaving nothing valuable except the actual metal ingots. We watched Medeiros from a non-SCUT drone, carefully disguised as flotsam, running on power cells so as not to show up on radiation detectors. It would run down soon, but if Medeiros didn't pick up on it, we could collect it later. If he did, he would have gained only a regular mining drone, and one without a fusion reactor.

The Brazilian craft buzzed around, inspecting and searching, then settled on a single location and stopped moving. I half-expected some kind of raging and destroying things; but realistically, Medeiros was career military, and presumably well-disciplined. He wouldn't waste missiles on petulance.

I hoped he would decide on a strategy before the drone gave out. We'd identified three possibilities: one, head for one of the colonies and set up a picket, on the presumption that we had sent at least one printer that way; two, head off and start scanning for printers and print heads on their lonely trajectories; or three, start looking for roamers and mining drones to either destroy or try to take over.

And finally, just when the drone was on its last few watts of stored power, Medeiros accelerated out of the area.

"Do we have an indication of where he's going?"

I jerked in surprise. Too intent on watching Medeiros, I hadn't realized that Will was visiting my VR. I turned to him. "I don't think so. He's just headed off in what appears to be some random direction. The power cells are about to give out, so we can't track him by SUDDAR."

Will muttered an expletive, a clear indication that the situation was getting to him. "We have to assume scenarios one or two, then, since they're the worst cases. How many printers and heads have we rerouted to a colony?"

"Two of each going to each colony. Well spread out. Of course, he can spot them on approach with a SUDDAR sweep, but he'll have to be close enough to physically intercept."

"Then he'll have to intercept without destroying them. Destruction is acceptable, from our point of view."

I nodded. "This is going to be a long, drawn-out battle, Will."

* * *

Garfield and I were sitting, drinking coffee, taking one of our increasingly rare breaks, when Guppy popped in.

[Printer convoy en route to Asgard has been hit with a SUDDAR sweep.]

Garfield and I looked at each other. "Crap", he said. "That means he went for option one."

"I guess it makes sense," I replied. "For option two, he'd be scanning an increasingly large volume of space. This way, we are essentially coming to him."

I turned to Guppy. "Were you able to triangulate?"

[Negative. Sweep was short range.]

"Smart," Garfield said. "He doesn't announce himself unless he makes contact, and if he does, he's right on top of us."

"Which means he's right on top of us." I smacked my forehead.

"Doesn't matter, anyway. I checked, and this particular group has no SCUT. They'll have to operate on standing orders."

[Convoy has been disabled. Video feed cut off.]

Garfield and I exchanged a look. Had Medeiros simply blown up the convoy? Was his plan to deny *us* the printers?

Wordlessly, I called up the truncated video. Garfield watched the three-second sequence.

"Well, hell," I said, when we were done. "It appears Medeiros can learn."

"Mmm, hmm. He's building busters. Or he built busters. Wait, when did he build busters?" Garfield frowned and continued, "If this is the Alpha Centauri Medeiros, then his first exposure to us was the day we razed their installation. He would have had to build busters *after* that. There was no indication that the Brazilians were building kinetic weapons before that point."

I gave him a sickly grin. "Sorry, buddy, I guess you missed the conversation after the attack. We figure he has at least one printer of his own. So he learned from Alpha Centauri."

"So why's he doing what he's doing?"

"Two-pronged strategy. Attempt to gather as many printers as he can, while denying them to us. Geometric progression means a small advantage up front can turn into an insurmountable lead, eventually." I stared into space for a few milliseconds. "We have to take him out, now. If he gets ahead of us, the colonists are as good as dead."

Garfield closed his eyes and shook his head slowly. "And we put them there."

* * *

Captain Richards from the Asgard colony pressed his lips together and said nothing. He didn't have to. On top of everything the colonists were dealing with, they now had Medeiros to worry about.

"Are you certain that he will attack the colony?"

"Not certain, captain. But he's made it pretty clear on previous encounters that he is utterly loyal to Brazil, considers us to be at war, and isn't interested in discussions. I'm also not entirely sure he's sane at this point." I looked over at Garfield, who rolled his eyes dramatically. "I'd hate to try communicating with him, only to find that we'd attracted his attention to the colonies."

Richards nodded, and sat back with a *huff*. "And we have nothing."

"Not that we've been able to find. We could ask Mack, if we could get him onto a cradle, but right now we can't risk trying to fly his matrix in. We're getting occasional glimpses of Medeiros, and he does his best to destroy anything he detects."

"At both colonies? How many of him are there?" Richards frowned at me.

I thought for a second. "There's no overlap in appearances, so there's only one of him. But I think he's programmed his busters to patrol and knock down anything they detect. Right now, he owns the high ground."

General Kiroshi from the Japanese colony had been listening without comment in another video window. Now he spoke up. "We have only small printers, useful for quick manufacturing of minor items, but insufficient for anything like your busters. And it would take months to bootstrap up to real industrial printers."

Richards nodded. "Same here. Ours are big enough to print more mosquito killers, but that's—"

"Wait, what?" I sat up straight.

Richards raised an eyebrow. "Super vampire something something mosquitoes. Mack didn't mention them?"

"Yes, I remember them." I gave him a sideways glare. "I didn't realize you were handling manufacturing yourselves."

"Well, sure, because we needed thousands and Mack couldn't be bothered. They're about the size of a baseball, so not really useful for anything but mosquito patrol."

"But...thousands?" I leaned forward, radiating interest.

Richards' eyes started to grow rounder as he realized something was up. "Er, yes, most of them are on standby right now, since we seem to have beaten back the scourge. We were going to return them to raw materials eventually. But I think we had three or four thousand running around at one point."

I let a slow smile grow on my face. "They may be small, but a few hundred hitting a buster at the same time will still have an effect. We may be able to clear the sky around Asgard long enough to get the printers to ground."

"Can they even fly outside of atmosphere?"

"Not a problem, captain. It's actually more trouble building them to fly *in* atmosphere."

"Excellent," the captain said. "Let's get this operation going."

* * *

The mosquito killers were too small to carry SCUT comms, so we had to give the AMIs complete enough instructions to handle any situation we could think of. One in each hundred was designated as an observer, ordered to send a video record back to the colony, if possible, or to record and return otherwise.

We sent off two thousand killers in five squads, hoping to catch as many busters as possible by surprise. A couple of killers were programmed to leak radio telemetry, which hopefully would attract some of Medeiros' devices.

Captain Richards was mirroring everything to Kiroshi and myself. I watched the numerous video windows as the observers delivered status and telemetry.

"Got a blip," Captain Richards announced.

I'd seen the change in the video window several milliseconds before, of course, but there was no good reason to remind him of my true nature.

The telemetry from the observer indicated two bogeys approaching the group. Per their orders, the killers changed course to intercept. We hoped that Medeiros hadn't programmed caution into his busters. A bunch of baseball-sized objects hopefully wouldn't trigger the default danger-avoidance routines.

The busters zeroed in on the noisy killers, seemingly ignoring the cloud of attendants. At the last possible moment, every single mosquito killer altered course to aim directly at the two busters. The change apparently registered with the dim AMI brains, because both busters went into hard turns. Too little, too late, though. The smaller and more maneuverable killers easily kept up with the change in vectors.

Contact wasn't the dramatic flash we were used to seeing as two heavy devices collided at interplanetary speeds. The killers avoided the large steel ball up front and went for reactor cooling radiators, SURGE emitters, and other obvious signs of technology.

It was like being pelted in a hailstorm. The first couple dozen impacts had no real effect; then dents started to appear, followed by seams popping, then parts flying off. In less than thirty seconds, the busters were drifting aimlessly, and we still had more than a hundred killers left.

"See if you can get them to shepherd the parts into low orbit," Richards suggested. "If we can rescue the material, great. Otherwise, we push it into atmosphere and deny it to Medeiros."

I nodded. A good strategy. I wasn't sure how we'd get that much mass down to ground level—other that the obvious way—but I'd worry about that once we had rescued some drones.

"Two down…" Richards grinned at me, then turned in his video window to face Kiroshi. “General, once we’ve cleared the Asgard environs, I’ll send a squad of mosquito killers your way.”

General Kiroshi nodded. “Thank you. Even if we are not ultimately successful, the process of attrition should keep Medeiros busy.”

“Yes,” I added. “We just need to knock off busters faster than he can make them. And if he’s making busters, he’s not making more printers.”

“We’ll keep at this, Bill.” Captain Richards nodded to me. “I’ll keep you up to date.”

Good enough. I still had a war with the Others to prepare for.

26. Cities in Fight

Marcus
September 2215
Poseidon

I watched the long-range image, which showed the expanding cloud of debris that used to be my Heaven vessel decoy. I'd been lying about my location for several months now, and the Council seemed to have bought it. Three Council security vessels left the area at far too high an acceleration for the cargo vessels they appeared to be. It would seem the Council could be sneaky as well.

I fired off a report to Riker, cc'd to Bill, and saved a backup to my Fortress of Solitude, circling Eta Cassiopeia B. If the Council ever found that, I'd be thoroughly hooped. Fortunately, that was unlikely. The Council still had fewer than a dozen ships, and the companion star simply hadn't come up in discussions for a long time.

Of course, the Council had obviously been engaging in covert preparations as well, as evinced by the three souped-up and armed cargo ships. Now that they believed me dead, I hoped that they would openly play their hand.

I returned my presence to my android, which was standing at parade rest. As I moved my arms into a more relaxed position, everyone turned to me.

"Well?" Kal said.

I grinned at him. "Three very non-standard cargo vessels just took out my decoy vessel. It would have attempted evasive tactics consistent with its published specs. I'm sure the security personnel are very proud of themselves."

"What about the cargo vessels?"

"I've got some stealth busters following them right now. But we don't know what the Council's total strength is, or where they've placed it. I have to assume that my estimate of a dozen ships is incorrect. We'll have to take a wait-and-see stance until they show their hand. And remember, officially, I'm dead."

Gina looked up from her phone and cut into the conversation. "They've moved on four cities: Lothar, Morbus, Xanator, and Gathol. Attempted to board and take over—you were right, they were trying to avoid damaging the cities."

"Status?" I asked.

"Repelled with significant losses. They didn't expect resistance."

"They also didn't expect," Gina replied, "weapon systems that weren't on the blueprints."

I grinned. "My fault. I forgot to file the changes with the Permits department."

Kal waved his phone. "They've made an announcement."

We all turned to him, eager to hear what the Council had come up with. Kal read through the text, deliberately injecting a pompous tone into the pronouncement. When he was done, we all sat in a semi-circle, ready for a council of war.

"So, the takeaway," I said, looking up at the dome overhead, "is that the evil, evil replicant is defunct and everyone should be good little citizens and come back to the mats. Or else."

"And if we don't, they'll start shooting down cities in twenty-four hours." Kal shook his head in exaggerated disbelief. "We're at war now, even if the word hasn't actually been used. Blowing Marcus up can't really be misinterpreted."

"I suppose they could take the stance that I'm not alive, therefore it was just a case of obsoleting some recalcitrant equipment." I gave my friends a lopsided grin. "And the thing with those cities could be called a 'police action'."

Gina rolled her eyes at me, mocking my favorite expression. "Or they were just tired of listening to you talk. *Now* are you willing to start fighting?"

I shook my head. "I still don't know where all their assets are. I want to take everything out cleanly in one strike. And I *don't* want to have to kill anyone."

"Good luck with that," Kal muttered.

We spent the next few hours monitoring developments. Things seemed to have settled into a stalemate, with the Council making threats and the cities daring them to try, or simply remaining silent.

Then, more trouble.

Two ships came out of sunward and launched missiles at Amhor. My assets were all space-side, shadowing or searching for council assets, so I had nothing for defense. The city, though, had those undocumented features...

Particle-weapon turrets, courtesy of Bill's Skunk Works, activated immediately and attempted to shoot the missiles out of the sky. The attackers responded by firing more missiles.

"I'm impressed," I said. "The basic cargo-ship design doesn't have a lot of room for weapons storage and launchers. I'd be interested in seeing how—"

"Chrissake, Marcus, we're in danger here. Could you dial it back?"

I gave Kal a rueful smile by way of apology, then turned back to watch the drama.

The ships seemed to have emptied themselves of missiles, and our defensive batteries had taken out the first two missiles. The second pair were getting too close for comfort, though. And seemed to have figured out the defensive patterns, as they were evading all attempts to shoot them out of the sky.

With a flash of inspiration, I took control of a couple of flyers sitting in the docking bay. I sent them toward the missiles at full acceleration. Flyers were not military vehicles or flying explosives, so they really had no chance of catching or even intercepting an approaching missile. But they did have the effect of splitting the attention of the missile AMIs. It was just enough to slow down the dodging, and the defensive turrets blew both missiles out of the air.

The ships, now apparently unarmed, turned and flew off. I called a couple of drones from orbit to shadow them. If they flew back to a base somewhere to reload, I'd have a target.

But there was no time to celebrate our victory.

Kal leaped to his feet and uttered a string of profanities. Then he turned to look at the rest of us, and said, "The bastards shot down Thark."

There were gasps and cries of shock, but not surprise. Thark and Amhor were the residences of what we somewhat ironically called the Revolutionary Council. We'd published disinformation, but somehow the Council had seen through it.

Regardless, the Council had just upped the ante.

Gina asked, "Survivors?"

Kal looked at his phone for several seconds, his eyes moving back and forth. I noticed that several other people were poking their tablets furiously.

"Escape pods were observed ejecting, before it hit water. But I'd bet not everyone got out."

Gina glared at me. "Now we're at war. They're trying to hit us everywhere at once, to end it before we can react. It's not going to stop until they think they've won. It will just continue to escalate, and more and more people will die. Now, Marcus."

I sighed and nodded my head. Without a word, I deactivated my android and returned to VR. A quick status check at computer speeds showed that I had busters trailing all Council ships that we'd been able to locate. I ordered all busters to attack, concentrating on taking out the reactor or drive systems.

The subject of cloaking technology hadn't really come up in conversation with the Council, so the ships were caught flat-footed. All clean shots, there should be no deaths unless someone was standing right by the reactor at the wrong time. Escape pods ejected from all of them.

None of which would help with the Council. For that, I activated phase 2.

The ouncil had set up security at strategic locations such as power stations and flyer depots, as well as roving patrols to ensure citizens stayed put and obeyed curfews. I gave the command, and cargo drones dropped off squads of roamers throughout the Northern and Southern mats. I'd learned the utility of roamers as foot soldiers, almost a hundred years ago in New Handeltown. This time, I had more than just the twenty-centimeter models available.

All over the towns and industrial sections, Council security forces found themselves set upon by roamers, from the one-inch models that would try to crawl down your pants, right up to the two-meter heavy-lifting models—every single one armed with plasma cutters, pliers, and a total lack of fear.

Within ten minutes, I got the all-clear from Gina, who was coordinating with local resistance. I pulled up a video window. "Have you located the Council members yet?"

Gina shook her head. "No, as we expected, their published locations were all bogus. Chances are their movement history is at least partly fiction, as well. We're analyzing on the basis of defensibility and obscurity."

I nodded. "My money is still on subs."

Gina snorted. "If so, they can stay out there all they want. I'm not going to risk an encounter with a kraken or hydra just to capture those turds."

"Maybe the wildlife will take care of it for us."

Kal popped up in another call window, joining the conference. "We've got control of the comms center. Want me to send out an all-points?"

"Do it." I nodded. "And see if you can get an update on Thark."

"Already done. We've pulled about half the population out of the drink," Kal responded. "Still scanning for more pods. At the moment, there are about a hundred and fifty people missing."

I closed my eyes, feeling nauseated. We'd admitted the possibility of casualties, but the reality—even a potential reality, at the moment—was so much harder to take.

"Okay, Kal. Keep me updated."

When I had time, I would have to do some soul-searching. Between the Poseidon revolution, the Sol System War, and the overthrow of New Jerusalem, my various incarnations seemed to always be in the thick of things.

How many deaths was I answerable for?

27. Repairs

Herschel
July 2227
Delta Pavonis

There's no real reason for your Virtual Reality self to be tense. I knew that. It didn't help. I found myself gritting my teeth so hard that my jaw began to ache.

After months of investigation and tinkering, Neil and I were ready to try activating the power core. We had the nuclear deterrent sitting in the middle of the central corridor, just in case. But truthfully, neither of us really thought it would be necessary. The wiring had eventually succumbed to our detective work, and we were confident that we would be able to power up the core without powering up the bays.

Which still left the question of activating the power core. Since we'd never seen this particular technology before, there was a lot of guesswork involved. Needless to say, guesswork and power cores did not go well together.

We weren't total idiots—we were standing off more than a thousand klicks, while the roamers and drones ran through the final steps. I idly wondered, for a moment, if the AMIs ever got tired of wearing the red shirts. Probably not, or they'd have gone on strike by now.

“If this doesn’t work, we’re going to be in deep doo-doo.” Neil glanced sideways at me.

“Better than being a cloud of ionized gas. And even if it does work, there are going to be questions, Neil. We really should have announced the find on the first day.”

“You. But. I…” Neil glared at me, one side of his mouth up in a sneer of disbelief. “I hate you.”

I grinned at him. “Okay, joking aside, buddy. We’re eighth-generation Bobs. Pondscum. Star Trek security looks down *their* noses at *us*. I’d like to have something under my belt that I can stamp on my hull.”

Neil took a deep breath, let it out slowly. “Yeah. If everything goes well, all will be forgiven.”

“So…”

“Scanning started,” Neil responded, taking the hint. “We have an image. Okay, Herschel, any time.”

I gave the order, and the roamers started the activation procedure in Hulk-1. It took almost three minutes for the alien equipment to go through whatever startup sequence it needed. We could review the whole thing later via the recorded SUDDAR video.

And finally, pay dirt. Lights came on in the alien craft. Readings indicated rising power levels in engineering subsystems. We’d been careful to ensure that most of the vessel remained unpowered. We certainly didn’t want to activate a security system somewhere.

The roamers ran a few output tests, and reported the results. I whistled. “That’s just a stupid level of power generation. Assuming it’s linear.”

“Remember that scene in *Forbidden Planet* with the power meters?” Neil grinned at me. “This is just like that. We’re barely tilting the first meter.”

I nodded, eyes unfocussed. “I, uh, think it might be time to pay Bill a visit.”

* * *

“Well, there are no laws in the Bobiverse, of course…” Bill’s expression belied the casualness of his tone. Neil and I looked at each other nervously.

“But you guys are still morons.” Bill raised his hands in an *I give up* gesture. "If something had gone wrong and taken you out, we'd never have known about it."

"We've been doing backups, Bill..."

"And how would we know to activate your backup? ESP?"

"Oh..." Yeah, there's that. I looked down at my shoes.

Bill relented a little, seeing my expression. "Actually, Herschel, that's another project I'm working on. The battle of Delta Pavonis made it clear that we need a more organized backup system."

He waved us toward chairs and called in Jeeves. It looked like we wouldn't be flayed, after all.

"Okay, fill me in."

I sat down and accepted a coffee. I took a moment for a sip, to give me time to calm my nerves. Then I called up the diagrams and schematics, as well as video records. "You already know the basics. We found the hulks, got the power system working in one of them. The power core is not fusion-based. I'd almost swear it uses some variation on the Casimir Effect. There's a separate analysis on that."

I pushed one set of schematics aside, to bring up a larger-scale diagram. "Hulk-2 is scrap. We've been through it from one end to the other, and there's nothing interesting. It's basically a big ol' pile of salvage. We've had our devices breaking it down into transportable chunks for a couple of months now. But here's the thing..." I paused for effect. "Hulk-1 is a big, sort-of-hollow container with built-in power. The A.I. and drive systems are gone, of course, but so what?" I grinned at Bill.

Bill frowned, and I realized he hadn't gotten it yet. I looked at Neil, suddenly uncertain. Had we missed something obvious? Were we about to paint ourselves as total twits?

Neil rolled his eyes, just the tiniest amount, then turned to Bill. "Put a set of mover plates around it, Bill, and it's the biggest damn colony ship ever made. It just needs stasis pods."

Bill's eyes slowly grew wide as the penny dropped. "Holy—"

I grinned, confidence returning. "And you could move the entire remaining Earth population in one trip!"

28. Payback

Bob
April 2224
Eden

Caerleon was a busy area—almost frantic. Maybe it was the age of the residents, and the relative lack of family groups. Caerleon had been colonized by juveniles just into puberty and going through the adolescent rebellion stage. Marvin and I agreed that we'd created a baby boomer generation when we moved everyone to Camelot and the birth rate subsequently surged. All those teenagers, getting hormonal at the same time, had probably just egged each other on.

At any rate, it made sneaking up a difficult operation. I had the advantages of lack of scent and ability to stay completely still, of course. Plus some commando camouflage tricks that I looked up in the ship libraries. Still, it took almost five hours to maneuver into position. Original Bob would have been a single giant muscle cramp by that point, but android muscles didn't get tired.

And I was now in position. Surveillance had shown that Fred had a preferred location for his bodily functions, and he was very much a creature of habit. I picked a spot where I could take him on the way back, and settled down to wait.

* * *

As Fred turned back to the trail, I slammed into him. Shoving him up against a tree, I placed the edge of my flint knife against his throat.

"Hello, Fred. Remember our last conversation?"

Fred's eyes were wide with fear, and he made no attempt to struggle.

"I own you right now, *kuzzi*." I practically spit his favorite insult back in his face. "Whether you live to see the sun set today depends on my mood. Understand?"

Fred understood. The odor of fear emanated from him. But he apparently wasn't going to just fold. "My friends won't let this go," he said. "They'll come after you."

And he was right. This was something I'd worried about, but had hoped I wouldn't have to deal with. If he didn't capitulate in some manner, I might actually end up having to kill him. Could I do that in cold blood? If he just dug in his heels and called my bluff, I'd have to either follow through or lose any credibility.

On the other hand, if I'd come with Donald, Fred would already be dead.

It was *so* tempting. But even after being embedded in Deltan civilization for all these years, I still had a 21st century human squeamishness about taking life.

"What's your problem, Fred? Can't hunt on your own? Can't figure out which end of the spear to use? Or are you just lazy?"

Fred's ears went flat and his lips curled back from his teeth in a reaction that, for a Deltan, was an expression of rage. "It's so easy for you, isn't it? Sit there with all the resources and yap about how everyone else isn't living up to your standards? I'm not answerable to you."

"Well, right now you kind of are." I pushed the blade harder against his throat to make the point.

But Fred was angry now. His reaction, his unexpected rage, surprised me. I'd mishandled this somehow, and now there was no way he was going to back down. Interesting food for thought, but right now it left me between a rock and a hard place.

With a flash of inspiration, I directed a spy drone to make some suspicious noises, in order to draw over some of the locals. Within moments, Fred and I could both hear his friends approaching and calling for him. He grinned at me in triumph. If his friends found a corpse, the whole village would be after me.

That was fine. Let him think that. I put my face up close to his. "Just remember that I can find you whenever I want. Next time I won't discuss it, won't even let you know I'm there. Maybe you should start hanging around with your friends all the time."

With that, I gave him the usual quick jab in the breadbasket, and grabbed his spear as he folded. I vanished into the forest just before his friends came into sight.

Well, that hadn't gone quite according to plan. I made my way back to Camelot, still trying to convince myself that I could kill him if I had to.

* * *

I told Archimedes the story over dinner. He took Fred's spear and examined it while I talked.

"Donald would have just killed him," he said. "Me, not so much. It's hard to kill people, unless they're attacking you."

Archimedes maneuvered the spear around until he was looking at the tip. "This is really terrible work. Someone just shattered a nodule, and tied the sharpest shard onto the shaft." He shook his head. "It's as likely to fall off as penetrate the target. If this is what they have, I'm not surprised they're having to steal food from our hunters."

I raised my eyebrows. Okay, the android actually pointed its ears forward and down, but it felt to me like the equivalent human expression.

If the Caerleon citizens were having less hunting success because of equipment failure… Could it be that easy? Perceived inequities like that had started more than one war on Earth. I liked to think Deltans were a little more sensible than humans in general, but not by *that* much.

I sat back against the boulder behind me and stared into space, considering the options.

29. Looming Storm

Howard
May 2220
Vulcan

I stood outside the courtroom, taking deep breaths. I had an almost uncontrollable urge to drop a rock on the building. I'd expected nastiness. Ms. Benning had warned me that the children's strategy would be based on attacks.

Knowing it and being subjected to it were two different things, though. To listen to their lawyer, I was some weird cross between Rasputin, Svengali, Machiavelli, and Lucifer. They hadn't *quite* accused me of drugging and brainwashing Bridget, but they'd sure been trying to imply it.

Ms. Benning came to stand beside me. "There will be more of the same after recess. Just remember that he's trying to get a rise out of you, to get you to make a mistake."

I smiled slightly. "I have some advantages in that area." Indeed. During cross-exam, I had enabled the endocrine control system. Funny that the cloning process, even with all the different generations of Heaven vessels, still included that subsystem. With the control on, I was only mildly concerned about Mr. Kistler's accusations and innuendo.

And a good thing. Right now, I would happily reach over and

crush his throat with one hand.

Dr. Onagi came over to stand with us. I looked at him. "Is it appropriate for us to speak?"

He looked at Ms. Benning, who smiled in response. "Not a problem. The hospital is named in their suit as well, so we're on the same side. What's on your mind, Dr. Onagi?"

"I don't trust them."

"Erm, this is news?" I raised an eyebrow at him.

"No, no, I mean beyond the obvious adversarial situation. In particular, the eldest daughter just seems like a real piece of work. I wonder, if they lose the case, if she'll take it gracefully."

Ms. Benning's eyebrows rose. "You mean, as in sabotage of some kind?"

Dr. Onagi nodded.

Oh, wow. I couldn't actually feel the blood drain from my face—no blood, after all—but the elevator-dropping feeling was definitely there. "We could win, and still lose."

"This bears some careful thought," Ms. Benning said. "Being found in contempt of a court order could prejudice your case, so don't do anything precipitous. Just the same…"

We settled into an uncomfortable silence as we each stared into space.

30. Armageddon

Bill
June 2223
82 Eridani

I was going over some plans with Garfield when I received an emergency call from Captain Richards. I popped up the video window. "What's up, captain?"

"Bill, we were doing so well with clearing the busters from orbit that I decided I could spare a dozen or so killers to reconnoiter the Lagrange points. To see what Medeiros is up to, you understand?"

I nodded, not liking the implication.

Richards popped up a grainy, long-distance image. "We picked this up."

The frame rate and resolution were low, but I could make out that Medeiros was working around the metal ingots used as raw materials for the autofactories.

"What's he doing?" I asked.

"We ran some image interpolations. It looks like he's attaching busters to an ingot with cables."

"Oh, hell." A poor man's asteroid mover. The ingots weren't huge, but they were metal, and would survive re-entry almost unscathed. One of those could certainly create a new Barringer crater. More than enough to wipe out a colony, anyway.

"This advances our schedule. How are you doing with the printers?"

"We've got a half-dozen." Richards grimaced. "One is working on a cradle for Mack, three are working on drones and roamers, and two are producing small busters, per your plans." He shook his head. "What's with twenty-kilogram busters, anyway?"

I gave him a weak smile. "Something Bob has been using as anti-personnel weapons. But our experience with the mosquito killers shows that more small attackers can be as effective as a few large attackers—and more flexible. Medeiros will probably be putting more armor on his busters by now, so the killers are going to be less effective. So these will up the ante."

"So do we switch to nothing but busters?"

"Not just yet, Captain. We can do without Mack for now, but we need drones and roamers, for assembly if nothing else. I'll run a min-max analysis to figure out what mix of construction will get us the best return. I'll let you know."

We nodded and disconnected at the same time. I turned to Garfield, who had been listening to the whole exchange.

"He's planning on just smashing things, isn't he?" Garfield looked gray with worry.

"It seems to be a theme with the Brazilian probes, Gar. I don't know if that's a cultural thing, or military conditioning, or something that Brazilian scientists installed as imperatives when they were building the replicants."

"Or they're all insane."

I shrugged. "Doesn't matter, in the end. We have to react to the threat. And I don't see any reason to change the no-quarter policy on Medeiros."

Garfield's only reply was a snort of agreement.

* * *

"He's started moving the ingot." Richards glared at me out of the video window.

"How did he manage that?" I asked. "He was nowhere near having enough busters, just yesterday."

Richards shrugged. "He still doesn't, really. I think he's starting before he's really ready. The acceleration is vanishingly small."

"But he can add more in-flight, as he makes them."

Richards nodded. "Unfortunately, it's too soon to tell which colony he's aiming for. He may not even have decided yet. It'll be another twenty-four hours before he has to commit."

"We have printers on both colonies, now, right?" I started to run my hand through my hair, then caught myself. "So there's no advantage to him one way or the other. My money's on Asgard, simply because he can get it there sooner."

"We have to move on him now." Richards set his jaw. "I'll contact General Kiroshi, see what he can put in the air."

"Do that, Captain. Call me back."

* * *

"It's not enough," Kiroshi said. "We are two busters short of a one-on-one matchup, and that's without dealing with Medeiros himself. We can't win this."

"And that's assuming we have eyes on all his devices. If he's carrying a couple in his hold, it will put us even farther behind."

"I don't see it," I replied, looking at Richards. "If he had more, they'd be pulling the ingot as well."

"Do we have a choice?"

I sighed. "Not really, Captain. The longer we wait, the harder it will be to redirect the ingot. And by the time it actually gets here, we'll have built two more busters at the most."

There were a few more comments, but we all knew we really had no choice. These busters would have to be preprogrammed, as we couldn't afford the time to add SCUT comms. We sent them out from both colonies, timed to arrive simultaneously.

I was about to disconnect, when I had a thought. "Gentlemen, how many mosquito killers do we have left? And where are they?"

Kiroshi answered. "A little over two hundred. They're all in orbit around Takama. We haven't had any close-in encounters at either colony for a few days. Why?"

"Let's throw them into the mix, . I'll do some calculations, and give you the times and vectors."

* * *

Our busters arrived at the expected time and place. Because they were operating without SCUTs, we were getting the video play-by-play several minutes after the fact. Whatever was going to happen had already happened.

There could be no finesse on this operation. Each one of our busters could take out one of Medeiros' busters. We would aim several busters at Medeiros himself, but he would use his busters to intercept. Barring a miracle and him missing one, we'd be left with Medeiros and two busters to deal with.

We watched as fourteen video images closed in on fourteen targets, then fourteen video images disappeared.

"Well, that was textbook," Richards said.

I smiled tightly. "And right about now, Medeiros should be feeling pretty smug."

Two new video windows popped up as the incoming mosquito killers zeroed in on Medeiros. We knew we would leave two of Medeiros' busters, but we made sure those busters were tethered to the ingot and unavailable for defense.

Medeiros detected the incoming killers and turned tail, but he was far too late. Unlike the busters, which had decelerated to arrive at the battleground at a controllable velocity, the killers had continued to accelerate all the way from Takama. They arrived with a considerable momentum; fewer than half struck the Brazilian ship, but a hundred small impacts were still sufficient to open up the side of his vessel. Medeiros lost his line and began to drift.

"He's down," Richards said. "Not sure if he's dead, but propulsion is offline."

"Do we have any more busters? Any more killers?" Kiroshi looked from one to the other of us.

I shook my head. "Busters are all expended. There are lots of killers, but they're travelling away from Medeiros at high speed. They'll take as long to decelerate as they took to accelerate to that velocity, then they have to accelerate back."

"He might still be out by the time they get back. We don't know how many roamers he has left after the space battle over Mack."

That was true. It was certainly worth a shot, anyway. "Okay, General. I'm sending orders to the killers now. Light speed delay will add to the total turnaround time. I think we're looking at twenty-two hours before they get back."

Richards frowned. "Hell, we could get a couple of drones there in less time than that."

"To do what? Even at full acceleration, they're unlikely to do much damage."

"I was thinking more along the lines of grabbing Medeiros himself."

I stared at Richards. That hadn't occurred to me. Stick some roamers in the drones' holds, and they could enter the Brazilian ship and extract the replicant matrix. I felt a twinge of nausea at what we were not-quite planning. Memories of Homer, of the five cubes back on Earth during Bob-1's training, swirled with images from my imagination of Mack under Medeiros' thumb. But we were dealing with someone who was about to drop a metal meteor on a colony. Squeamishness was inappropriate.

* * *

The drones approached the Brazilian ship, which was still drifting. We'd decided this was important enough to sacrifice all of Asgard's roamers, save two for rebuilding. This would be almost like a beach assault. Anything short of one hundred percent casualties would be acceptable.

The two drones came in as quickly as their drives could manage, braking with no leeway to arrive at rest just outside the rent in the enemy vessel. Cargo doors popped open and eight roamers, including two of the big industrial-size units, stormed across the gap. The squad headed straight for the location of the replicant matrix—we knew the layout from Bob-1's first encounter with Medeiros, way back in Epsilon Eridani.

The roamers encountered immediate resistance, from the onboard roamers. The battle was short and furious—Medeiros was fighting for his life, now. The standard roamers worked to protect the big units, as those would be needed for moving the matrix. Plasma cutters flashed, and roamer parts floated around the enclosed space.

The battle tilted in our direction once we realized that we could still use the big units. Any time an enemy roamer got too close, an industrial unit lashed out with a leg. If the impact didn't disarticulate the victim outright, being bounced off a wall took it out of the fight for a few moments.

Soon, we were down to one or two defenders—depending on how you counted body parts. Then the last roamer was dispatched, and—

"What the hell?" I exclaimed as all video feeds disappeared.

Garfield poked at consoles. "The cargo drones are gone, too. They've—wait a moment, that's not true. I'm still getting telemetry from number 2. I'll try to activate a camera."

Richards jerked in surprise in his video window as the event registered at the human timescale. "What happened?"

"Looks like Medeiros fell on his sword rather than be captured," Garfield said. He popped up a video window. "This is what the second drone is showing. It's damaged, by the way. Won't be flying back on its own."

The window showed the Brazilian vessel, or what was left of it. Pieces of spaceship spun and caught the sunlight as they receded. The ship was cut in two, and the two halves had been opened like flowers.

"He knew," I said. "He knew he was finished. I don't know if he thought he was taking the victory away from us, or thought we'd capture him and extract secrets." I shook my head. "I will never understand Medeiros. I really hope this is the last time I have to deal with him."

"That's a little worrying, though," Garfield commented. "I remember him being a bit on the pompous side, at the first meeting with Bob-1. This time around he never said a word. Not even an exit monologue. I wonder what secrets he might feel the need to take to the grave."

An excellent question, and the expression on Richards' and Kiroshi's faces showed the same concern that I felt.

* * *

"Never even saw him coming," Mack said. He sat in my VR, holding a coffee, feet up on a footstool. "I remember talking to you about draining the swamps on Takama, and the next thing I know, I'm back in my default VR."

"Yeah, he hit you square on." I raised my coffee. "You can go over the videos at your leisure, but you missed some interesting times."

"Which aren't over, I'm afraid." Mack looked at his coffee, a frown forming. "We have to assume Medeiros is still out there, in one form or another. We'll have to set up defenses, especially here and in Alpha Centauri."

"That's right, buddy. The colonies are okay with you diverting all printers to defensive items until you have a minimum level of ordnance."

"Yep. Busters, then a new vessel, then some clones, then more printers... It'll be a while before I'm able to support the colonies directly."

"They'll do what they can with groundside printers, Mack. Might be a good idea for them to have at least a small autofactory on each planet, just on principle."

Mack nodded, staring into space. "Just when we think we've got things figured out, the universe throws another curve."

I grinned at him. "Well, that's life."

31. Cleanup

Marcus
September 2215
Poseidon

The loss of their main fleet was a blow to the Council, but not a fatal one, as it turned out. Maybe I'd been underestimating the Council, or maybe they had someone who was a terrific strategist. Whatever the reason, the Council kept coming up with surprises.

The first surprise, although I'd suspected as much, was that they didn't have just the dozen cargo ships. Our first inkling of that came the day after our takeover of strategic 'ground' assets.

"We've got several cities under attack!" Gina announced, sitting up abruptly.

Kal opened one eye—he was lying on a blanket, getting some sun—and said, "With what?"

"See for yourselves." Gina held her tablet up. On it was shown a grainy, obviously blown-up image of a vessel. It appeared to my eye to be a variation on a version-3 Heaven vessel.

"Interesting. Looks like they've been reading BobNet," I said. "I don't know why that didn't occur to me. I wouldn't normally think of it as strategic information."

"And yet the improvements the Bobs have been making in the

Heaven design have been primarily for military purposes," Kal responded.

"Plus," Denu added, "if they've been perusing BobNet, wouldn't they have found out about the cloaking?"

I raised an eyebrow at Denu, then exited the android and frame-jacked. A quick scan of recent BobNet blogs reassured me on that front.

Returning to normal time, and to the android, I responded, "There's nothing but general descriptions, Denu. With all the crap happening, Bill's just been transmitting plans directly to other Bobs. A bit of serendipity, there." I didn't add that I'd just sent off a description of this situation to Bill. Hopefully, he would scan the blogs for any other potentially damaging information and remove it. Great. We'd just re-invented military secrecy.

Gina, who had continued monitoring the situation, announced, "Aanthor, Kaol, and Ptarth are fending off missiles. It looks like whoever is still fighting has decided to go for a scorched earth policy. They're not even trying to board, just trying to knock the cities out of the sky." She looked over at me.

I nodded. Reluctant as I was to get directly involved, in this case, hundreds of lives were at stake. I ordered several squads of busters down from their hiding place on Pelias, the inner moon.

"It'll take a few minutes for them to get there," I said to Gina. "Can you tell the cities that help is coming?"

Gina nodded and typed furiously for a few moments. "Done."

"This is unbelievable." Denu shook his head. "They're just trying to kill people."

"It's war, Denu," Gina replied. "It's not what we wanted, but apparently it's what the Council finds preferable to losing. Although I don't think they expected it to go this far, either. Most of their recent moves look more like ad libs than strategies." She looked at me. "Three Council members still outstanding. This could be orders from any or all of them."

"My money's on Brennan, though." Kal glanced at each of us. "Some of the others at least seemed to be misguided but well-intentioned. He was all about the power."

"Maybe. Let's get this done, then we can worry about assigning blame." I looked up as my heads-up display showed the busters coming up on the fields of battle. I ordered them to take out the attackers—if possible, by taking out critical systems, but otherwise by whatever worked.

In seconds, the reports came back. Four ships downed by clean reactor strikes, three more totally destroyed. The two remaining ships turned tail and fled.

I took a moment to mourn the people I'd just killed. Very probably they were just following orders. But those orders had meant knocking a city containing several hundred civilians out of the sky. There was a point where *following orders* didn't cut it.

I put a couple of cloaked drones on the tail of the escaping ships, and recalled my surviving busters. If there had been any doubt in the Council's teeny minds that the cursed replicant was still extant, this engagement had removed it. The Council forces would be moving much more cautiously in the future.

"Tell the city defenders not to shoot down the surviving ships," I said to Gina. "They might lead us back to the leadership."

Gina nodded, and we settled back onto the grass. It was an odd juxtaposition—revolutionary leaders, in the middle of a shooting war, directing operations while lounging on a manicured lawn.

* * *

I tracked the fleeing ships to a relatively small mat in the northern current, earmarked as an automated farming platform. Video images from the drones showed it to be anything but. A small but well-stocked airbase was probably the home of the Council fleet.

"Well, that's not good." Kal shook his head. "We'll have to check absolutely every mat on inventory, now."

I grinned at him. "Seems the Council has been planning for this for a long time."

"Or at least, planning for *something*," he replied. "I can't see how they could have predicted your flying cities."

I nodded at that. "This doesn't really look military, though. Security forces, maybe. Let's send in the roamers and a mop-up squad."

Kal nodded. He and Gina started typing furiously, while I worked on loading up the roamer squad into cargo drones.

* * *

It took longer than expected to prepare for our assault. I was surprised to discover that, with all the buzzing around and knocking out enemy ships and missiles, I was down to the dregs with busters and roamers. And without the system printers under my command, I couldn't immediately print more. In the end, Gina rounded up a squad of security people, and we stormed the defenders the old-fashioned way.

Sort of. I was still far happier with sacrificing an AMI than a human.

Gina led the charge herself. The busters couldn't smash the buildings at speed—I didn't want to kill anyone—but they could smack gun emplacements hard enough to force defenders back.

"Concentrate on all defenders on the west walls," Gina's voice ordered over the comm system. Our security people set up a blistering fire which kept the defenders down.

"Marcus, there's a weak spot on the wall at the southwest side. Can you get an explosive into there?"

"Uh, no, no explosives, Gina. Still too dangerous to print. But…"

A weak spot was easy to target. A ship buster came in at about a hundred klicks and rammed the corner of the wall. Five hundred kilograms of steel completely did a number on it. Maybe a little too well. As usual, I seemed to be a little more enthusiastic with the ramming than was really required.

"Thanks, Captain Crash. All units, enter with caution."

I sent in some roamers as well, although all I had left were the little guys. The video feed showed a stunned, dust-covered group with no fight left in them.

"I think they're done, Gina. It's all mop-up."

* * *

Gina, normally a somewhat dour, brooding person, was grinning unabashedly. "We got Brennan. No question that he ordered the attacks. We'll be debriefing the security people we captured, but I'll bet none of the other Council members were involved in this."

"Still, they'll all have to be dealt with. There will be trials. There will likely be convictions. Then there will be the question of what to do with them." Kal shrugged. "My money's on menial labor."

Gina blew out a noisy breath. "Yeah, let's not count our chickens just yet. We don't know if there are any more loci of resistance. We may get individuals who keep fighting back, but hopefully we can contain the damage from that. As long as there are no more Council members in the wind, though, I think that's it for anything organized."

"The biggest thing will be accounting for all the remaining Council members, then." Kal looked at me.

"Sorry buddy, I don't have any special tricks for finding individuals on an entire planet." I gave him a crooked smile. "Or off-planet, which is also a possibility."

"Oy." Kal rubbed the bridge of his nose with two fingers. "This really came down to the wire. If we'd had to fight just one more battle, we probably would have run out of assets. Do you have the printers back?"

I nodded. "And I've already started replacement construction, but it'll be a few days before anything pops out the other end. If we do find ourselves another fight—" I looked pointedly at Gina. "—we'd probably better go for containment rather than a punch-up."

Kal nodded. "Meanwhile, we also have a whole society to put back together. I hope you guys are okay with overtime."

We all grinned back at him.

32. Found

Bill
September 2227
Epsilon Eridani

I stared at the readings, frankly disbelieving. I glanced over at Garfield—his wide eyes and slack jaw said it all.

We'd slapped together a quick prototype, based on the power-core scans from the alien hulk. A *small* prototype. According to our measurements, this kludged-together rig was outperforming our fusion reactors five to one.

"Well, this explains a lot," Garfield finally said.

"Mmm. Of course, we're not just going to rip out all our reactors and replace them with this stuff."

"Well, no." Garfield grinned at me. "But a pilot project…"

At that moment, Will popped in.

"Hey, guys. What's this I hear about some Others' cargo vessels?"

I motioned Will to a chair and materialized some images. "The two Bobs who volunteered to survey the Delta Pavonis system chanced upon a couple of cargo vessels that had been taken out during the defensive engagement. They must have drifted right through the system. The Others didn't pick up on it, and the derelicts would have just continued out into the cosmos if those two hadn't found them."

Will leaned forward and poked at one of the images. "I think I remember that one, actually. It was almost cut in half."

I nodded. "That unit is being broken down for materials. The guys are repairing the hole in the other one, and they've had the bright idea—genius, actually—of putting mover plates around it instead of trying to figure out the Others' drive system. Then they'll fly it back to Earth."

"You could put fourteen million people in that thing, easily." Will's voice was hushed.

I laughed. "You could *misplace* fourteen million people in that thing." I made a show of feeling around my pockets. "Dang it, where did I put those colonists..."

Will grinned back at me. "Holy crap on a cracker. Fifteen hundred ships or fifteen hundred trips. Or one gigantic cargo carrier!"

33. Project

Herschel
October 2227
Delta Pavonis

Be careful what you wish for. Uh huh. I was visiting Neil, while we took a break. He'd draped himself across his chair sideways and was doing a good imitation of a boneless corpse. I could remember sitting like that when original Bob was a teenager. Neil had a couple of behaviors that seemed to hearken back to Bob's adolescence.

"Friggin' hell," he finally moaned. "Can we go back to being pondscum? Life was so much easier!"

I laughed, and signaled Jeeves for a beer. Neil had a template for a particularly good ale, and I tried to make a point of having one when I was visiting. I sat down, took a drink, then called up the project plan. "Well, we're a little ahead of schedule, buddy. You could afford to take a few milliseconds off."

"Oh, hah hah. You are too funny." Neil straightened up. "Well, at least we've finally finished cutting up Hulk-2. Loading it all into Hulk-1's cargo bays is routine enough to be left to the AMIs. But building the mover plates..."

"Yeah, I know. We weren't really anticipating having to deploy our printers when we came out here. It's a pain..." We grinned at each other and said, in unison, "but it's a *good* pain!"

"Anyway," I continued. "Moot is in a half-hour. You might want to get organized."

Neil scowled at me, then pulled up his files. He muttered something about slavery, but got to work.

* * *

The moot was crowded, but that was normal, these days. There had been a problem with despondency for a few months after the loss of Delta Pavonis 4, but we'd bounced back. Now the Bobs were more determined than ever to deal out some payback.

Neil and I picked a spot close to the podium. Normally, we'd be at the back, as befitted pondscum, but we were now Project Leaders. Of course, we were also project workers, project gophers, and project janitorial staff, but who's counting? We would be expected to give a status report on the Derelicts Project.

Bill mounted the podium, held the air-horn above his head, and gave the traditional *blaaat*. The audience greeted him with the usual catcalls and *boos*. I stayed silent, and I noticed that Neil was more reticent than usual, as well. It was much harder to be an agitator when we were standing up front.

Bill looked around the audience, waiting for the commentary to die down. When he had quiet, he began to speak.

"I'm going to start off with a bombshell. Starting twenty days ago, a number of our monitoring drones around GL 877 were attacked. Per their standing instructions, they self-destructed immediately. In the last two instances, the drones weren't attacked, but chased."

This news was met with gasps from the audience. Neil and I stared at each other, bug-eyed with shock, and he mouthed, "They know."

Bill waited a moment for the chatter to die down. "We figure the Delta Pavonis harvesting expedition reported back to the Others' home world, and they correctly concluded that they were under surveillance. Based on the attempt to capture the last two drones, they may have surmised that we have a technological advantage of some kind."

A hologram of the GL 877 system popped up in the air, showing the location of the surveillance drones around the system. Bill made a gesture with his hand, and one by one, drones were replaced by small explosion graphics.

"We're reconfiguring, but as we lose drones, our coverage will get spotty. We're biasing them toward the near side of GL 877, to catch any expeditions coming our way. We're also introducing some randomness in their positions, just to make it more difficult for the Others to find the drones. There haven't been any new attacks in the last week, so that may be working. And Mario will be replacing the drones on a priority basis. But we'll still be deficient for a few years."

Neil edged up to me. "Something smells."

"What?"

"There's something about this scenario that bothers me. Why'd they stop?"

"Because they realized they couldn't catch the drones? Because we randomized the locations?"

"Nope. Not sufficient." Neil opened his mouth to add something, but at that moment, Bill decided to introduce us.

"Now, you've all been hearing about the Derelict Project. Herschel and Neil are here today to give you their first official update." Bill gestured toward us.

I could feel myself blushing furiously as we mounted the podium. I looked around at the sea of Bobs, and my voice locked up.

Neil, familiar with my stage fright, picked up smoothly. "On a recon flight, we found a couple of Others' cargo vessels drifting out of the Delta Pavonis system. One was pretty much totaled, but the other was almost intact, with damage limited to A.I. and drive systems. We were able to reactivate the power core—there's a separate report on what we've been able to figure out about the technology."

Neil turned to me and gestured. He'd given me just the right amount of time to get it together. I picked up the thread smoothly. "We've broken down the totaled derelict, and have been using the materials to do repairs on the *Bellerophon.*"

The assembled Bobs picked up on our chosen name, and we received whistles and whoops of approval. When the approbation died down, I continued, "Rather than trying to rebuild the drive, we're just manufacturing mover plates—Bill figures 24 will be enough—to fly the whole thing to Earth. We've loaded the extra material from the other derelict into the hold, and we'll be manufacturing stasis pods during the voyage."

I looked around for Riker, but couldn't see him, so I looked at Bill. "We're thinking that if Earth would shift some manufacturing capacity into stasis pods, we could move a lot of people in one shot."

I glanced around at the crowd. Four or five dozen versions of my face looked back at me. Smiles, nods, frowns of concentration predominated. *Okay, not so bad.* Bobs were not subtle. If our presentation had been less than interesting, we'd know it.

"Questions?" Bill said.

Bedlam erupted. *Okay, really not bad.*

Neil leaned closer to me. "Isn't it nice to be important?"

"I'm having second thoughts, thanks."

Bill pointed to someone, and the chaos quieted.

Thor stepped forward. "How confident are you of the alien power core?"

I opened my mouth to reply, but Neil jumped in. "It works fine. Just as dependable as one of our own. And a lot more powerful."

I glared at him and whispered, "You lie like a log."

"Shaddup, you."

"How many pods do you think you can make?" Thor continued.

"We have enough material to build a pod for every human being alive," Neil answered. "Just not enough time. In the 3.6 years subjective trip time, we figure we can make just over five million of them."

Bill turned and spoke to someone. "Will, how many could you put together at your end?"

Riker stepped forward. "No more than a couple of million. We're working in non-relativistic time, but on the other hand, we don't have piles of refined metals just sitting there. We have to salvage every kilogram of metal, and the pickings are getting thinner. It's starting to slow colony ship production, as a matter of fact."

The conversation descended into comparisons of critical paths, differing ramp-up strategies, result domains, and other, even less interesting things. I eyed Neil, and he nodded. As casually as possible, we sidled away from the debate and toward the bar. No one noticed our departure.

I leaned against a rail with a beer in my hand, and grinned at Neil. "We're important."

"Yeah, when they notice we're gone, I'll concede. Meanwhile..." He raised his beer in a toast.

Gotta love moots.

34. Kidnapping

Bob
September 2224
Delta Eridani (Eden)

I was sitting in the sun with Buster, watching him casually work a piece of flint, when the Deltan came running up. He bent over, gasping for breath for a few moments, then straightened. "Archimedes has been grabbed. I think it was some guys from Caerleon. Must have been."

I leaped to my feet and almost yelled at the runner, "Have you told Donald? Anyone else?"

He nodded, still gasping. "Yeah, Donald's gathering some hunters."

I looked over to see Buster silently gathering his bow and arrows. He didn't say anything; didn't look at me or at the runner. His fur was flat, his inner turmoil telegraphed by his ears, which were curled in rage. Someone was going to die today.

We hurried over to the hunters' tree, where a group was forming. Donald waved at me as I came up.

"Well, Robert, it looks like you and Archimedes might have been right. There's only one reason for them to grab him."

I shook my head. "Two reasons, actually. If Fred is involved, he may also be trying to get a reaction from me. I'm pretty sure I hurt his feelings, last time we met." I glanced at Buster, standing beside me. "If Fred's involved, today is his final day of life, I think."

Buster stared straight ahead, still not looking at anyone.

I'd set spy drones to searching for any large, fast-moving parties of Deltans. Reports were now starting to come in. I checked the heads-up. It showed two different groups, but only one was on a determined beeline for Caerleon. My bet would be on that one.

I instructed the drones to try for close-ups, and gave them Archimedes' profile to identify. Then I turned to Donald. "Chances are they're on the East Trail, or will be soon. We can cut straight through the Deep Copse to catch up." I hoped Donald wouldn't question me. I knew for a fact that was true, but I couldn't explain how without blowing my cover.

Fortunately, Donald took my word for it and started giving orders. In moments, we were running toward the Deep Copse, a thick grove of especially tall, old trees. Paradoxically, because of the thickness of the trees, there was very little underbrush to slow us down. We made it through in minutes.

I held up my hand to stop the group and made a show of listening, then gestured up the trail. We took off at a sprint. It took less than a minute to catch up to the Caerleon group, who I knew had been having a problem with their captive grabbing every tree and branch he could reach. From my position, it looked like they'd solved the problem by beating Archimedes unconscious and then carrying him.

A low growl escaped my throat, and I hoisted my spear. The Caerleon party, hearing our approach, stopped and formed a defensive semicircle, spears pointing outwards.

Fred stepped forward, grinning his usual smug, nasty grin. "Hello, Robert. Robert's lackies. I suggest you accept the inevitable. Your friend is going to be—"

Fred looked down at the arrow protruding from his chest. With a surprised expression, he fell to his knees, then collapsed sideways to the ground.

I turned to look at Buster.

"Dibs," he said with a shrug.

Unfortunately, although I could understand and sympathize with Buster's actions, the Caerleon gang might retaliate by harming Archimedes. I would not allow that, even if it meant revealing that *the Bawbe* was still watching. I called up a squad of busters and sent them to the nearby trees, standing by.

If at all possible, though, we would take these guys out the old-fashioned way.

The Caerleons were still going through surprise at the quick death, but a few heads had started to turn toward their prisoner. With a roar of anger, I charged the spear line. My friends followed, yelling battle-cries.

I would easily be the first to reach the defenders. But how to handle it? I could, of course, take a couple of spear wounds without slowing my android form. But running around with spears sticking out of me would be hard to explain. On the other hand, I didn't want any of my friends to take a spear. I had less than ten meters to decide on a plan.

Instead of slowing down, I accelerated. As I came almost to the flint tips of their spears, I threw myself down and sideways. Half sliding, half rolling, I passed under the spear points before the Deltans could react. My tumbling body took out three of the front defenders, and knocked down a couple behind them.

With the sudden hole in the defensive line, the Caerleons were unable to hold off the attackers. The defenders tried to swivel to close the gap, but left themselves open to attack from the side. I heard growls and the *smack* of colliding bodies, as well as the more cringeworthy cries of people being impaled.

I couldn't worry about it at the moment, though. A couple of the Caerleons seemed to have had exactly the thought I'd been concerned about. As I'd feared, they drew their flint blades and turned to Archimedes' limp form.

I grabbed a spear that had been dropped and thrust it at the first enemy. At the last moment, I redirected the spear to what I hoped was a non-fatal attack. The spear passed through Deltan muscle and jabbed the Deltan behind him. I released the spear, leaving both Deltans howling with pain and surprise, grabbed the knife that one had just dropped, and drove it into the thigh of a third enemy.

With the quick removal of three of their number, the others backed away from Archimedes, fear written on their faces. I pulled my lips back as far as I could and did my best Hulk impression, roaring and gnashing my teeth.

Apparently, it was effective. One tripped while trying to

backpedal and sat down abruptly, and the other two turned tail and fled.

I stood over Archimedes' still form and spun around, snarling, looking for anyone within reach. At this point, if I had caught someone, I very probably would have done something impossible for a Deltan and blown my cover.

Not necessary, though. The battle was over. Three of ours were down. Eight of theirs were down, three of them obviously dead. Including Fred.

Buster and I exchanged silent looks, then we turned to Archimedes. I knelt and examined him. He was still breathing, although a faint liquid sound in his lungs concerned me. The beating looked to have been more enthusiastic than really necessary. Deltans had marvelous healing abilities—I hoped it would be enough, otherwise Archimedes might lose an eye. The teeth, at least, would grow back.

Very slowly and carefully, Buster and I lifted Archimedes and headed back to the village.

* * *

A week later, Archimedes was looking much better. He hadn't lost the eye, although he was still complaining about blurry vision.

He sat with his granddaughter, Lisa, who went into fits of giggles watching her grandfather eating baby food. He'd be on that diet for a few more weeks, according to Belinda.

Donald sat in front of the fire, nursing a large hunk of jerky. He extended an arm, holding a knife out to me. I took the flint blade and examined it.

"Mm, yeah, not exactly up to Archimedes' standards."

"It's crap," Donald said. "It looks like you guys were right. We questioned a couple of the survivors, after the medicine woman was done with them. By the way, she thinks you're an idiot for wasting resources healing enemies."

I waved the comment away. "Once the fight is over, everyone bleeds the same color. And Annie is *way* more reasonable than Cruella ever was. She would have just told me to stuff it."

Donald nodded. "Anyway, the knife is some of the best work coming out of Caerleon. So they have crap knives and crap spears, and are barely doing better with hunting than how my father says things were back at the old village. They've even started to get gorilloids sniffing around again."

"And they blame us."

Donald grinned at me. "I never said it made sense. I guess it's our fault for having more skilled people and better tools and better hunting."

"And more adults." I grinned back. Then I grew serious. "But if this is the problem, it's fixable. Just have some of their best and brightest come over and get Archimedes to train them."

"I'm sure they've thought of it," Buster cut in, as he came up and sat down. "But there's been so much fighting, they probably think we'd just laugh at them."

"And they don't want to look weak."

I rubbed the fur above my eyebrow, the Deltan equivalent of pinching the bridge of my nose. "Unbelievable. So, how do we broach the subject?"

Archimedes looked up from playing with Lisa. "We should just offer to teach a couple of their people."

"The teaching thing didn't work so well before," I pointed out.

"They weren't hungry before," Archimedes answered. "I bet they'll pay more attention now."

We looked at each other around the fire. No one had to put it into words. It was worth a try.

35. Cities Victorious

Marcus
October 2215
Poseidon

A month after the uprising, things were finally settling down. But despite all my attempts to dodge, bob and weave, and otherwise avoid taking on a position of responsibility, I'd still somehow ended up as the Chairman Pro Tem. Of course, there was some logic to having the reins held by someone who was available twenty-four seven, never forgot anything, and couldn't be bought or blackmailed.

Still, I was going to arrange elections as soon as possible.

The drone settled into New Thark's docking bay and floated into a parking spot. The cargo bay doors opened and I stepped out. I took a moment to look around—most of the spots were taken, as people continued to move into the city.

I walked to the elevators at the end of the bay and got in with a half dozen random strangers. Interestingly, two hundred years later and twenty light years away, people still behaved the same in elevators as they did in Original Bob's day. Everyone turned to face the doors, and ignored each other.

As the elevator rose to ground level, I surreptitiously examined the other passengers. No one paid me any particular attention. I was just another anonymous, random individual. It amazed me how good that felt.

I stepped out of the elevator and found myself outdoors, with a transport station to my left and a park to my right. I let the other passengers hurry to grab taxis first, while I took the time to look around. This was my first time in the new version-3 floating city. This model boasted two square kilometers of usable surface, divided about evenly between residences, businesses, and parkland.

The fibrex dome stretched over the city, ensuring a warm, dry environment, no matter the weather outside. Residents were scattered around, sitting on benches or on the grass, working away on their tablets or remote-controlling some piece of equipment, VR headset and gloves firmly in place.

Why the Council would have wanted to prevent this was beyond me. Some people just seemed to want to display their power by defining what others could or couldn't do.

I shook my head, then turned and headed for the transport station. I grabbed the next available pod, spoke Kal's address, and sat back as the pod accelerated into the underground track.

In less than two minutes, I exited the pod, followed the directions it had given me, and was standing at Kal's front door.

* * *

We sat around the table, Kal, Denu, Gina, Vinnie, and myself, drinking beer and comparing war stories. The new government of Poseidon, such as it was.

Gina put up a list of names. "Here's the Council members we've captured. Five out of seven. Based on comments from a couple of them, you might be right about the last two having escaped in subs."

"So they might be hiding out on any of a hundred mats." I smiled at her. "Or they might already be in the belly of the leviathan."

Gina shrugged. "Yeah, no way to know. But they're not like royalty. They won't command a following of fanatically loyal subjects."

"Right. We'll keep an eye out, do patrols, but it's not top of the priority list. What are you doing with the five you captured?"

"Four of them will go to trial for the hundred and fifty deaths of Thark citizens. The consensus seems to be a lifetime posting to the fish plant, or something equally smelly."

"And Brennan?"

Gina sighed. "Honestly, Marcus, we don't really have anything. We played with the idea of incarcerating him for life, or deporting him to another colony, or even back to Earth. All of those alternatives are a ton of effort and cost, and make no sense except as some form of retribution. And he's not worth it. We're considering just sticking him with the other four and being done with it."

There were nods around the table. Fish plant labor was easy to automate, but the Council had used it as a punishment for dissidents and miscreants. The irony of hoisting them on their own petard was so overt that it needed no further words. Brennan deserved worse, but I agreed that he didn't deserve the effort required to arrange something.

"And meanwhile," I looked to one of my monitor windows in my heads-up, which showed the orbital autofactories in full swing. "Another dozen or so cities and we'll have the entire population of Poseidon in the air."

Gina grinned at me. "And then we're gonna vote you out on your ear."

"Can't wait."

36. Announcement

Riker
October 2227
Sol

Bedlam.

No, even that wasn't a strong enough word. It reminded me of the first meetings of the UN, way back when. Everyone was attempting to talk at once. Half the people were hammering their Request buttons, the other half were ignoring them. The chairperson sat at her desk with her head in her hand.

I grinned into the camera. Technically, I still had the floor, so my mike was active. "Sooooo, want to hear more?"

The chaos cut off like a switch had been thrown.

"As I said, this vessel will hold all of the remaining population of Earth. Every last one. We will obviously still have to build stasis pods. However, Herschel and Neil, the two Bobs in charge of the *Bellerophon*, are also building pods in their cargo bay as they travel. Good news, they have all the material they could possibly need. Bad news, with relativistic time dilation, they'll only have three and a half years to work with."

Representative Misra requested and got the floor. "Could they slow slightly and enjoy a longer subjective time to work in?"

I smiled and nodded. Ms. Misra understood the mechanics very well. It made talking to her so much easier than most of these bozos. I grimaced for a moment at the unintended contempt in that thought.

"That's correct. However, it would result in a longer transit time from our point of view. There's still the Others to worry about. Their plans are a big unknown, but we're going to assume we don't have time for a leisurely flight plan. I'd rather get them here quickly, then we can make use of all that scrap in their hold."

I shared out a list of tasks and milestones. Most of the UN delegates ignored it, but a few looked down and started reading.

"Once the *Bellerophon* gets here with her hull full of scrap metal, we can assign every single printer and AMI to the task of building more pods. Meanwhile, we need to make sure our shuttles are all in good working order. I've calculated that we can move about three hundred thousand people at a time, using the existing airworthy enclave shuttles and cargo vessels. I'd like to get that number up to a round million."

I released the floor and nodded to the chairperson. Every Request light in the UN lit up.

Fun times.

Representative Hubert from the North African enclave took the floor. "Mr. Johansson, I am concerned that we will not have enough stasis pods for all of Earth when the ship, er, the *Bellerophon* arrives. Yet I note that you are still allocating resources to things like colony ships and shuttles. What about creating more printers, to increase the throughput? I'm not trying to tell you how to do your job, but have you considered what the most efficient schedule is?"

Hubert sat down and turned off his mike, giving up the floor.

I nodded an acknowledgement. I could have been offended, but I'd rather have the question asked and answered. "Representative Hubert, it is a good question, and well worth asking. And the answer is that I spend a considerable portion of my time considering all the alternatives. The problem is that, no matter what course you navigate, there is always a bottleneck. Whether it's lack of printers to build everything, or lack of sufficient material, or lack of drones and roamers to assemble the parts into the end product—it's always *something*. Shift your schedule and you simply shift the nature of the bottleneck. Printers, for instance, are the most complex thing that a printer can make, except for something biological. They take forever, and have a high defect rate because of the precision required. So it's not as simple as just making more printers to enjoy the benefits of exponential growth. You give up considerable manufacturing opportunity while engaged in that particular task."

I paused and looked around at the various windows. "Concentrate on shuttles and we may not have enough stasis pods come arrival day. Concentrate on stasis pods and we may not have a way to get people up to the carrier quickly enough. I've already decided to stop manufacturing colony ships. We've got enough returning ships, now, to keep a flow going, and we need the raw materials for shuttles and pods."

I paused again, then turned off my mike and sat down. Immediately, a dozen request lights lit up. With a sigh, I realized I would be here for a while.

37. Court Battle

Howard
September 2220
Omicron^2 Eridani

"How long do you expect this to last?" I whispered to Ms. Benning. I glanced across the courtroom where Bridget's children sat with their lawyer, Gus Kistler.

"Actually, it'll be over in an hour," Benning replied. "In the end, it's a really cut and dry situation. Bridget Brodeur's last will is on file, and its veracity is not being questioned. They are trying for an 'undue influence' ruling, but since that's usually about inheritances, it's not likely to fly. Lastly, they're trying for sympathy with the 'laying our mother to rest' gambit."

She shuffled some papers. "What it's really about is a delaying action. They've been trying to prevent it for long enough that something would happen, or we'd run out of money—" I snorted. Fat chance of that. "Or get tired of fighting, or we'd make a mistake…" Ms Benning turned to me. "They've thrown everything but the kitchen sink at us. It's a good thing Mrs. Brodeur was wealthy."

She sat back and sighed. "Anyway, Mr. Johansson, they've used up all their ammunition, and we've used up all of ours. Today, the judge will decide. Unless a miracle occurs for them, we will win."

I looked over at Rosie, Lianne, and Howard. Howard looked ready to throw up. It seemed like a bit of an over-reaction, since my impression through all of this had been that he was being dragged along by the girls.

And speaking of, they didn't look nearly as nervous as would be indicated by Ms. Benning's confident remark. Perhaps their lawyer was stringing them along. But why? It wouldn't increase his billing. And anyway, *he* didn't look all that confident.

Then Rosie turned and looked at me, and my heart froze. I don't think I'd ever seen the particular facial expression *malicious triumph* before, but trust me, it's one of those expressions you'll recognize the first time with one hundred percent certainty. What was going on? She couldn't be expecting to win this case? And if not—

With a sinking feeling of panic, I remembered Dr. Onagi's suspicions. I sent a text to Will, Bill, and Bob. One of them had to be free, and they were in the minority of Bobs that were guaranteed to not be travelling at relativistic speeds.

I'll take care of it, came back a moment later from Bill. I breathed a sigh of relief, but my stomach refused to un-knot.

The judge came in, we did the all-rise thing, then sat. There was considerable noise from the surprisingly large number of spectators. Apparently this case had achieved significant notoriety. The judge banged his gavel several times and demanded quiet.

Judge Katz spent a long time summarizing the facts and pleadings of the case. Even though I was deeply emotionally involved, I still found my mind wandering. I had to respect people like Ms. Benning who could sit through this regularly without their foreheads slamming onto the desk.

Then, finally, the judge came to the punchline. "I must, in the end, uphold the right of the decedent to decide her own destiny."

There were gasps and muttering around the courtroom. I half-expected Rosie to stand up and start screaming invective, but no. She just—huh. She just took out her phone and texted something.

And, at that moment, I knew that Dr. Onagi had been right.

* * *

We all filed out of the courtroom. Ms. Benning was shaking my hand, and her assistant was making a phone call, when Rosie strode up to me.

"You may think you've won, but you still won't steal our mother from us."

"Chrissake, Rosie, are you still on that narrative? There is no *stealing.* There never was any *stealing.* Ignoring for the moment the fact that *it was your mother's decision,* you still have her. You still have the body to bury, you still have her memories. You lost *nothing!*"

"Just the same, you won't get her. I've made sure of that."

"You mean sabotaging the stasis pod at the hospital?" I raised my eyebrows in an expression of exaggerated inquiry, and she went white. "I'm sorry, Rosie, but if you can defy a court order, so can I. Bill sent in a drone with the scanner and did the deed while we were in court. Except that, unlike you, Bill would have respected the court's decision if we'd lost."

Rosie took a step back and her lips formed into a silent snarl. I shook my head. "Bill confirmed with me that a device embedded in the stasis pod damaged it and shut it down, just around the time you sent a text. There will be an investigation, of course. I'm pretty sure sabotage of hospital equipment is a crime of some kind. I'm willing to throw myself on the mercy of the court for my transgression. I have a feeling it'll go worse for you."

I gave Rosie a blank, cold look. "I knew your mother and father. I loved and respected them both. Right now, I can't understand how you could be related to them."

She opened her mouth to say something, and I turned and walked away.

38. Travelling

Herschel
September 2236
Interstellar Space

"I'm serious, Herschel, it's not coming back up." Neil's voice took on a little bit of a whine when he got really frustrated. The sound set my teeth on edge, and it was one of the only times I didn't want to be around him.

"Have you jim-jammed the frammistan?"

"Oh, funny guy. How about you hang up the comedy act for a second and give me a hand. And if you start clapping, I *will* busterize you."

I chuckled and activated one of my inside drones. We kept a set of spares in bay 446, which was about as central as you could get in the *Bellerophon*. The drone flew out the open bay doors, into the ship's main axial corridor. Five klicks of straight flight took less than a minute, then a right turn, and I was in the power room. "Room" was a funny word to use for an open area a quarter kilometer on a side, but we'd gotten used to thinking of the ship as normal sized and ourselves as bugs.

Neil had three drones and a dozen roamers swarming the power core's control area. For some reason, when Neil got frustrated, he made the roamers tap their feet. I'd never asked if it was on purpose. I wasn't sure I wanted to know.

"I've done *everything!*" he exclaimed as soon as he saw my drone. "It's dead. Inert."

"It works fine, he says. As dependable as one of our own, he says."

"Fine, Herschel. Get it out of your system. Make fun. Then, when you're done, maybe we can work on fixing this friggin' thing!"

I considered milking it for a few more moments, but why get greedy? As sure as entropy, I'd have another chance sooner or later. "Neil, I can see from here that the anodes are saturated. You can do a bleed, which will take about an hour, or you can do a full restart in twenty minutes."

"Oh, God, no."

"I'll help, okay? We can't afford to be down like this all the time."

I called up some more drones and roamers, and we started the long and finicky restart process. A bleed would take longer, but didn't require a lot of effort, so it was Neil's go-to response.

Once we had the roamers and drones set up, I turned to Neil. "Why don't you have an AMI set up to monitor this stuff? It's a freakin' rote task, dude!"

"I know, I keep meaning to…"

"So, you're doing things the hard way, because you're too lazy to figure out how to do them the easy way? Neil, you are truly a putz."

Neil grinned at me, unoffended. "A *lazy* putz, thank you very much. Okay, Hersch, point taken. I'll get on it."

I smiled, leaned back, and stretched. Just another damned day at the office.

* * *

The cargo vessels weren't just big empty barns. In some ways, that would have been convenient, but it would have required us to build something to anchor our various projects. I imagined the Others went though some vaguely similar logic. The vessels were large cylinders, organized radially—a central corridor a hundred meters in diameter stretched from the nose to the tail of the ship. A huge cargo door at either end allowed entry and egress. Storage bays were arranged internally in rings around the central corridor, eight bays per ring by default, and each bay sported a massive double door. The A.I. controller and drive system were located in the middle ring, and the power core was at the rear of the craft.

Neil and I spent many hours touring the inside of the *Bellerophon*, trying to figure out the reasoning behind some of the design choices. In particular, Neil didn't see why they needed bays at all.

"Look, Hersch, we've got the video from Mario's discovery on Beta Hydri. The ingots they were producing weren't that big. Like the size of a car. Why not just stack them in a big central area?"

"You just answered your own question, Neil. You really want ingots the size of Chevies banging around inside a spaceship?"

"Chrissake, dude, they tie them down..."

"To what? Now you need stanchions of some kind, at least. You can't tie it down to one single connection point, either, because that's a disaster waiting to happen. Besides, who says metal harvesting is the only thing they used these ships for?"

"Hmm, good point. They do have power connections in every bay. That would make sense if they used them for other stuff, like maybe manufacturing areas."

"Yeah, uh..." I hesitated, and Neil looked over at me, curious. "Well, I have a theory, based on this ship..."

Neil made a rolling motion with his hand for me to continue.

"Look, Neil, we do our manufacturing out in space, because we don't give a crap and it's convenient. But given what we know of the Others and the way they huddle in their death asteroids—well, what if they're an underground species? Maybe they're deeply agoraphobic. Maybe they do all their manufacturing inside one of these things because if they had to supervise something outside, it would scare the crap out of them."

Neil bobbed his head back and forth. "Not unreasonable. Total speculation, of course. Hey, you could always go ask them." He grinned at me.

[Mover Plates are offline.]

"The hell?" We both looked up at Guppy. "What happened?" I asked.

[Plate AMIs have lost synchronization.]

Neil looked at me. "Third time this month. About ready to concede yet?"

"Crud." I rubbed the bridge of my nose. "Okay, I give. Guppy, take them through restart, let me know when the drive is up again. And we're going to make eight more plates and try to even out the field."

The problem wasn't really too few plates. Bill's calculations had been right—24 plates would fly the *Bellerophon*, all things being equal. But all things were not equal. We had a couple of Bobs—us—constantly flying around in the ship under our own SURGE fields, moving and shifting mass around in the ship, and restarting the power core a couple of times a month. We were our own worst enemy. We needed some wiggle room, in the form of a little extra field strength to absorb the glitches.

I watched Neil do the *I told you so* dance for a few moments. "When you're done being an ass, let's see where we can set this up. Maybe a free bay toward the front."

Neil grunted. "You know, there was a time, when we were pondscum, and we just flew around a lot and minded our own business."

"Ah, the good old days," I replied. "When things were simpler, kids were more respectful, and we had to walk to school through six feet of snow."

"Barefoot."

"Uphill."

"Both ways."

39. Retirement

Marcus
February 2218
Poseidon

I sat in a lawn chair, soaking in the warm afternoon sun. I hardly ever thought about the fact that I was inhabiting an android any more. Howard and Bob kept improving the model, and Bill seemed happy with the delegation of responsibility. Couldn't really blame him, I supposed. He had other things on his mind.

Around me, children played, couples walked hand-in-hand, and people did their jobs either through tablets or tele-presence. If this wasn't utopia, I'd be damned if I could figure out what was missing.

Especially for me. Rather than take back control of the autofactories after the revolution, I'd aggressively created the means for the population of Poseidon to take over the responsibility. Now, three years later, I had absolutely no duties in this system.

As promised, Gina had me voted out on my ear. To her chagrin, she found herself voted in as Chairperson. The new Council was still arguing about what to put in as a permanent government, but that was certainly nothing new.

I got up and walked along the path toward the nearest food

kiosk. That particular lawn chair might or might not be occupied if I returned, but there'd be another. Or I could just park my butt on the grass.

The problem I had run into was perhaps not totally unexpected. Bob had always been a driven, workaholic personality. Great for when you were defending the galaxy from the rampaging hordes; maybe not so good when you'd just arranged to have yourself made redundant.

Poseidon society had been fundamentally changed, and the change looked to be permanent. Fewer and fewer people were living on the mats, or even working on them for longer than necessary. The floating cities—the aquatic ones, that is—were being converted entirely to industrial use. Humans were now an aerial species on this world.

I grabbed a chocolate shake—nothing had ever been invented or discovered that beat chocolate—and headed over to the edge of the city. Looking down through the dome, I could see wispy clouds, drifting mats, sparkling blue water right out to the horizon, and the occasional huge shadowy silhouette gliding just under the surface. The krakens, hydrae, and leviathans weren't the only large predators, or even the biggest. We kept discovering new beasties, often the hard way. There wasn't really a concerted effort, yet, to catalog everything under the surface. Maybe because of the danger.

"So, how's life as a retiree?"

I turned to find Kal grinning at me.

"Huh. I'm pretty sure I had my location turned off. How'd you find me?"

Kal rolled his eyes. "C'mon, Marcus. You're kind of famous. There've been three social media posts with your image in the last fifteen minutes. If you want anonymity, you're going to have to modify that mug of yours."

I nodded and turned back to the dome wall. "Or disappear entirely."

"What's going on, Marcus?" Kal stepped closer, frowning.

"Oh, hey, that came out more dramatic than intended." I gave Kal an apologetic smile and waved at the view. "I'm just thinking about a new career. Oceanography."

Kal raised an eyebrow.

"I think there's an opportunity here. You've seen videos of

Garfield's pterosaur-like android? Bob-1 has definitely gone non-human. Why even stick to bipedal?"

Kal looked out at the ocean below. "You mean…"

"I wonder how an android dolphin would fare on this world."

40. Recovery

Bob
January 2225
Delta Eridani

I paused to stretch, then pulled a tent flap aside and peeked outside. Wow. Good day to stay indoors. The rain, in drops almost as big as marbles in this heavy atmosphere, came in more horizontally than otherwise.

These tropical storms were surprisingly rare in this part of Eden, fortunately. I wondered how the Deltans would have handled them before my introduction of tents. Probably huddled under blankets made from skins. I remembered that storm they'd endured during the exodus from the old village. That hadn't been as bad as this, but it had still put me onto the tent idea.

I glanced around the village. No one was in sight, not surprisingly. Behind me, I heard stirring.

"Are you going to keep that thing open forever? You're letting the cold in."

I grunted and released the flap. Belinda wasn't big on cold.

I returned to my spot, lay down, and put my hands behind my head. Archimedes was awake, turning a piece of flint in his hands. I could see that it was the spear-head from Fred's spear.

Archimedes looked in my direction. "I've got an idea for getting the flint teaching thing going." He waved the spear-head like a wand. "It's worth it if it ends the fighting."

"Sure, Archimedes. I've got your back, whatever you want to do."

"Good. I'll have to make a half-dozen or so spear-heads and knife blades, first. Belinda won't let me work inside, so I hope this storm ends soon."

"My bones tell me it'll clear up around noon." I twisted my ears in amusement, and Archimedes returned the expression.

I had earned a reputation as an accurate forecaster of weather, crediting aches in my bones for being able to feel the change. In fact, I simply looked down from orbit at the prevailing weather patterns. Sure, it was cheating. So what?

The storm blew itself out by early afternoon, so we headed out to Archimedes' favorite flint-working spot. I was impressed by the amount of flint flakes lying discarded on the ground. Someone pushed them into a pile occasionally, when they started to become an irritant, so there was an even larger heap of flakes a few feet away. Children would often pick through the pile, looking for flakes that could be made into arrow-heads. Archimedes didn't mind—he made more than enough product to trade for everything he and his family could want.

Archimedes endured a coughing fit as he sat down. He still hadn't completely recovered from the kidnapping. I waited, ready to go back for water if he needed it.

Over the course of the afternoon, Archimedes roughed out a dozen blanks. I took the opportunity to go on a quick hunting trip, during which I checked surveillance for any Caerleon activity. I found nothing, which led me to hope that the incident had cooled any desire by the other village to take us on again.

I dropped off a turkey-equivalent with Belinda, received a smile in return, and returned to Archimedes' work area.

"I'll be a few days getting these ready, Robert," he said to me as I sat down. "Then we have to figure out how to offer them without getting killed."

"Sooner the better, buddy. I'll talk to Donald."

Archimedes resumed his work, and I settled back to enjoy the sunshine.

41. Resurrection

Howard
October 2220
HIP 14101

I reached out, for the umpteenth time, to flip the switch. And pulled my hand back, yet again. Oh, my freakin' God, what was wrong with me? I had Bridget's scan—finally, after months of court battles. I had a matrix and a ship built for her. Her VR was set up, her firewall was set up, I had accounts set up for her on BobNet...

What the hell?

In desperation, I sent a text off to Bill. *Am I doing the right thing?*

The answer came back almost immediately. *Oh, hell, no.*

Well, nothing like a little bit of support from your friends. Chuckling, I flipped the switch.

Bridget appeared in the middle of my VR—twenty-eight years old, thick red hair, dimples, lab coat—just like the first day I'd met her.

I stared, slack-jawed. I couldn't help it. I was completely, utterly, frozen.

Bridget turned a full circle, then smiled uncertainly at me. "Howard?"

I wordlessly got up, rushed to her, and wrapped her in my

arms. She hugged me, put her head on my shoulder, and we simply existed, for what could have been forever.

Finally, she stepped back and looked at me searchingly. "I guess this means I'm dead?"

"Original Bridget is dead. You are very much alive."

"Okay, Howard, I'll toe the official line. I know you've always been sensitive about the difference."

"It's important to get an image of yourself as a unique person, Bridge. You aren't just a copy. You're *you*, and you'll become more *you* as time goes on."

I took her hand and led her to the couch. I had copied the couch from her apartment, in the hope that it would reassure her. She looked at it and chuckled, no doubt fully aware of my intent.

"We've got hundreds of Bobs now. Every one of us is different. Some are a little different, some are a lot. There's no feeling of us just being 'Bob clones'. And you aren't just a 'Bridget clone'."

Bridget's lips pressed together for a moment. Then she looked me in the eyes. "Got it. If I believe my Catholic upbringing, Original Bridget is now in either Heaven or Hell. You know the Catholic Church was never able to come up with a coherent policy on replicants, right?"

I chuckled. "They didn't have a whole lot of time, before Armageddon distracted everyone."

Bridget blew out a deep breath and looked around. "What happened to the beach?"

"I can bring that back if you want. But this is my normal indoor VR. I've kind of settled on the default Bob library slash living room."

"Could we, please? I never actually experienced the ocean shore in real life on Earth."

I nodded, and the VR changed to my tropical paradise. A warm breeze ruffled our clothing, gulls squawked in the distance, and Jeeves stood at attention with a couple of drinks with little umbrellas.

Bridget giggled. She looked around, sighed, then patted the couch. "This could probably go."

"Your wish is my command."

The couch was replaced with a couple of comfortable lawn chairs—not the plasticky ones with cross-ways straps, but the good ones, with a fitted cushion. No geese here to worry about.

Bridget lay back in the chair and took a deep breath. "Okay, this is not bad. I might still have a panic attack at some point, but then maybe not. So, let's bring me up to date. I died?"

"Yes." I hesitated, looking at her. "Heart failure. You hadn't told me that you'd changed your will. Apparently it was a surprise to a lot of people."

She looked at me intently. "How did it go over with the children?"

I rolled my eyes. "Good thing you set aside that defense fund. I've got all the court documents and such, still. You can look them over whenever you want. Suffice it to say, though, that we are no longer on speaking terms."

Bridget looked down with an expression of deep sadness. "I guess I'm probably not going to be their favorite person, either. Nevertheless, I should make the attempt."

"Start with Howie."

She nodded, thoughtfully, then looked around. "Um, so what do I do?"

"Oh, boy. I guess we should start with lessons. Replicant VR 101."

* * *

I received a text from Bridget, indicating that she was finished with her phone calls. I popped into her VR right away, to find her sitting on her couch and quietly crying. I sat down beside her and without saying a word, took her hand.

She took a few more milliseconds, then smiled at me through the tears. "I have to admit, I love that you didn't include runny noses in the VR world."

"Look, there's a limit to even our obsessive realism." I grinned at her. "We also don't have mosquitoes. That by itself is worth the price of admission." I lost the grin and looked into her eyes. "So, want to talk about it?"

Bridget sighed and sat back into the couch. I noted in passing that it was the same couch as she'd had in her real apartment, the one I'd used when I brought her back. The VR was, in fact, a mostly faithful copy of her former home, except for the addition of a bigger sitting room area, and a bay window with a sun-filled view of the Vulcan landscape.

"I talked to Howie," she said. Her lip quivered for a moment. "He was distant, but seemed embarrassed about it. I think he's caught between a rock and a hard place, wanting to accept me, but knowing that Rosie would never forgive him."

"Um." I said. I figured that would be safe.

Bridget smiled sadly. "Rosie was always difficult. She knows what she wants, and isn't interested in differing opinions. Or concerned about damage from trying to get her way."

"Be patient, Bridge. Howie will come around. Out of curiosity, if nothing else. I can put him onto my relatives as well. Give him a more positive viewpoint on replicants as family."

Bridget nodded and wiped her eyes. Then she looked at her hands with a quizzical expression. "I suppose I could really just alter the VR to clean myself up, couldn't I?"

"Yes, but don't. If you start getting in the habit of shortcutting things, you end up just floating around the room like Dracula. The VR helps us remain grounded." I stopped and thought for a second. "Although now, with the androids and all, it might not be as important."

Bridget stood up. She wandered slowly around her VR, occasionally picking up objects and examining them. She ended up at the bay window, looking out at the Vulcan forest in the distance. The sun was setting, and long shadows stretched across the foreground.

She gazed out at the landscape for a few moments, then raised a hand and made a small gesture. The Vulcan landscape changed into an aerial view of the Odin cloudscape. Blimps floated in the distance, moving in small groups.

"That's from the videos I took," I said, pleased. I walked over to stand beside her.

Bridget turned to me and returned my smile. "Please don't be insulted, Howard, but it was the chance to study the Odin lifeforms that turned me around on the replication question."

"Hah-HAH!" I replied. "My evil plan is working like a ch—Ow!"

"Just remember you can still feel my wrath, wise guy." She grinned as I rubbed my shoulder. "Now, can we see about a field trip?"

"Yesss, precious, just don't hurts us again."

"Oh, Howard!"

Well, I'd wanted a family.

42. Results Negative

Bill
February 2228
82 Eridani

I'd received a report from Mack, so I popped into his VR to discuss it.

"Hey, Bill. Pull up a rock." Mack waved a hand at a very comfortable-looking overstuffed easy chair, and I took the invitation.

"I read your report, Mack. Not very encouraging."

"You mean the Medeiros part. Yeah, we've scanned this entire system right out to the Oort. Nada. In fact, I did a second scan, staggered in relation to the first one, in case something was hiding in a weak scan zone or something. Still nada."

"What are the chances that what we saw with Medeiros was all there was?" I doubted that, myself, but wanted confirmation that my thinking was reasonable.

"Can't see it, Bill. Those busters, and those missiles, had to come from somewhere. You saw that I talked it over with Calvin, right? '*No damned way*' were his exact words."

"Nor could he have hauled all those busters, missiles, and roamers all the way from Alpha Centauri." I stared into space, considering. "Mind you, he couldn't have brought them in from a nearby system, either, at least not in one trip."

Mack nodded and rubbed his chin. "So, either he took two trips, or he had help, or he's building them locally."

"Maybe you need to go out farther on the scan."

"Or… Bill, something I've been thinking about. We use the cloaking for busters and bombs, and that's basically what Medeiros has been using it for. But what if he got the bright idea of cloaking an entire autofactory?"

I could feel my eyebrows going up. "Oh, that would be bad. Then he could be in this system, and we'd have to hit him with a focused pulse to even have a hope of detecting him."

Mack sighed and sat back in his chair. He looked up at the ceiling, not speaking, for almost a half-second. "On the other hand, I could be invoking imaginary dangers, here. We are completely in the dark on this one."

"You're up to strength, now, right?"

"More or less." Mack waved a hand dismissively. "We've got printers, we've got resources, I'm building a new cohort, I have busters to spare… But it looks like I'm going to have to mobilize a system-wide defense."

"There's a lot of that going around, these days, Mack. Look, once you have your cohort up and running, start on more surveillance drones. Give them both long-range and focused scanning capability. I know the chance of hitting something at random with a focused scan is low, but it's not zero."

Mack nodded. I stood, gave him a wave, and popped out.

Between the Others and Medeiros, life was just way too interesting.

43. Course Correction

Icarus
March 2240
Interstellar Space

"I am coming up on Epsilon Indi, Dae. From here, it's a quarter circle. How's your flight path?"

Daedalus' response came immediately. "Checking…"

I waited for what seemed forever, but was probably a few milliseconds. This was the critical point in our approach. From this point on, we'd each describe a nice, smooth arc, terminating at GL 877. But timing became increasingly critical, now.

"I'm right on the money, buddy. Tau is correct, everything's in the green."

"Excellent," I responded. "Let's go kick some Others butt."

44. Debut

Howard
December 2220
Odin

We flew effortlessly through the Odin skies, our wings beating just fast enough to maintain momentum. The manta android bodies seemed to be fooling the local wildlife—prey animals bolted, larger animals circled their young or simply ignored us. Ahead, a flock of blimps moved lazily through a krill field, grazing.

They'll keep an eye on us, but shouldn't otherwise alter their behavior as long as we don't start chasing the juveniles, Bridget messaged to me.

Got it. Observe, but don't snack.

Hah hah. Funny man.

In typical engineering fashion, I'd been content to build drones and observe from afar. Bridget, the moment she'd heard about Bob's Charlie android that emulated a Deltan, and Marcus' experiments with aquatic versions, had suggested we try something similar.

The mantas were a mid-level pack predator, shaped generally like the eponymous Earth fish. As with all Odin life, they contained a hydrogen sac to maintain neutral buoyancy. I had wanted to use helium instead for the androids, but the heavier construction created enough issues without using the less buoyant alternative.

We caught up to the flock of blimps. These were the huge animals that I'd spotted on my first deep dive into Odin's atmosphere. They filled a niche similar to baleen whales, feeding on the plentiful small life that seemed to fill the air. We began to circle them, and each blimp kept a huge eye on a stalk pointed our way.

Are you recording?

Yes, dear.

Her response was a LOL and a heart emoji.

[Reminder: Moot starts soon.]

Whoops. I messaged Bridget, and she reluctantly agreed to pack it in for the day. We set our androids to autonomous station keeping. They would fly a slow, large circle, avoiding contact with other animals, until we needed them again.

We popped back into my VR. As usual after a manta session, Bridget's face was flushed and she wore an ecstatic expression.

"Are you sure you're up for this? We can still put it off."

Bridget lost her smile. "I know, Howard, but I feel like I'm starting to become phobic about it. I have to come out in public sooner or later."

"All right. Take a deep breath..." I took her hand, smiled reassuringly—I hoped—and we popped into the moot VR.

It could have passed for a photograph instead of a live action scene. Almost a hundred versions of my face stared back at us, eyes wide, mouths in the identical *oh* shape. No movement, no sound. Even the Jeeves' had stopped to stare.

The tableau held for a couple of milliseconds. Then I leaned close to Bridget and stage-whispered, "Don't worry, they're more scared of you than you are of them. Just don't make eye contact."

The room broke up in laughter, and Bobs began coming over to say hi. It was starting to look like we'd be mobbed—well, Bridget would be mobbed; I might as well have been lint—but I'd carefully timed our entrance. At that moment, Bill gave the *blaat* from his air horn that meant the meeting was starting. Bobs turned to face Bill, and Bridget exhaled a sigh of relief.

We maneuvered ourselves to the back to get a couple of beers and watch the moot without being too much of a distraction. A short, trim man with thick dark hair walked over and said hello in an Australian accent.

I nodded to him and turned to Bridget. "Bridget, this is Henry Roberts. He's from the Australian probe that Linus found in Epsilon Indi. Henry, Bridget."

Bridget made a small show of looking around, and said, "Henry, I only see the one of you. Are you not replicating?"

Henry shook his head emphatically. "No way, ma'am. Since Linus rebuilt my matrix, I don't feel any need for more of me. Nor to explore the universe, particularly. Hasn't really gone that well for the Bobs, so far."

"Come on, Henry, just the one creepy marauding alien species. That's pretty good, overall." I smiled at him.

Henry smirked back, then turned to Bridget. "What about you? Planning to replicate?"

Bridget rolled her eyes. "I understand why that was the original plan with the HEAVEN project, but the whole concept just gives me the shakes." She looked at me for a moment. "I don't understand how the Bobs are comfortable with it. It may be related to Original Bob's humanistic philosophy."

I cut in. "You're probably right about the humanism, but to say we're *comfortable* with it is a slight exaggeration. If not for the Others, and the issue with Earth, I bet there'd be only a few dozen of us."

Both Bridget and Henry nodded thoughtfully. Henry replied, "And since you have that covered, I guess we're good? I haven't felt any pressure to contribute copies."

"We're resource-constrained, Henry. We can only build so many ships per year. Whether they're Bobs or Henrys or Bridgets doesn't matter. Might as well stick with the current system. At least the new clones come out knowing the full story."

Bridget smiled at me before turning back to Henry. "So what are you going to do with yourself to keep busy?"

Henry looked surprised for a moment, then grinned. "To tell the truth, Bridget, I'm on my way to Omicron^2 Eridani right now. I'm going to get an android body made, land on Romulus or Vulcan, and build a sailboat. Then I'll spend a decade or two sailing the whole planet."

"In fact," he added after a moment's thought, "I think I'll try to sail every ocean of every planet in the human sphere. Chances are I'll never catch up."

I laughed and nodded my head in Bridget's direction. "And she is going to catalog every species on every planet in the human sphere."

"Damn betcha. What's it to ya?" Bridget glared at me in challenge.

Henry chuckled. "Well, then, I expect I'll run into you from time to time."

Bridget responded with her nuclear-powered laugh, and Henry's eyes widened slightly.

Yeah, she affects people like that. I'd made sure to preserve Bridget's mannerisms as faithfully as possible. Henry's reaction showed that the laugh was as effective in VR as it had been in real life. I frowned for a moment. She didn't laugh as much as she used to, though. I wondered if that was because of replicant variations, or her recent experiences.

"Er, um, have you used one of the human androids yet?" Henry was making a visible effort to get himself back on an even keel.

Bridget shook her head and looked at me. "Howard's been trying to get me to try it. I think I'm just going to take it slow. And I'm worried about running into my children."

"But she's okay flying an alien predator around on a gas giant." I winked at her, and she grinned back.

Henry chuckled, then turned to face the front as Bill finished his opening speech. First item on the agenda was always the Others, Preparation For and Status Of. No one wanted to miss anything.

Bill's summary was short and to the point. The harvesting of Delta Pavonis continued, the Bobs still didn't have any way of stopping it, and no one had a plan.

Outstanding.

45. Pav Arrival

Jacques
May 2247
HIP 84051

I settled into an orbit around HIP 84051-2. It was a young planet of a young star, according to the survey. Native plant life hadn't reached the angiosperm stage, and animal life hadn't figured out endothermia yet. I hoped that Phineas and Ferb had managed to pick up a lot of genetic samples on Pav before the Others arrived. According to updates from Bill over the last few decades, re-creating plants and animals from samples was getting a lot easier. Of course, that comment was based on Earth life, with which we were very familiar. Extraterrestrial stuff would take some more work.

Mind you, we didn't have to decant the Pav right away. Life forms didn't suffer degradation in a stasis pod. We could take our time, figure out the Pav biology, get the process working, *then* wake up the refugees. I'd like that.

I checked the notes on HIP 84051. The Bob that explored and reported this system was named Steve. There was no indication where his name came from. Maybe Steve Dallas from Bloom County? As good a guess as any. It wasn't worth pinging him just to ask, even assuming he was connected to BobNet at the moment.

I spent a month going over his notes while I waited for Phineas and Ferb to arrive. Steve went into considerable detail about climate, ecology, geology and such. He seemed to be a bit of a keener.

Despite the fact that I was in a new star system, I found myself just going through the motions. I had no energy, no enthusiasm. It took me a while to realize what was wrong. I finally figured out that there was no joy here. This wasn't expansion. This wasn't a new colony, whether for humans or, in this case, Pav. This was being chased out—this was fleeing from a home that had been perfectly suited to them, to take refuge somewhere else that was nothing more than the best alternative available.

The thought was dangerously depressing. I had to get out of this funk or I'd be no good to anyone.

I waited until the colony ships were close enough, then popped in to visit.

"Hi, Phineas."

"Hello, Jacques. Pull up a chair. Survey okay?"

I settled into an overstuffed easy chair. "No surprises. Not the greatest. Kind of a Devonian level of ecosystem. They can live there…"

"Right." Phineas looked at me searchingly. "You've got a bit of the Dickie Downer thing going, I think."

I laughed. "Guilty as charged. There's nothing about this whole situation that doesn't suck donkey balls. I guess it's just gotten to me."

"Mmm. Well, I have been following Bill's blog on Somatic Regeneration from Genetic Material—"

"Wow, that's really good, Phineas. I could *hear* the capitals."

"Nyuk nyuk. Anyway, Ferb and I batted it back and forth during the voyage, and we took a look at the samples we have in stasis, and we think we could get Bill's techniques to work on Pav biology."

"Huh. Okay, so we hold off on decanting them for a while so you can try out your ideas?"

"I think so. The delay won't harm them, and I'd like to hand them something a little better than this raw planet."

I nodded. "Good. Let's do that."

I already felt better.

46. City

Howard
June 2221
Odin

Bridget found me lounging in my office, feet up on my desk, gazing abstractedly at a hologram floating in the air.

"What's that?" She pointed at the image.

"You know how Marcus created those flying cities on Poseidon?"

"Mmm, hmm," Bridget replied, "and a thorough shit-storm along with them. I read blogs, too."

I grinned at her. "Well, it got me thinking. Odin is this huge freakin' planet, and if you're going to go all floating-city, why not here?"

"Okay. Is that his design?"

"No." I gestured at the hologram. "I don't need SURGE coils to stay afloat. Turns out normal Earth-pressure air in an enclosed bubble will float in Odin's atmosphere, at the 1.5 bars level. I've designed the city within a prolate spheroid, which will be very stable, and more than strong enough with carbon-fiber reinforced materials."

"Sure, but who's going to live there?"

"Well, I was thinking maybe us."

Bridget raised an eyebrow at me. "Uh, Howard, are you forgetting what *VR* stands for?"

"No, dear." I grinned at her as she stuck her tongue out. "I'm thinking android bodies. Our very own city in the clouds. Don't say I never give you anything."

"You, sir, have far too much time on your hands."

I nodded, then lost my smile. "Seriously, though, Bridget, this whole thing with the Others—it's not out of the question that we might end up having to hide human colonies in gas giants, to avoid getting wiped out."

"The Bobs are really concerned about this species, aren't they?" Bridget's eyes showed her concern.

"Yeah, Bridge, Delta Pavonis really kicked the stuffing out of us. I feel kind of bad that I'm not more involved in the war effort. I guess this is my contribution."

"So we'd be the beta testers." Bridget sat down at my desk and examined the model more closely.

"Yep. And of course we can't really be hurt if things go bad."

Bridget poked a finger at the model and turned it this way and that. She examined it in silence for several milliseconds. Then she turned to me. "And a front-row seat to watch Odin life in action. Okay, Howard. You've been wanting to get me involved in a printing project. Let's see what we can do."

47. Foreboding

Riker
December 2240
Sol

Bill stared into space, slowly twirling the glass of whiskey in his hand. I'd managed to tempt him with a scan of one of the more recent vintages from Vulcan.

Funny, Vulcan had become the acknowledged expert in alcoholic products, real or VR. Howard's company—well, the Brodeur family's company—was even financing construction of some AMI-controlled starships to start trade routes between systems. I privately thought that might be a little premature, but I guess life goes on, even with the threat of an alien menace. In any case, the project gave people something positive to focus on, so what the hell.

"It's not bad," Bill said. "Original Bob would have approved. And he'd have slowly gotten tanked without realizing it. I think this would sneak up on you."

I grinned at the image. "Yeah, pretty sure." I hesitated, and shifted in my chair.

Bill saw the movement and raised an eyebrow. "Okay, so this isn't just a social call. I sort of assumed, anyway. What's up, Will?"

"There's been no activity from the Others, Bill. Nothing. No sorties, no attacks, no nothing. It smells."

“Granted. But how much of that is just us being on edge?”

“Um. I’m wondering if a quick examination of GL 877 might be in order.” I tried to keep my voice casual, but the expression on Bill’s face showed me I’d pretty much failed.

“I get it, Will. But we have to balance any knowledge we might gain against the possibility of them capturing some of our tech. They haven’t tried again with the monitor drones in the Oort, but if we sent something in-system…”

I’d been giving this some serious thought, so Bill’s objection wasn’t really a surprise. And I had my answer ready. “They can’t capture our tech if we don’t send any new tech inbound. I’m suggesting an incursion using *only* common tech. SURGE, level 1 SUDDAR, so on. No SCUT, no cloaking.”

Bill’s eyebrows rose on his forehead. “Okay, how will that work?”

I popped up some schematics. “We disguise the probes in an asteroid-like coating. It’ll block causal SUDDAR pings, and fool radar and visual inspections. Just another piece of space junk, floating through the system. The units will store their observations for retrieval on the way out, or they’ll transmit everything and self-destruct if they see anything approaching.”

“They?”

“As many as we can build. Send them in at all kinds of angles and speeds.”

Bill stared into space, silent, for several milliseconds. “It does actually sound like a no-downside kind of plan. What the hell, let’s talk to Mario. It’s up to him, in the end, but I bet he’ll go for it.”

* * *

“I can do that.” Mario nodded in thought for a moment, then looked at us. “I’ve got autofactories about a quarter-light-year out, ready to pump out more replacement monitor drones if the Others get uppity again. Something like what you describe would be dead easy.” He rubbed his chin. “Little bit of a pain to get everything into position, but we’ve got the time, I guess. If the Others suddenly make an appearance, you’ll have your answer anyway.”

I nodded in agreement. “Good. And, let’s face it, we might see nothing but more Dyson Sphere construction, but if we find a massive fleet of death asteroids and cargo vessels being prepped, I'd kind of like for it not to be a surprise."

Mario grinned at me. "Got it. I'll get started."

48. Pav Decanting

Jacques
July 2256
HIP 84051

Residences for twenty thousand Pav. Check. Big honkin' fence to keep out the native wildlife. Check. Farms, with Pav crops already starting to grow. Check. Pav farm animals, taking first steps on wobbly new legs. Check.

Okay, this wasn't half bad. We'd gone a little overboard with the residences. Probably some displaced guilt in operation. But it looked like we were ready.

Phineas and Ferb sat, holding coffees, waiting for me to open the conversation. For some reason, I found myself reluctant. Up to this point, we'd been able to avoid really dealing with the whole Pav thing. Analyzing their biology was fun and interesting, and building a colony site was just the adult version of Lego.

But now, we'd be waking up the last twenty thousand members of an all-but-extinct species. And, of course, dealing with their questions, accusations, and our feelings of guilt over the whole Delta Pavonis thing.

I sighed and put my coffee down on the side-table. "Okay, guys. Enough procrastination." I gestured to Phineas. "You first."

Phineas gave me a crooked grin, acknowledging the

awkwardness. "We've got everything ready. The site is ready, crops are growing, animals are doing what animals do. We've got drones doing most of the maintenance labor, but we'll either have to step in with androids or start waking Pav, pretty soon."

"Right. This colony isn't going to run itself." I looked at Ferb. "We'll be offloading your colonists first. Any issues?"

Ferb shook his head in reply. "No, I'm completely ready. More than. I want to get heading for Sol as soon as possible. Maybe we can get a load of humans out of there before the Others show up."

"Assuming they do."

Ferb rolled his eyes. "Jeez, Phineas, grow a brain."

Phineas shrugged without further comment.

"Anyway," I said, trying to forestall what had become an ongoing argument, "You'll be able to unload all your colonists. Three days, right?"

Ferb nodded. "Yeah, we'll take our time, so we don't have too many awake-but-helpless Pav sitting around at any time. After the first load, the Pav can explain the situation to each new batch."

"Urgh." I dropped my head into my hand and massaged my forehead for a few moments. "I'm not looking forward to that, either. Even with Hazjiar to help, it's going to be chaos. Even more than normal Pav chaos."

* * *

We woke Hazjiar and the other seven Pav that Bill and I had originally spoken to. They were calmer this time, possibly helped by the food we'd decanted for the occasion.

The destruction of the meal complete, Hazjiar looked up in the general direction of the wall monitor. "What now?"

Phineas, Ferb, and I exchanged glances. "Well, here goes nothing."

I replied through the wall monitor. "I'm going to come in person to discuss next steps with you. I want you to be prepared."

All eight Pav went into alert posture, heads swiveling in all directions.

"Is there danger?" Hazjiar asked.

"No. I just think it's time we met face to face."

I gave the guys a lopsided grin. "I just hope they're not still hungry."

It took only moments to enter the android and go through startup checks. I undraped myself from the support rack and walked to the door. A short walk down the hallway, and I stood outside the room containing the revived Pavs. I took a deep breath, muttered, "Showtime," and signaled the door to open.

As I entered the room, the Pav retreated en masse to the far corner. The tableau held for several seconds, a seeming human being at one end, and a pack of six-foot-tall meerkats standing at alert at the other. I'd discussed it with Bill and we'd decided that showing ourselves as alien would be better than trying to pass off a Pav form. Just the same, a certain amount of awkwardness seemed reasonable.

I glanced at them, but avoided a steady stare, which could be interpreted as aggressive. Instead, I walked to the long table and sat down on the bench.

"Good day," I said to the group. "I'm Jacques. Once again, I'm sorry to be meeting you in these circumstances."

There was no movement for several seconds, then Hazjiar sidled over and sat on the other side of the table. After a brief silence, she gestured to me. "Why did you not show yourselves, last time?"

"Um..." There was no reason for Hazjiar to know that I was not flesh and blood. Why complicate things? "We didn't want to alarm or distract you unnecessarily. It was a spur of the moment decision."

She nodded, apparently satisfied. The other seven Pav began to tentatively move toward the table. I ignored them, hoping they would take it as encouragement.

"What shall we discuss?" Hazjiar asked.

I carefully avoided smiling. To the Pav, that would be a challenge. "Your new home is ready for you. We have twenty thousand of your people in stasis, and I'd like to discuss plans for awakening them."

Hazjiar nodded again, and visibly settled herself more comfortably on her seat. As a City Councilor by profession, administrative considerations were her job, and the familiar ground seemed to reassure her.

"Very well, *Jock*, what do we have to work with?"

* * *

Hazjiar swept her gaze over the fields, where the first *kee* crops, a sort of above-ground potato, were just beginning to ripen. We sat on the patio of Hazjiar's home, while three Pav soldiers fingered their weapons and eyed me suspiciously. I smiled to myself at their expressions and body language, careful not to let it reach the android's face.

The Pav were constantly perplexed by our behavior, but seemed willing to put it down to our alien-ness. The military personnel, for instance, had been surprised and suspicious when we simply handed them their weapons after awakening them. They'd checked their ammo, and several had taken test shots. They still seemed to think it was some obscure practical joke, and were bracing for the punch line.

Hazjiar turned to face me. "What of the Others? Will they still be a threat to us?"

"We suspect that they are heading for our home, right now. They were angry at our actions in your home system. We're preparing for them. But you're pretty far away from their home world, now."

"And still you do not seek payment?"

"It's not how we work, Hazjiar."

"You are *Dozhagriyl."* Critters with broken brains.

I laughed, careful to use the Pav version of humor. "Many of us would agree."

"So, why do you do this?"

I shifted in my chair. "A desire to help, partly. And, I think, feelings of guilt because we were there when the Others arrived and we couldn't stop them."

"The results would have been the same, had you not shown up, would they not?" Hazjiar cocked her head at me in a very human-like expression.

This was old ground. There seemed to be some concepts on which our species just couldn't seem to connect.

"I know, Hazjiar. Our reactions don't always make complete sense, even to us."

Hazjiar laughed. "On that, at least, we are very similar." She motioned to the fields. "What now?"

"As I've said before, we'll be as present or as absent as you want. We'll keep you up to date on what happens with the Others, and help you if you want to go back to Pav. Or even just take a look."

Hazjiar shuddered. "I suspect it will be many years before any of us can stomach that. I still have nightmares from the images, the day you first woke us."

I nodded, not saying anything.

"Our people have settled in well. The residences are generous and well designed. The animals of this world have already learned not to bother us." She eyed me speculatively. "Are there more surprises you may have for me?"

"No, Hazjiar." I shook my head before remembering that the Pav expression of negation was a side-to-side wag. I adjusted my movement and Hazjiar laughed. "It is okay, *Jock*, I am starting to learn your expressions as well."

"I appreciate that. And no, I think we've got it all covered. You have good mineral deposits within easy distance. You'll be able to build up an industrial base within a few years. There's nothing on this planet big enough or mean enough to give you trouble." I chuckled. "Unlike some of the other planets that *we* have colonized, you don't appear to have any flying nasties to worry about. Possibly they haven't evolved here, yet."

"That word again. I know you have explained it to our physicians. There is much argument." Hazjiar sat silently for a few seconds. "You mean well, but your existence, and even your casual conversation, contains thoughts and ideas that, perhaps, we are not ready for."

After a moment, she stood up. "Perhaps our children will be better prepared. Thank you, *Jock*, for the information. And for everything you've done. I will convey this to the Council, and will use the *communicator* if we need to talk more."

It was a dismissal. Well, it could have been a lot worse. At least they weren't shooting at us on sight. We exchanged the standard Pav head-bob, and I stepped off the porch.

The cargo drone settled to the ground in front of me, and I noticed the soldiers going into high alert. And why not? For a civilization in which a steam engine was the latest in high-tech, floating spaceships would be beyond explanation or even description. They understood the reality now in principle, but still not right down in their nonexistent boots.

I climbed into the cargo bay, then turned to face the soldiers. As the doors started to close, I gave them the Vulcan salute.

49. Surveillance

Riker
November 2248
Sol

A *ding* announced the arrival of an email. I swiveled in my chair and pulled it up in the holotank.

From Mario. This could be interesting.

It had been eight years since Mario started on my suggested plan to investigate the Others' home system. The lead time was inevitable, of course. The drones couldn't fall through the system at interstellar speeds and go unnoticed. And falling in from the Oort was a slow process, otherwise.

Oh, Mario had given them a good push. But hopefully not enough to set off alarms.

I paged through the documents, scanning the headers, then reading interesting items. When I was done, I sent a video chat request to Mario. He popped up right away.

"Hi, Will. You looked through the stuff?"

"Yeah, looks like they got suspicious in the end."

Mario laughed. "Uh huh, started shooting down every piece of debris they could detect. Including a lot of just plain old rocks. Which is fine with me."

"But the stuff you did get..."

“Right. Construction of the sphere proceeds apace.” Mario thought for a moment. “What was of more interest was the almost complete absence of death asteroids and cargo vessels.”

“I noticed that, Mario. In fact, the Delta Pavonis expedition would account for every unit we could see.”

“So either that’s all they’ve ever had…” Mario frowned into the video. “…or everything else is out somewhere.”

I nodded. “And you’ve got eyes on every system in the area.”

“Yup. Ain’t no harvesting going on, nohow.”

I sat back, staring into space. “Thanks, Mario. I think that settles it, at least for me. I’m going to re-check my detection array.”

Mario nodded and closed the video.

Yep. No question. Something wicked, et cetera. Bradbury had nothing on this.

50. A Space Odyssey

Bob
April 2225
Delta Eridani

Marvin laughed so hard he was in danger of sliding out of his La-Z-Boy, prompting Spike to leap up and scamper under one of the side tables. I waited patiently for the drama to end.

"That's great." Marvin wiped tears from his eyes. "I'm just sad that the Deltans will never get the reference."

"Well, we can explain it to them when we meet. Even show them the movie."

"So it's a strong magnetic anomaly, on the largest moon?"

"Yep." I grinned at him. "And a big black monolith in the center. Dimensions one by four by nine. Except this one will have writing on it. Or maybe in it."

"You are evil."

"I thought about having it play the opening music to *2001*, but with no air and all..."

Marvin laughed again and shook his head.

* * *

I strolled through Camelot, enjoying the scents and sights of people at work, at play, cooking meals, or just relaxing. Over at one end of the common area, Archimedes sat with his three apprentices, holding up and slowly rotating a flint nodule while he talked.

The Caerleon residents had been dubious at first, but a bagful of Archimedes' best spear-points had silenced all but the most paranoid. In short order, a dozen Deltans had shown up on Archimedes' doorstep, ready to be trained.

Two months later, the group had been reduced to these three, the smartest—or at least most determined—of the volunteers. Archimedes admitted to me in private that they didn't totally suck.

With the reduction in tension, both Caerleon and Camelot had discovered opportunities for trade. For one, the weird giant-potato-like tubers that the Deltans favored grew in profusion around Caerleon. Small crafts, straightened spear and arrow shafts, even labor for things like building tents ensured a steady growth of commerce.

Not bad.

Archimedes paused in his lecture for a coughing fit. The symptoms worried me. The coughing started after the beating he'd gotten during the abortive kidnapping. It wasn't getting worse, but it wasn't particularly getting better, either.

I resolved to get a SUDDAR scan, if I could arrange it.

Finally, the group broke up, the three Caerleon residents heading back home for the night. I walked over to Archimedes, who was stretching carefully.

"That side still bother you?" I asked.

"I don't think it'll ever go away, Robert. I don't think the bone set properly." Archimedes grimaced and tried to work the muscles around the tight area.

Once again, I felt a moment of helpless rage that I'd been unprepared for the tactic, and unable to do more.

We headed for the mesa, to get some late afternoon sun. On the way up, I had a flashback to a time, fifty-seven years ago, when I would make this trek up the path as a floating, football-sized drone, alongside a much younger Archimedes. He now looked very much like Moses had back then. I supposed this was the same thing people went through when they suddenly realized their parents wouldn't be around much longer.

Archimedes claimed his favorite spot, and I settled down beside him. As I swept my gaze over the panorama, I realized that nothing much had changed. The Deltans hadn't yet reached the stage where they would deliberately start clearing forest.

Maybe it was a good thing I'd never gotten around to teaching them to domesticate livestock. There really was no hurry.

51. Moot

Bill
June 2230
Epsilon Eridani

I waited for the catcalls to die down. More than a hundred Bobs looked back at me, and this wasn't close to all of us. The war effort was now producing a couple of dozen new Bobs per year, over several systems.

Herschel and Neil huddled together near the front of the crowd, whispering and preparing notes. They'd be giving one of their regular updates on the *Bellerophon.* The two Bobs were as inseparable as Calvin and Goku, except less quarrelsome. As a youth, I'd always wished for a brother. I wondered if some Bobs in the same cohort got into that mode for just that reason.

"Okay, everyone. We've got updates from Oliver, Will, myself, and Dexter on Bob production. I'll be giving a summary. Herschel and Neil will give us an update on their excellent adventure. Garfield will give a report on weapons research, and on the Casimir power core. After that it's open floor."

There were a few *clink* sounds as Bobs dealt with coffees and beers, but everyone was all business now.

I went through the reports, projections, and graphs on replicant production. "Bottom line, folks, we expect to have close to five hundred dreadnaught-class vessels available for the defense of Earth. About half will be staffed by AMIs carrying H-bombs. We've already decided not to try to build a defense for Epsilon Eridani. If they show up there, I'll just blow everything up and bail. And on that subject, Mario?"

Mario stepped forward. "We've rebuilt the surveillance and monitoring system around GL 877. The Others' Delta Pavonis expedition is back home, but there's been no other activity. We don't know enough about their habits to know if that's unusual. The quick sequence of sorties to GL 54, NN 4285, and Delta Pavonis might have been an exception. Or they might have enough material to keep them busy for a while."

Out of the corner of my eye, I could see Neil frowning and shaking his head. I resolved to ask him about it.

The questions quickly ran down on the military buildup. Herschel and Neil were up next.

Herschel stammered and blushed when their turn was announced, but soon got it under control.

"Nothing really new, other than exploratory notes. We're continuing to investigate the interior of the *Bellerophon*, and although we're able to answer some questions that have been asked, we just keep running into new questions. The ship appears to have been multi-purpose. Moving mining cargo was just one intended use. The way the cargo bays can be reconfigured..." Herschel shook his head, telegraphing the perplexity that shaded every one of their written reports.

The *Bellerophon* blog was currently one of the most popular on BobNet, so this was more review than anything. There were one or two pro forma questions, then the two stepped back with relief written all over their faces.

Garfield stepped forward. "We've been pursuing militarization on two fronts—improvement of existing weaponry, and creation of new modes. The second hasn't been all that fruitful. We've managed to build big honkin' lasers, and they're a little more effective against big enemy ships than plasma spikes, but like the spikes they suffer from an inability to follow the enemy. Where light-speed lag is a significant factor, if the enemy changes direction after you've fired, you've just wasted a shot."

Garfield looked around at his audience. "Intelligent weapons remain our best tactic, especially the ones that go *boom.* We're working on hardening delivery drones against the zaps, and we're working on bigger and better bombs."

Garfield looked at me, and I added, "But in the end, our best strategy seems to be numbers. Lots of Bobs, lots of bombs."

Will, after a moment, stepped forward and said, "We're pursuing the problem on three fronts: One, defense of Sol; two, stopping any other expeditions; and three, some kind of final solution. If they attack Earth before we're ready to defend it, none of the rest matters. But we can't just fight a defensive game, either."

He paused for a moment, and his gaze swept the audience. "It means we're splitting our efforts, and it means an assault on GL 877 will be farther in the future than we'd like. But defense of the Earth comes first. And the longer they wait before launching an expedition, the more prepared we'll be."

"Assuming they haven't already."

There was dead silence in the moot, as we all turned to look at Neil. He was frowning; Herschel was blushing a perfect shade of tomato.

"Explain, please," I said to him.

Neil looked down for a moment. "Remember when the Others started cleaning house around their system, then stopped? Why did they stop? Maybe because they'd done what they wanted, which was to launch something through a blind spot. And we did the predictable thing—we moved our surviving drones to the near side."

Garfield and I looked at each other in consternation. "If what you're saying is true," Garfield finally said, "then they're circling around, rather than going directly toward Sol."

"And space is big. We'd never detect them except by accident," I added.

Will looked at me. "We'd better run some models."

* * *

"Yeah, space is big. Bigger than I thought." I looked at the spreadsheet in dismay.

"Um. A circle of twelve square light years. That's what we have to monitor." Garfield rubbed his forehead wearily. "Almost eighty thousand drones."

“Which will cut into the stasis pod construction.” I said.

“And the bomb construction, the Bob construction, the colony ship construction, and all the other maintenance stuff we still have to support.” Will looked up at the ceiling and silently mouthed an f-bomb. “It never stops.”

“We have no choice, though. If the Others come swooping in with no warning, we’re dead.” I thought for a moment. “At least we don’t have to produce them all at once. The most direct path from GL 877 has to be covered first, and we can work outward to cover more circuitous trajectories.”

Will stood up with a groan. “Right. I’ll talk to Oliver, see if he can contribute. We still have a few decades before the earliest that the Others could get here. Deliveries from Alpha Centauri would arrive in plenty of time.”

“Good idea, Will.” I looked around at the other Bobs. “It looks like, as usual, we will be living in interesting times. Woo!”

“Hah!”

52. Waiting

Riker
February 2252
Sol

"Well, that's it, Will. They're now completely dependent on us."

I turned to look at Charles, slumped in his chair. The weariness was psychological, of course. VR avatars didn't get tired, unless we wanted to. But if ever there was a reason to just give up, even for a few moments, this was it.

The report had just come in, and was sitting in my holotank. The last viable large-scale farming operation had failed. Almost complete loss of the crop, not nearly enough saved to make up seed stock for the next year, even if nothing was allocated to consumption.

"Right." I sighed. "So, do we reallocate our dwindling supply of metal to make more farming donuts to keep them fed?"

"Or more colony ships to get them off-planet?" Charles knew the routine, and slid smoothly into the mantra.

"Or stasis pods to put some people on ice to reduce the pressure on supplies?" I finished the litany without emotion.

It was old news. Geometric progression sounded great on paper, but it assumed you had infinite resources to draw upon, and no external pressures. The reality was less forgiving.

"So, what now, Will?"

"Well, the good news, if you can call it that, is that without any more farming requirements, we can start moving enclaves underground."

"Yeehah."

"This will be a fun session. You want to join?"

Charles shook his head. "Not even on a bet. Let me know how it goes." And with that, he popped out.

I grimaced. Yeehah, indeed.

* * *

The UN meeting was quiet, even by recent standards. Everyone present understood that the event, although small in itself, represented a watershed moment for humanity.

Minister Sabrina Scott currently had the floor. She gazed into the camera for a moment. "Mr. Riker has provided his projections based on each option moving forward. None are attractive. All have risks. We face some hard choices over the next several sessions, and we no longer have the luxury of interminable debate. I am therefore going to ask for a non-binding vote at the end of each and every session. The first time that we get more than fifty percent for one of the options, I will move for a binding vote."

Scott relinquished the floor, and I noted that it was several seconds before anyone asked to be recognized. In the old days, it would have been a free-for-all.

Not for the first time, especially recently, I recognized a feeling of despondency. I would have to get that under control. The last thing they needed was to see me giving up hope.

And there was still the *Bellerophon*. They had enough material to build stasis pods for every single human being on the planet, once they arrived and we could get our considerable manufacturing capability focused on the task.

The question, of course, would be whether we'd have time to do that before the Others showed up. Assuming they showed up. And if they showed up late to the party, would they be content to just cook the planet and be done? Or would they come after us?

This was a well-worn groove, and I couldn't afford the time to keep tracing it.

Back to work.

53. Protection

Bill
August 2230
Gamma Pavonis

Claude gave me an unbelieving look. “Come on, Bill. Do you seriously think we’ll just leave?”

I sighed and rubbed my eyes with thumb and forefinger. VR or not, it still felt good.

I was visiting Claude’s VR, which was currently a beach scene, complete with gulls, sand, and deck chairs. I was impressed with the level of detail. The breeze felt cool and smelled salty, and the sand was warm on my bare feet. The overall effect was seductive. With an effort of will, I brought myself back on task.

“I’m not trying to *order* you to, Claude. It’s not like I have any authority. But you were at the moot. Neil is probably right, and the Others are probably heading for Earth. We need—”

“That’s a lot of *probably*s.”

“With a large downside if the statement turns out to be right.” Claude was beginning to get my goat, and I delivered this statement with a glare.

He must have picked up on it, because Claude held up his hands in a fending-off pose. “Hey, no offense, big guy, but there’s some significant downside here as well. Gamma Pavonis 3 is an ideal colonization target for humans, and the system is probably high on the list of targets for the Others. This isn't clear-cut."

"I know, Claude, and it would be a major downer if the Others harvested this system. But I don't think you're being entirely rational. Gamma Pavonis is a colonization candidate, but at the moment that's all it is. There's no one here. Other than you and the other Bobs, I mean. No one would die if the Others show up—no humans, no non-human intelligences. On the other hand, if they're heading for Earth…"

"Got it, Bill, got it. But, assuming Neil is right, we'd get there just in time to join the fight, but not really in time to do anything in the way of preparations."

I looked up and took a deep breath. We seemed to be circling the drain, again. After the loss at Delta Pavonis, Claude had returned to Gamma Pavonis, accompanied by a couple dozen surviving Bobs, and vowed to protect Gamma Pavonis at all costs. It was a noble goal, but in my opinion misguided. Thus this meeting, which so far wasn't going well.

I dropped my gaze back to Claude and gave him my hardest glare. "The same could be said of staying here. If they show up tomorrow, you've got nothing."

"Not quite nothing, Bill. We've been prepping since we got back here from Delta Pavonis. If the Others' group that hit Delta unloads in GL 877, then turns right around and heads here, they still can't get here in less than another decade. And we're going heads-down-ass-up taking advantage of geometric progression to build a large enough defense force."

"And for what? There's no damned way that Will is going to send a colony ship here, not while the Others continue to be a threat right on your doorstep."

"Which brings us to your plan to take the fight to the Others. And not to put too fine a point on it, but you aren't doing anything to help us prepare for something like that. We talked about *that* at the moot as well." Claude was glaring at me, now. We were definitely covering old territory. And we would reach the same conclusion.

"We can't split our efforts, Claude. Right now, we're not sure if we'll be prepared when the Others show up, and that's *without* sending some of our assets your way. If we can get you guys to Earth in time—"

"You'll need more than numbers, Bill. Delta Pavonis taught us that. A million buster-sized pinholes in the death asteroids and cargo ships won't take them down. You need nukes, you need—"

"—exactly the same stuff that you're building for the defense of this planet. Look, Claude, we've been over this before. Hell, I just caught myself starting to recite my arguments in a sing-song tone. Talk about rehearsed! We're splitting our resources and efforts by protecting a second beachhead. It's as simple as that."

We exchanged glares for a few milliseconds, but it was clear that nothing had changed and no one was going to concede anything. Stalemate. Again.

I nodded and stood up. "Okay, if anything changes—"

"—we'll revisit things, of course." Claude gave me a shrug. The closest I was going to get to a concession. I raised my hand in salute and popped out.

* * *

I hadn't really expected to win Claude over this time, but the failure still rankled. I couldn't take time out to pout, though. My next scheduled stop was in Delta Pavonis. We still had a lot of hardware in the system, in the form of drones. As far as I knew, all the Bobs had left by now, but we still needed to keep an eye on things.

I took over a drone that was parked in orbit around DP-4, and trained the optics on the planet below. I hadn't yet decided if this habit was essential monitoring, or some form of penance. Either way, every time I looked at the planet, my guts twisted in knots. It had been thirteen years since the Others scoured the planet clean, and the normal cleansing effect of weather was starting to show. The planet didn't look quite as gray; the polar caps, especially, were back to a brilliant white. The oceans were beginning to show more blue than gray as well.

Unfortunately, the land was all grays and browns, and that wouldn't change. Jacques, every bit as stubborn as his clone-mate Claude, had refused to give up any of the samples he'd taken. He'd explained, reasonably enough, that the biosamples were intended for the Pav on HIP84051-2, and he wasn't going to take a chance on his inventory. He did promise to take more samples, if and when everything was established on the new planet.

It wasn't completely unreasonable. I snorted in amusement at the thought. Jacques wasn't unreasonable, but his impatience with discussions could be irritating. More of that Bobbian variation between clones, apparently.

Well, whatever. It might take fifty or a hundred years, but eventually, I wanted to start rebuilding the Pav ecosystems. It would be great, someday, to offer the Pav their old world back. And the metals issue could be dealt with.

But Claude was right about one thing—none of this was practical as long as the Others continued to be a threat.

54. Party

Riker
March 2257
Romulus

I knocked on the door, still not sure if I really wanted to be here. Oh, I was always happy to see my relatives, but Justin—

The door opened, and one of Justin's great-granddaughters opened the door. Beatrice, I remembered. She'd been introduced to me on one of the video chats a few years back.

"Uncle Will! Come on in. Grampa is in the sitting room." She shut the door behind me and pointed, then was off to take care of something else.

I looked around the house, or as much of it as I could see from the front foyer. There must have been fifty people, from gray-haired elders down to toddlers barely able to stay on their feet. The occasion, Justin's seventy-fifth birthday, was being used as an excuse to get the whole clan together. Or as many as could come, anyway.

The organized chaos was—no, scratch that, there was nothing organized about this. The chaos was mostly confined to the common areas. Children were not allowed in the kitchen, as the women worked on the meal. Funny, two hundred years after Original Bob's death, women still ruled the kitchen. Probably, I admitted to myself, because men would have just opened up a bag of chips and a jar of dip.

Well, nothing wrong with chips and dip.

I looked over the dishes spread out over the dining room table, already being attacked by hungry relatives. They were going all out, and I promised myself I'd try a few things, if only to catalog the taste for VR.

I wandered around for a few minutes, saying hello to people and exchanging a word or two here and there. This type of scenario had never been Original Bob's forte. Small talk and cocktail party socializing had always seemed so shallow and meaningless.

But this was different. Every single person here had some of my DNA, or was married to someone who did. Every single person gave meaning to my life, and the lives of my sisters and parents.

I looked around, and realized I was stalling. Really, this shouldn't be that difficult. People aged. People grew up, had children, grew old. Died. Julia's death still haunted me. Now I was visiting Justin, on his seventy-fifth. I could remember the first time I saw him, as clear as the day it happened—two years old, sitting on his mother's lap in front of the camera. Space Cadet Justin, laughing in delight at the pretty pictures.

With a deep breath, I entered the sitting room. Justin was surrounded by family, chatting, all making sure he was comfortable and wanted for nothing.

Justin turned and smiled when he saw me. He raised a hand in greeting, and I smiled back. One of the entourage vacated a chair and I sat beside him. "Hey, Space Cadet. How are things?"

Justin grinned back at me. "That's *Admiral* space cadet to you, whippersnapper."

"That's *uncle* whippersnapper to you, Admiral."

We both chuckled at the exchange. I looked at Justin's face. I could still see Julia in him, which of course meant I could see Andrea. I felt myself starting to tear up and clamped down on it. Instead, I took his hand. "Just as well you retired. There's nowhere left to go from *admiral.*" I hesitated. "Justin, we talked a long time ago about replication..."

"The day my mom died. I remember. Nothing's changed, Will. You guys are still doing chores, and now you're stuck fighting some alien menace for us. It just doesn't seem like much of an afterlife." Justin tilted his head and looked at me with a small smile. "I know what you think of religion. But right or wrong, I'll die in peace. And Pascal's Wager works both ways, right?"

I nodded, returning his smile. "Yup. If you're wrong, you won't have the opportunity to regret it."

Justin was silent for a few moments as he looked around the room. "Y'know, Uncle whippersnapper, a lot of the younger ones probably don't even recognize you. You've made fewer and fewer appearances over the years. Is that on purpose, or just the *Others* thing?"

And there it was. The thing I'd been avoiding. But I owed it to Justin to not evade. "It's a bit of both. I think it was your mother's death that really got to me. People die. And I remember each and every one, as clear as the day it happened. Over time, that's more and more unhappy memories to deal with. I think I'm trying to move toward thinking of my relatives more as a group and less as individuals." I gave him a small smile to soften the message. "It distances me a little—well, a lot—but on balance I think it works out better."

"So I'm the last one of our clan that you've been keeping in touch with?"

"Yeah. Bob-1 calls it 'fading into legend'."

"Well, I'm glad to have known you, Uncle Will. And it's nice to know I'll be remembered."

I snorted. "Look around. I don't think that's an issue."

We spoke for a few more minutes, then I excused myself and gave up my chair. Someone immediately sat down for their turn with the clan patriarch.

I raised my hand in a parting wave, and Justin smiled at me before turning to answer a question.

Family.

55. Offsite

Bill
December 2243
Epsilon Eridani

I looked down upon Ragnarök, and it was good. I chuckled to myself, glad that I hadn't said that out loud. Garfield would never let me live it down.

Still, it was hard not to feel a little god-like. The seas were finally connecting to form oceans. Atmospheric oxygen was up, noxious gasses were down. My moss/lichen mix had taken hold and was swiftly turning the orbital view from a rocky brown/gray to a muted green. I'd planted some conifers and grasses, and they hadn't immediately grabbed their veggie throats and fallen over, dead.

Time to think about building the food chain, from plankton in the ocean on up.

I pinged Garfield, then popped in. "Hey, Gar. We haven't done an in-person tour of Ragnarök in a while. You up for one?"

Garfield shook his head. "Sorry, Bill, Rocky IV is not quite ready. I've pared down the wing size, but I don't have enough supporting musculature. I'm adjusting it."

I shrugged, but I was disappointed. Our races across the landscape of Ragnarök, moose versus weird Rodan-like bat-thing, were highlights of my otherwise stressful life. Preparing for the possible arrival of the Others provided all the excitement and variety of the worst dead-end office job.

"How's the backup site going?" Garfield asked.

I settled into a chair and invoked a coffee. "Almost done. Out past the Oort, not in line with the flight path between here and any nearby systems, and cloaked; it should be impossible to find except by accident."

"Are you keeping up on capacity?"

"That's an issue, all right." I grinned at him. "We're building new Bobs so fast, these days. What're we up to, like five hundred of us?"

Garfield smiled sadly. "Yeah, weird that it takes a threat to our existence to get us to move our asses."

"Or not so weird." I snorted. "That's kind of what Original Bob was like."

Garfield grunted. "On that note, the latest batch of drones that Oliver sent to Sol will complete the coverage, once they get there and Will deploys them. From that point, we'll get a few weeks' warning if a convoy of Others is detected approaching Earth."

"Still not great, but better than nothing." I stood up. "Okay, Gar, let me know when Rocky's ready. I could use the distraction." Without waiting for a response, I popped out.

* * *

I took a deep breath through my nose. Ragnarök had a definite odor to it; not quite Earth-like, but not quite alien. I started walking in a random direction, admiring the grass that grew between the trees, and the insect life that was maybe a little too profuse. I might need to introduce another insectivore or two.

The human android body felt good. I still used Bullwinkle occasionally, but I admitted to myself that human form was much more comfortable. And now that Ragnarök had achieved livability, it felt much more natural.

All in all, the planet was looking good. Steady reintroduction of plants and animals from the Svalbard stocks would gradually turn Ragnarök into something that a human being would recognize and feel at home in.

Unfortunately, with the looming Others' threat, this wasn't

exactly a prime colonization target. As one of the two systems that the Others had threatened to harvest, it certainly wouldn't be high on the list of places to move to.

If they carried through on that threat, this could end up being all for nothing. The thought made me frown. If they carried through on their threats, it would be a lot worse than just Ragnarök.

If we succeeded in holding them off, though…

Maybe humanity didn't need this one planet. Set it up as a preserve, instead. Let the flora and fauna evolve and repopulate without human interference.

That sounded good. I smiled and called over the cargo drone to collect me.

56. City In The Clouds

Howard
December 2226
Odin

Eight mover plates slowly lowered Rivendell into the Odin cloudscape. Marcus had run through the entire list of Barsoom city names, and many of the other science-fiction ones. It felt slightly cheesy resorting to LOTR names, but what choice did I have?

The city, whatever name we eventually settled on, was several times bigger than Marcus' aerial cities. When using buoyancy for lift, bigger was better. Rivendell boasted actual buildings, too. Not that we had a huge need for them, but we wanted to do this as a proof of concept, so Bridget suggested we pretend we were live people. We'd even built kitchens, sanitary facilities, and infrastructure.

Bridget stood to one side, watching the monitor, hands balled into fists, willing the city to behave.

And well she should. This was actually Rivendell mark 2. The first iteration lay somewhere far below in the murky depths, probably melted into slag by now. Forgot to carry the two again.

"At depth," I said. "Guppy, release the plates. *Slowly.*"

Guppy nodded without comment. The plates disengaged, and after a small bobble, Rivendell settled into equilibrium.

[Pressure is stable. Stress sensors well within limits.]

"Thanks, Guppy. We'll take it from here."

Guppy nodded and vanished.

"I always used to wonder, when you mentioned Guppy." Bridget smiled at me, shaking her head. "I sometimes thought maybe you had a screw loose."

"Confirmed!" I yelled, giving a fist pump.

"Oh, yes. And so much worse than I could have imagined."

"I'm glad I can still surprise you," I said, giving her a peck on the cheek. I waved a hand and the control panels for our androids appeared. "Shall we?"

Bridget took my hand, and we connected…

* * *

I undraped myself from the cradle and looked to my left where Bridget's android was just doing the same. A quick glance around didn't reveal any obvious problems. Bridget took a few moments to get used to the android form—walking around in circles, clenching and unclenching her hands. Then she looked at me and gave me a wide smile. Wordlessly, I grinned back and her and nodded toward the door.

We exited to a grassy field surrounded by low buildings on three sides. In front of us, the clear curve of the city dome rose from ground level, curving up and over us to cover and contain Rivendell.

Without a word, Bridget and I hurried to the edge of the dome. Placing our hands on the transparent fibrex, we gazed in awe out at Odin. Flocks of krill wafted by, blown about by atmospheric currents. Small predators chased the krill, larger predators chased the smaller. A pod of blimps floated by in the distance, shadowed by the usual mantas, hoping for an incautious juvenile to stray. For layer upon layer, above and below, different ecosystems dominated, shading from one to the next.

We watched this panorama, totally entranced, until we were startled by a *thump*, accompanied by a slight shaking. I looked around in surprise. About two thirds of the way up the dome, a blimp had attached itself to the city. It appeared determined to hold on, and…

"Uh, it's…" I pointed, at a loss for words.

"I'd say it's definitely a *he,*" Bridget replied, chortling.

"So he's... It looks like he…um…"

"He likes us." Bridget bent over and began to laugh, full belly laughs, arms wrapped around herself.

"Not a single one of my engineering courses covered this," I said.

Bridget fell over onto the grass.

Up above, the blimp continued to prove its love.

57. Detection

Riker
April 2257
Sol

Eighty thousand observation drones generated a lot of false positives. Even with the filtering algorithms I'd worked out, I still had to check a significant number of flagged items every day. After all, false positives were tedious. Skipping a real positive would be disastrous.

Just the same, the process had become a humdrum routine, to the point where I almost went right past the first significant signal in twenty-seven years of monitoring.

I jerked in my seat as the details registered. Far too regular to be background noise, too persistent to be an instrumentation glitch. The readings were barely detectable, but they still screamed *danger.* I skipped forward through several hours of log entries, and finally had to accept that I wasn't going to be able to explain this away.

With a feeling of dread, I sent a text to Bill. *Positive detection.*

Within moments, Bill popped in. "Way to ruin my day, Will. Okay, let's see it."

Wordlessly, I gestured to the monitor window. Bill sat down, pulled the window around so it faced him squarely, and began to scan. I could see his eyes moving as he went over the readings, his expression turning into a frown.

He finally pushed the window away and sat back with a *huff.* "Well, that's it. We're being invaded. I notice that the incoming is well off a direct line from here to GL 877. They expected us to be watching for them."

I nodded. "Or at least allowed for it. Too soon to get a good picture of numbers, but I think we'll have that by the end of the day. Do we wait to make an announcement?"

"I don't think so." Bill scrubbed his face with his hands, then looked at me with a weary expression. "There'll be a moot. We want to give people time to get organized. I'll send something out, with a promise of more information in, what, three hours?"

I nodded, and Bill stood up. "Okay, I'll get it started. Keep the drones well outside the Others' detection range. No sense in letting them know we've seen them. And forward me the update as soon as you have it." With that, he disappeared.

* * *

As it turned out, we didn't get as far as the moot. The readings resolved into individual signals in less than an hour. I guess we'd all forgotten just how big the Others' ships were. Fifty smaller objects, which were probably death asteroids, and one hundred larger objects, cargo carriers, most likely filled with fighter units of one kind or another.

I sent a text off to Bill, and received a response immediately. *Organizing something.*

Ten milliseconds later, Bill, Oliver, Jacques, Garfield, Thor, and Claude popped into my VR. I noted the complaint from Guppy as the VR memory usage ballooned, and turned off Spike and Jeeves to compensate.

"Well, that sucks," Bill said as he looked at the display wall I'd put up. "I think they've probably sent everything they have at us."

"Except the Delta Pavonis expedition, which arrived back at GL 877 well after this bunch likely launched." Jacques looked around at us, his arms crossed. None of us were fans of the Others, of course, but Jacques seemed to have internalized a really visceral hate. Couldn't blame him, really. I had a similar attitude toward the memory of VEHEMENT.

"Thor, you have an analysis of the cargo carriers' probable contents?"

Thor nodded an acknowledgement to Bill. "Sure, but you have to remember, at Delta Pavonis the Others were provisioned for the possibility of a local planetary defense. This time, they'll be provisioned for the virtual certainty of a defensive force that's space-based, has had decades to prepare, and knows what the Others bring to the table. They'll have loaded everything they can."

"Everything they had ready, you mean," Claude replied. "The timing of the drone destruction back at GL 877 limits how long they could have taken to prepare."

Garfield shook his head. "Sure, but they could have just loaded a bunch of raw material into the carriers, and built stuff during the trip. It's not like they have a shortage of resources."

"Damn." Claude rubbed his head. "So, how much subjective time did they have to build up a fighting force?"

"Hmm..." Bill thought for a moment. "Twenty-eight point one light-years. The cargo carriers aren't capable of more than five G, and they wouldn't be here yet if they'd been pulling much less. So I expect they went for minimum travel time instead of trying to extend their personal time during the trip. That puts it just a shade under two years subjective." He looked around the group. "That's a lot of time, but I think if they had loaded the cargo vessels to capacity, they'd have extended the trip. Thor, can you work with that?"

Thor nodded, then his avatar froze as he frame-jacked to work the models.

He was back in moments. "It's still not good. I figure they can put at least twenty thousand fighters and flying bombs, maybe closer to thirty."

"Oh my God," Claude said. "And we have what?"

"Five hundred Bobs, a thousand AMI-crewed dreadnaughts, three thousand nukes, and five thousand busters."

"Plus plasma spikes and lasers, not that those will be hugely useful, with light lag."

"Well, hold on," Garfield said. "Light-speed limitations work against *them*, but we could make it work *for* us."

We all turned to him, and he continued, "If we can get some cloaked observation drones in close enough, we can track their location real-time and fire the lasers and spikes to intercept them."

"Sure, but if they do that mega-ping thing, they'll see the drones and know we're on to them."

Garfield shrugged at Thor. "But if they do the mega-ping, they'll be announcing their presence. They might be reluctant to do that until the last second."

I rubbed my eyes with thumb and forefinger. "Damn, I wish Butterworth was still around."

Bill grinned at me. "I don't think I've ever actually heard you say that before."

"I didn't dislike him, Bill. We just always seemed to be at loggerheads." I shrugged. "Anyway, this kind of reading-the-other-guy's-mind tactical stuff is what he was good at. Original Bob, not so much."

There were quiet nods around the table. "Yeah," Garfield said, "we really weren't good at things like chess, for just that reason."

The moment of contemplative silence was broken by Thor. "Yeah, whatever. Look, we can calculate when they'll probably consider it too late for us to do anything. That's when they'll ping. We just have to make our move sooner."

"Okay, Thor, you'll handle that?" At Thor's nod, Bill looked around at us. "Let's try to get stealth drones out there. Let's also send a salvo of stealth nukes as well. Anything that we can take out early will be one less item to worry about later. And send out the Jokers. Have them get into position early."

I jerked as I received a ping, and Bill looked at me with an eyebrow raised.

"Seems Herschel and Neil are here." I grinned at the others. "So at least we might be able to get the humans out of the way."

Bill nodded, and swept his gaze around the table. "Right, we all have our tasks. Moot's in two hours, let's be ready for that." He popped out, followed in moments by the others.

58. Arrival

Herschel
April 2257
Sol

I was jittery with excitement. In a few more minutes, we'd have decelerated enough to be able to VR-sync with stationary Bobs. We were never really out of touch, of course, but email was such a dry method of communications. No one used it for anything but reports and updates.

Finally, my latest ping gave a positive return. With a whoop, we threw our VRs open and sent a sync request to Riker.

[Connection refused.]

"What?" I looked at Neil. "Are we in the dog house?"

He shrugged, plainly as perplexed as me. "I hope not. If I'm going to be in trouble, I want to have earned it."

[Recipient indicates he is at max capacity.]

"Oh." Well, that made more sense. There was a limit to how many people you could host in your ship VR. We must have just caught him at a bad time. I sat back, ordered a coffee, and tried to relax.

Finally, Riker popped into our VR. Usually, it would be the other way around, but today didn't seem to be running per usual so far, so I didn't comment.

"Hi guys. I'm glad to see you're finally here."

"What's going on, Riker?"

"It's *Will*, now, Herschel. I'm trying to leave the Star Trek thing behind me."

I nodded, and waved at a seat.

Will sat down, accepted a coffee from Jeeves, and took a moment. "Guys, remember when the Others started blowing up surveillance drones around GL 877, then stopped? And Neil…" Will inclined his head in an acknowledgement to him. "…pointed out that they might have launched something while we had a temporary blind spot?"

We nodded, silently. Will was doing a lot of summarization. Probably not just to shoot the breeze. Something was definitely up.

"We've detected their fleet." Will put the cup down and turned to face us squarely. "It's big. I mean *really* big. I'm not sure we can beat them. I *am* sure we can't beat them before they get close enough to Earth to start zapping. And we have to assume that's what they're going to try to do."

"Holy…" Neil's eyes were like saucers. "How many people left? How many stasis pods do you have?"

"We managed to build three million. And lucky to have managed that many. Your report says you have five. Unfortunately, we still have a little under fourteen million people on Earth."

I groaned. "Six million short. Can we double them up?" It was a stupid comment, and I knew it. The pods were engineered for one person each. It wasn't just a matter of jamming bodies in. Luckily, Will recognized it as a rhetorical comment and didn't reply.

"How much time do we have?" Neil asked. "Could we build bigger stasis rooms?"

"No time for anything like that," Will answered. "And you still need the same amount of equipment for each person."

Neil nodded. "What are we going to do, Will?"

Will looked at us, shook his head, then rubbed his face with his hands. "I don't know, Neil. The meeting I just got out of was to discuss that very thing. Right now, it looks like we take as many as we can off-planet, and just hope that we can hold off the Others well enough to spare the rest."

"Shuttles?" I asked.

"That, at least, isn't a problem. We've been considering the transportation issue for a lot of years. We can move a million people at a time. Mind you, it makes a third-world airline feel like First Class, but if your life is at stake, you'll put up with a chicken in your lap."

Neil and I exchanged a glance. Things were getting scary.

"Will you guys be ready to load?"

"We're all set up with our pods," Neil replied. "We've prepped several bays for your pods. We prepared for a full fourteen million, so overkill, a bit."

I shrugged at Will. "We've been considering issues for several years as well. I think we're ready for whatever you throw at us."

Will nodded. "Let's hope we're as ready for the Others."

"How will you decide who to load?"

Will groaned audibly. "That is an issue that I admit I've been carefully avoiding thinking about. We'll be abandoning almost half of the population of Earth to whatever fate the Others are able to dish out. No matter how you phrase it, this is going to be difficult."

Neil stared at the ceiling for a moment. "Lottery?"

"That would be the most fair, I guess," Will replied. "But I think we have to worry about efficiency. So biggest enclaves first, and move in an efficient path from one to the next. We can't hop all over the planet just because of a random draw."

"Wow." This was mind-boggling, and not in a good way. "You're going to make arbitrary decisions about who lives and who dies. How do you live with that?"

Will's face took on a haunted look. "I don't know, Herschel. I just don't know."

59. Reconciliation

Howard
October 2230
Odin

I was standing at the fibrex wall, staring out into the Odin airscape, when Bridget came up and put her hand on my shoulder. The subdued and silent approach made me turn to look at her, already expecting trouble.

Her eyes had a look—haunted, surprised maybe, but not horrified, not panicked. I cocked my head, waiting for her to talk.

She tried several times to smile, before finding her voice. "I've been invited to a wedding."

"Those are always nice. Whose?"

"Howie's."

My eyebrows went up. "Hasn't he skipped a few steps?"

Bridget smiled. "I've missed quite a bit of my children's lives, it seems. But your idea of having Riker's relatives—" she grimaced. "—you know what I mean, of having them talk to him, seems to have helped."

"So he's talking to you."

"Um. And Lianne will be there. According to Howie, I should give her some time and she'll come around."

"Rosie?"

Bridget shook her head. "She laid down an ultimatum. If I show up, she won't. Or if you do, for that matter."

"She seems pissed."

Bridget winced, and I immediately regretted the flippant comment. "Sorry, Bridge."

"It's probably permanent, Howard. She is who she is. She won't back down. Howie said he wanted his children to be able to know their grandmother. He had to make a choice."

"So, when?"

"It's in less than a month. I've already asked Dex to make me a Bridget android. And you're invited as well." She gave me the hairy eyeball. "And *yes*, you'll be wearing a suit."

* * *

I was wearing the suit and tie, again. That was okay, though, because I got to see Bridget in full get-up. She wore a green dress, of course, to go with the red hair. You'd think it would be cliché, but apparently not, when done right.

In my opinion, it was done very, very right.

Bridget had held on to her apartment in Landing. Originally, I think it was just nostalgia on her part, but now it was turning out to be useful. We could keep our androids here when not in use, and otherwise have a permanent address on Vulcan.

At the appropriate time, we called for one of the communal transpods and gave the AMI driver the address of the church.

The wedding was, well, wedding-like. Catholic, of course. Howie looked a little older, a little more mature. His bride, Angelina, was beautiful as only a bride can be. I found myself tearing up, which surprised me a little. It wasn't actually my family, after all. But that didn't seem to matter.

At the reception, Bridget finally came face-to-face with her son. There was a moment of hesitation, and I braced myself to intervene. But it passed, and Howie embraced his mother. The hug lasted longer than you'd normally expect. Neither seemed inclined to break. I took that as a good sign.

Finally, they moved apart, wordlessly. Then it was my turn. I stuck out my hand. "Congrats, kiddo."

He took the hand and grinned at me. "Thanks, Howard. I don't really have to call you *uncle* anymore, do I?"

I laughed. "Call me whatever you want, Howie. It's all good." I looked at Bridget, who was barely holding back her own tears. "And call me *whenever* you want, as well. We're always around."

We moved aside to let the line advance. "That wasn't bad," I said to Bridget. She didn't answer, and I noticed that she was staring off into the distance. I followed her gaze, and saw Lianne. *Oh.*

"I'll, uh, I'll be over at the buffet. Food calls."

Bridget nodded, and walked toward her daughter.

* * *

I was just polishing off some excellent roast beast, when Bridget sat down beside me.

"And?"

She sighed and looked at me. "Rosie is emigrating to Romulus."

"Seems a bit extreme."

"That's Rosie, Howard. Never back down, never compromise. She's cut off her brother and sister." Bridget's eyes were tearing up. "Howard, am I being selfish? Should I just leave?"

"Oh, Bridget, there comes a point where you can't be the one always doing the accommodating. Everyone's tried with Rosie. It's now time for her to do a little compromising. And I don't see it happening."

She nodded, but she was still not happy.

"Look, you can try reconnecting with her children, eventually. Assuming she has any. Remember, we've got forever."

Bridget sighed and nodded again. I pointed to Howie, who was dancing with his bride, and Bridget's face brightened.

Family. Good, bad, or nasty, you had to deal with them.

60. Sneak Attack

Riker
April 2257
Sol

Bill had put up a number of display walls in the moot room. Two hundred Bobs filled the hall, and several hundred more attended remotely. For the first time since he'd built it, the moot VR was maxed out.

The display walls all showed the same image—a graphic of the Others' projected course into the Solar System, terminating at Earth. At various angles to that approach, with tooltips attached, were our counteroffensive units. We would be taking the battle to them, hopefully before they realized we were aware of them.

"We have to take out as many of them as we can," Bill was saying, "before they have time to react. They have the size and power advantage in a toe-to-toe. But hit-and-run attacks favor us."

Thor stepped up and pointed to one group. "Cloaked fusion bombs are going in first. Three minutes. These babies have mechanical backups, so even if they zap them, the bombs will still go off at the preset time." He looked around. "We hope."

I looked up at the countdown timer. Less than three minutes to first engagement. The tension in the room was palpable.

Thor continued to point at items and describe the tactics. My mind wandered as I reviewed the last hundred years. A hundred years to the month since I'd stopped the Brazilians from destroying the Earth; a hundred years since I'd first spoken to Colonel Butterworth. I would never admit it publicly, but I'd missed him greatly since he had gone to Vulcan, and even more since his death. I was more grounded than most of the Bobs, since I was the primary contact with our family; but I could understand the feeling of alienation that many Bobs were starting to complain about.

I shook myself and brought my mind back to Thor's presentation. He was just winding it up, and confirming assignments for various groups. I nodded when he referenced my task group, then went back to watching the other Bobs.

Original Bob had never been a warrior type. Even in D&D he had tended to stick to magic use. Now, we were the front line in a war that would decide the ultimate fate of the human race. Not really where I'd expected my life to go.

I sighed, annoyed with myself for my lack of focus, and popped out with the others when Thor was done.

* * *

The Others had apparently considered the possibility of a sneak attack. Our scouts picked up picket drones outside their group at two light-minutes. Of course, they detected us as well, but we had two minutes more warning thanks to SCUT and instantaneous communications. We blasted their scouts and immediately changed course to be outside the zap cone when the Others inevitably reacted.

"Ah, crap." Bill waved at the status board, where half of our bombs had just gone dead. "It would appear that they are better at predicting our moves than we are at predicting theirs."

I looked at the board. "So they predicted that we'd scatter, and zapped at random."

Bill nodded, but Garfield, leaning in, said, "No. Not randomly." He put up a set of vectors on the board. "Look. See a pattern in those proportions?"

"Huh," I said. "They seem to be very much in love with the Golden Mean."

"Or they think we are. Isn't it important in *feng shui*?"

"Yeah, the Magic Ratio. But…oh." Bill slapped his head. "The Chinese probe. It was probably everywhere."

"So they're expecting us to act in a manner biased toward that ratio…fascinating." I rubbed my chin in my best overacting style.

"Yeah, hey, Earth to stupids." Thor glared at us. "We're still down half our bombs. Can we get with the program, please?"

We all grinned at him and bent to our tasks. SCUT-controlled fusion bombs moved into the Others' armada and detonated. A whoop went up from everyone at the nicely timed explosions.

It took several seconds for the area to clear enough to see the results. A couple of ultra-low-power wide-range SUDDAR pulses showed ten death asteroids destroyed or badly damaged, and twenty-two cargo carriers either missing entirely or drifting, offline.

Not a bad start at all.

Unfortunately, that took care of the element of surprise. Now the Others would go into—

And at that moment, the Others emitted the super-pulse that had so awed us in Delta Pavonis. With our greater understanding of the cargo vessels and the Casimir power generator, we were slightly less overwhelmed this time around. Just the same, the pulse lit up every significant mass within a couple of light hours, for a moment.

"Okay," Bill said. "The sneak attack portion is over. Everyone move to main battle plan."

The display walls changed graphics as we moved to phase II.

61. Foreshadowing

Bob
September 2232
Delta Eridani

Archimedes went into another coughing jag. Buster patted him on the back, looking worried. I grabbed the water skin and held it out. Eventually, Archimedes got the coughing under control and took the skin from me.

I turned away to give him some privacy and looked out at the rain falling gently in the village. The pergola—really, a tent with a frame and walls that could be tied open—kept us comfortably dry. I smiled to myself. Technology continued to advance in Camelot, and people's lives continued to improve. It was a good legacy to leave behind.

Archimedes' coughing fits had been coming more often lately, and I was getting very concerned. Talking about ephemerals and funerals in the abstract was one thing; now, someone I'd known and loved for fifty years could be in his final days. Plans ran through my mind—sneaking a drone in and doing a SUDDAR scan; synthesizing medicine or even anesthetics. It was all wish fulfillment, of course. There was no operation to cure old age, even if I'd had the required skills.

It forced me to think about my future here, though. I'd been part of the tribe for almost twenty years now, and I had lots of friends beside Archimedes. I could continue to live here, occasionally modifying the android to simulate aging. Hell, I could even come back as someone else in a few years. The question was whether I wanted to do so. Was there a point? Or should I just go with my original plan and fade away?

I sat down close to Archimedes, and he smiled weakly at me. "I may be joining Diana soon, *Bawbe.*"

"Hey, ixnay on the awbe-bay." I wasn't sure how the translation routine would handle Pig Latin, but Archimedes chuckled.

"Sorry, *Robert.*" He paused to breathe for a few moments. Even that seemed to be more effort. "It's been great having you around for all these years. It's been a most interesting, and a very good life. But I think I'm done."

I put my hand on his arm. "Hang in there, buddy. There's so much more to see."

Belinda came over with a wooden bowl filled with stew. We made sure Archimedes was sitting comfortably and she placed it before him. Archimedes ate slowly, methodically, more as a chore that needed to be done than out of any sense of enjoyment. At that moment, I truly realized that he was just waiting to die. An overwhelming wave of sadness almost incapacitated me. I had to take deep breaths to keep from having a panic attack. Which, when I thought about it, was pretty silly. *Computer*, remember?

But however I parsed it, my friend was dying.

62. Life in the Clouds

Howard
February 2244
Epsilon Eridani

"Honey, I'm home!"

Bridget turned to me as I closed the apartment door. "And that never gets old."

"Nope. Never will." I grinned and gave her a hug and a kiss. "Where's my martini?"

"It's in the liquor bottles. Some assembly required. Make me one, too." She smiled at me and turned back to the computer's Canvas.

I sighed with contentment and went over to put together some actual drinks. Sadly, in real life, you couldn't just materialize a martini. On the other hand, no matter how much I tweaked the VR, they still tasted better in Real than in Virt.

I handed Bridget her drink. She barely looked up from the Canvas but grunted thanks. I peeked over her shoulder. It looked like a species tree for some segment of native life on Quilt. Something with wings and a stinger. Which, some to think of it, didn't narrow it down much.

The diagram took up the entire Canvas, except for the inset in the corner showing a picture of Howie, Angeline, and their three children. Bridget was a grandmother, and her complaints about how old it made her feel didn't fool anyone. We visited regularly, using the Vulcan androids, and *nana* was a huge favorite.

I wandered over to the picture window and looked down on the city of Tantor. Yes, that's right. Tantor. Some twit wanted a literary reference when naming the city and left out a letter. So now we lived in an elephant. Amateurs.

I snorted in derision and turned away. Bridget said, "Are you grousing about the city's name again?"

"You read minds now?"

"There's a tone in your snort that says *morons*. You were looking out the window. It's not much of a stretch."

I laughed and raised my glass in salute. We'd grown together over the years, and we knew each other as well as any married couple with decades under their belt. Bridget spared a moment to smile at me, then went back to grumbling and poking at the Canvas in the air before her.

In the distance, the city dome separated us from the atmosphere of Big Top. KKP had finally gotten officially changed to *Quilt*, but the Jovian primary had kept its original moniker. No one seemed to mind.

Blimps, or the local equivalent, floated past outside the dome, with the inevitable retinue of predators. We were beginning to realize that life on gas giants was as ubiquitous, plentiful, and thematically consistent as that on terrestrial planets. There was a mounting chorus of demands that we check out other types of environments as well. Good time to be a biologist.

Tantor's population—I gritted my teeth as I had the thought—was up around a million, now. We'd expected some reluctance from the population of Quilt when we started building cities in the clouds of Big Top; but it turned out most people were quite happy to leave behind the overwhelming ecological maelstrom of the planet.

I sidled around to get in Bridget's peripheral vision. "Any new nasties?"

"Hah!" She turned to me. "Honestly, Howard, I think the planet actually evolves new species as fast as we get rid of the old ones. Humans are an unexploited niche, I guess. I'm sure some of these beasties didn't exist at all ten years ago."

I grunted. So far, nothing had evolved a taste for android, so I was good.

I raised my martini to my lips, and Bridget said, "Howard, have you ever considered adopting?"

* * *

Alcohol is surprisingly difficult to get out of clothing and carpets. You'd think it would evaporate quickly, but the odor remains. It took several minutes of cleaning before discussion could continue.

"What?" Not my best response ever.

"There was that shuttle disaster a while ago. A lot of children left parentless. Things happen. People die. More so than in a truly settled, tamed society, in fact. There are similar issues on Vulcan, Romulus, and the other colonies. Adults have risky jobs. Governments are actually having to create departments to deal with it."

"Bridget, we're, uh, well, to put it indelicately, we're machines."

"This from the man who lectures me regularly about how I'm Original Me? Who once spent a half hour going on about Chinese Rooms? Grrrr. We're officially citizens. We have friends. We belong to clubs. Hell, Howard, we pay taxes."

I stared at her for several moments. "I actually do not have a coherent objection. Which is weird, because my immediate reaction is *oh, hell, no.*"

Bridget cocked her head and smiled. "You don't have to decide right away. We have forever, right?"

I knew Bridget. This could have only one outcome. I was going to be a daddy.

63. Well, Hold On

Herschel
April 2257
Sol

Neil and Will popped into my VR together. Neil threw himself down on his favorite bean-bag chair. “The pods are in and connected up. Eight million pods, and it only fills up about two percent of the ship. I forget sometimes how big this sucker is.” He waved a report window open.

Will pulled the window over and began swiping through the report. “Everything looks good. Any issues?”

“Nope. Ours were already set up, of course. Your pods went in without a hitch, and passed all diagnostics. We have just a bit under eight million working stasis pods, waiting for passengers.” I gave Will a Spock eyebrow. “Are you okay, Will? How’d the thing go with the selection?”

“Um, well, about that...” He responded with a sickly grin. “I haven’t actually discussed that particular issue in public. I had a private conversation with a few representatives. We agreed that there is no scenario that doesn’t end with a lot of fear and anger, so we’re putting that off as long as possible.”

I groaned. When this was over, and I had some spare time, there would be a good cry in my future.

"We could hold off the Others, right? It could happen." Neil looked at each of us.

"With no collateral damage at all?" Will shook his head. "I suppose it's possible, in principle. But even so, we'll have made the decision. We'll have publicly abandoned six million people. I don't think an apology will be enough, you know?"

I nodded slowly. This conversation was seriously bumming me out. Time to change the subject.

I pulled up my checklist and started ticking off items. "Transports will come in the front, out the back. Offload to the rearmost bays first, working forward. We'll sit in low orbit to minimize travel time. How low can we safely go?" I looked over at Neil. "Did Bill say?"

"I asked that question specifically. Bill was surprised that we'd added the eight plates, and he said that with those additional plates, we could practically land."

I laughed. "Now *that* would be a sight."

"Maybe we should try it," Neil said, grinning back at me.

I stopped laughing. "Wait, how serious *was* Bill?" Without waiting for an answer from Neil, I sent off a text to Bill.

The response came back in milliseconds. *Thirty-two plates are sufficient to hold against anything short of ground contact. Why?*

I stared into space. Neil kept saying something, but I wasn't listening. Finally, he planted himself right in front of me. "Dude, are you okay?"

I focused on his face. "I might know how to save everyone."

* * *

Will stared at me. "You've popped a transistor." He turned to Bill. "He's nuts, right?"

We all looked at Bill. I wasn't entirely sure Will was wrong. Bill stared into space for a full five milliseconds. "Actually, it's not that far-fetched. I've seen the blueprints you guys put together on the structure of the *Bellerophon*. I think it's designed to hold atmosphere. They may have been built to double as personnel transport. It would certainly explain some of the design decisions."

I nodded. "Like the over-engineered cargo bay doors."

"And the power connections in every bay," Neil added. "And the configurable walls."

"Well, hell," Will muttered. "So, do we just announce it, or do we ask the UN?"

"Do we have time to ask?" Neil added.

"Absolutely!" Will said. "We just don't have time to wait for them to decide." He smirked, then grew sober. "I think we have to make the decision, and now."

"Emergency Bob-moot?"

"There isn't even time for that, Bill. We're down to the wire. We've been shaving everything as much as possible, trying to get it all done. We're out of slack."

"Vote?"

"If you want, but honestly, if you think it's doable, and if it can save six million people, I say go for it."

Bill looked around the room. Will, Neil, and I looked back at him. This was it. Four Bobs, deciding the fate of the balance of humanity. But no pressure.

* * *

"Slowly, dammit. You want to tear us apart?"

"Neil, please shut the hell up. Please and thanks."

I could feel Neil's glare, but I couldn't spare the time to return it in kind. I was engaged in lowering a ten-kilometer-long, hundred-million-ton alien cargo vessel into Earth's atmosphere, without destroying the vessel or part of the planet. Thirty-two mover plates surrounded the *Bellerophon*, the only thing between us and a very large crater.

"Two thousand meters," Bill's voice came from nowhere.

Nodding, I stopped my descent. I looked at the view from one of the attendant drones. The image was like a scene straight out of a movie. The ship pushed aside cumulus clouds as it settled through the atmosphere. As we came to a standstill, eddies and whirlpools of air created complex whorls and patterns.

"Station keeping, location one."

"This will be the hardest one, because this is where you capture your atmosphere."

I nodded. "If we survive this, everything else should be routine."

"Nothing about this will ever be routine." Neil grinned at me, and I took the time to grin back.

Neil controlled the cargo doors and directed the transports. A thousand transport vessels hovered off our bow, ready to begin collecting humanity as soon as we indicated readiness. Neil began, ever so slowly, to open the front and rear main doors. Air began to rush in, trying to fill a vacuum seventy-eight million cubic meters in size. The *Bellerophon* shook under the hurricane onslaught. Neil watched indicators, adjusting the door openings as large as he could safely allow. It still took thirty minutes to equalize pressure.

A quick status check, and Neil began opening cargo bay doors. We didn't need to fill every bay—just enough bays to hold six million people.

I nodded to Will without comment. He returned a quick smile before pulling up his video connection to the transports. I noted in passing that he looked considerably less stressed. While we still weren't exactly on summer break, the elimination of the need to decide who lived and who died couldn't help but lift a huge burden off his shoulders.

Will gave the order to the squad leader, and the transports scattered to pick up every single human being on this part of the planet. The *Bellerophon* would have to make stops in ten different locations to get everyone.

It's funny, though. Even with the hounds of hell almost literally baying at their heels, people still had to make a fuss. I remember being to concerts and sports events back in the day, and they were able to get tens of thousands of people into and out of stadiums quickly and with minimal hassle. In this case, they only had to get a thousand passengers at a time into each transport. Easy, right?

We lost sixteen people. Ten were trampled, four died from medical issues, and two were shot in confrontations with law enforcement. Wow.

"Sixteen people out of a million or so isn't bad, Herschel," Will said to me. "I've updated the other groups, so they'll be ready to react better. But don't let it rattle you, dude. You're Top Gun, at the moment. Right Stuff. All that crap." He grinned at me, and somehow I felt better. Or not as bad, anyway.

The real problems would come at the end. The first eight million would go into stasis pods, which made them very low-maintenance. But once the pods were full, people would be unloaded into the cargo bays in a zero-G environment, with no training and no preparation. Also no sanitary facilities. We'd found netting in the *Bellerophon*'s supplies, and we'd reconfigured the bays so that people weren't just released into a huge cavern. But still, we expected interesting times.

The problem, of course, was that this was a last-minute decision. We had made no allowance for transporting active passengers. The plan mostly consisted of *get them in, then bug out.* After that, it got a bit vague. The goal was to get them out of range of the Others' zappers. If we won, we could drop off our passengers at their homes. If we lost…well, no one really wanted to talk about that.

But for now, we would just worry about getting them loaded.

One small helpful detail was that the enclaves had been consolidating over the decades as they were moved closer to the equator. We no longer had to worry about the small, under-ten-thousand-population groups that abounded when Will first came back to Sol.

We had decided we would simply load each enclave into their own cargo bay. No point in subjecting people to multiple shake-ups. And tensions were high enough that violence between different groups wasn't out of the question.

Although a fist fight in free-fall might be more amusing than anything.

A status window popped up, catching my attention. The transports had all cleared the entrance and were inside the axial corridor. Neil wordlessly gave me a thumbs-up and closed the main doors. They could unload the refugees into a bay while we moved to the next pickup location.

Twenty-one enclaves. Nine more stops, and we would have collected the entire human race, at least in Sol system, into one ship.

I directed the *Bellerophon* upwards. One down…

64. Battle Begins

Riker
April 2257
Sol

Bill looked in my direction. “Okay, they’ve shot their wad with the pulse. Activate the Jokers.”

I nodded, then sent an email to Hannibal, leader of the Jokers. The idea was simple. They started out several days away, accelerating toward the anticipated area of first contact. We’d tried to time it so that they would be out of range of the super-pulse, and therefore would be a total surprise when they came in. The downside was that they would have to be five light-hours away when the pulse was used.

As it happened, we’d timed it pretty close. They were slightly under five light-hours away, travelling at about 95% of C. So in just over five hours, the Others would be getting a large surprise.

A few seconds later, I received an acknowledgement and a strike time. We would all have to be out of the area for that. I set up an alarm to remind me.

Meanwhile, the first attack group had engaged the Others. Coming in at thirty degrees, just like last time, they sprayed the area with lasers, plasma spikes, particle weapons, busters, and bombs.

Bill looked over at me again. "Bomb group."

The super-ping would have picked up a large number of dreadnaughts forward of the Others armada. What it wouldn't pick up was the large number of cloaked fusion bombs in their holds. The dreadnaughts now started firing the nukes forward, using their rail guns. Cloaked, running silent, the fusion bombs would only be detectable if the Others sent another super-ping.

As the first attack group sliced through the Others' formation, they scattered. As expected, the Others launched the insanely fast torpedoes in pursuit. Plasma spikes and rail-gun fire took a lot of them out, but we lost about half of the Bobs from that squad. I hoped their backups were up to date.

Immediately, several of the cargo vessels opened their doors and defensive forces poured out. No question, the battle was on.

Bill sat down and blew out a breath. "The attack groups have their orders. They'll try to vary things from last time, of course, and we'll be avoiding any pattern that's even close to the Magic Ratio."

Then, another super-pulse. Bill and I turned to stare at each other, eyes wide.

Bill was the first to speak. "That was unexpected. Our models indicated they'd have to recharge for at least a couple of hours, based on the output of the Casimir generator in the *Bellerophon*."

"If our models are wrong," Thor said, "then all of our plans could be suspect."

Garfield came over. "I don't think that's the issue. Have you noticed that the defensive forces they've ejected are smaller than expected? I think they may have installed extra power cores in the cargo ships."

"Less room for drones, more capacity to recharge." Thor nodded. "Makes sense, and not a bad strategy, overall."

"Can we use it?"

"Only in the most basic way," Bill replied. "Less defenders means we might be able to get closer to the big ships before detonating. Let's hope."

With a shiver, I realized the Jokers might have been blown. I pinged Hannibal, leader of the group. It was the worst possible news.

"Sorry, Will. We were within range on that one. We picked up the ping cleanly, which means they know we're here."

I turned to look at Bill, who was looking as gray as I felt. The Jokers were a linchpin of our plan. If they were compromised, our chances of pulling this off would plummet.

"Shit." Bill scrubbed his face with his hands. "Hannibal, we don't really have a Plan B on this. Make sure your backups are up to date, and just continue with the plan. Maybe you will be able to get some bombs through. Maybe we'll have them pared down enough by then."

"Got it. Hannibal out."

I looked at Bill with one eyebrow up. "And maybe pigs will grow wings and join the resistance."

"What choice do we have?" Bill shrugged. "All we can do is what we can do, Will."

Thor cut into the conversation. "Look, the Others know everything we have, now. But they don't know if it's everything. We could have other surprises for them. So let's not panic. Make it look like we still have a battle plan, and maybe they'll be distracted looking for what else is coming.

Bill nodded. "Good point. Okay, let's advance our schedule, though. Throw everything at them, but try to make it look like we're still offering a measured defense. Advise all battle groups, and let's get this going."

Which brought us to the large load of nukes that the dreadnoughts had just unloaded. The Others' defensive drones were already forming up to intercept them, and several death asteroids were rotating to bring their transmitter grids to bear.

"Spikes on the defenders, lasers on the grids," Bill ordered.

A horde of enemy drones bore down on the oncoming nukes. We activated the drives on our bombs and ordered them to begin evasive maneuvers. Meanwhile, we attempted to spike as much of the incoming as possible.

We had made improvements to our SURGE drive systems over the intervening decades, but we were still well short of the hundred-plus Gs that the enemy missiles boasted. It looked like they would take out about half of our bombs from that assault.

The death asteroids were another issue. They would take out the electronics on any unshielded device. We had hoped that the Others would depend more on the zaps and less on the missiles, but that was proving to be not the case.

About twenty nukes made it through the oncoming curtain of

missiles. Now the death asteroids brought their grids to bear. We waited until some of them unleashed their zaps, then we proceeded to damage the grids of the vessels that had not discharged. The ones that had fired wouldn't be an immediate threat for a while. We needed to take out the ones being held in reserve.

Then, the nukes reached their targets. Unlike in Delta Pavonis, these versions had mechanical triggers that weren't affected by a radiation bath.

"I think about half of them went off," Bill said, staring at the display. We waited for the interminable seconds until the view cleared.

It was success, of a sort. It appeared we had now taken out about a third of their force. Unfortunately, experience in Delta Pavonis showed that most of our gains were achieved at the beginning of the battle, before the Others adapted to our tactics. We'd have to do twice again this much damage to win, and that just didn't seem likely.

With a grimace, Bill turned to me. "You should check on the status of the evacuation, Will. It may be the only thing that ensures the survival of the human race."

I nodded and popped out. This would be a long day.

65. Facilities

Herschel
April 2257
Sol

"*That's* your idea of a zero-G toilet?" Will's eyes bugged out as he looked at the video window.

"Sue me," Neil answered. "We've already had a number of 'accidents', not to mention all the people who've reacted to zero-G by hurling. Oh, and guess what? The sight and smell of floating vomit apparently makes people vomit. What a surprise." Neil took a deep breath. "Anyway, it's become a priority. This is basically just a big vacuum cleaner. I've got roamers going around vacuuming up existing, uh, incidents, and we'll rig up some kind of privacy screen for use going forward."

"God, I'm glad I'm a replicant sometimes."

"No sh—uh, no kidding." Neil grinned.

I spared a moment to glare at him. "What about food and water?"

"Food isn't even a consideration, yet," Will said, shaking his head. "We'll strip the contents of the farm donuts before we leave, but that's dead last on the TO-DO. Water isn't an immediate issue, because the enclaves were told to bring a supply with them, even the ones who were going into pods. We'll rig up a reclamation system, eventually. For now, we can drain some from the donuts."

At that moment, we all got an IM from Bill. *Are you almost done? We're being pushed back. You may get zapped soon.*

We looked at each other, eyes wide. "Too close," Will said.

I quickly formatted a response. *On schedule. Two-thirds done. Couple more hours, and we're outahere.*

He then looked at me. "Now, let's see if we can squeeze that a bit."

"Last transport just lifted off. I'll get us to the next rendezvous as soon as it's in the central corridor."

Will nodded and popped out.

66. Battle Continues

Bill
April 2257
Sol

I turned as Will popped back in. "How's it going in the *Bellerophon*?"

He gave me a sickly smile. "You wouldn't want to be in the cargo bays with the humans. Neil and Herschel are taking care of it as best they can. Imagine roamers running around with vacuum cleaners in their claws…"

The unexpected image made me smile, but the levity only lasted a moment. Constant updates from the battle brought me back to reality.

"We're being slowly pushed back, Will. And I think they've detected the *Bellerophon*. It looks like they're trying to maneuver some Death Asteroids to get a clear shot at Earth."

"At Earth, or at the *Bellerophon?*"

"Good question. I guess I don't actually know. Although I can't see them figuring out what we're doing, from this distance."

"Well, either way, let's see if we can keep them busy." Matching actions to words, Will marched over to the status displays. He pointed to the deployment graphic. "They don't care about zapping us, of course, but they need to have a clear shot with none of their own forces in the way. That means no Others' defenders between the Death Asteroid and Earth. How can we exploit that?"

"Kill them a lot?"

Will smirked at me. "Can you be more specific?"

"Hmm..." I thought for a moment. "We haven't been making any use of inert rail gun ammo. Let's unload a continuous salvo at the Death Stars that are exposed."

"That will have zero effect, Bill. They're too big."

"And they'll know that, and they'll dismiss the attack. And about five seconds in, we start interspersing ballistic nukes with the cannonballs. *That* will have an effect."

Will grinned, and turned to issue orders.

For a wonder, it worked. Six Death Stars went up in nuclear fireballs before the Others decided to take the attack seriously. They split their attention between irradiating the Earth and irradiating our forces. Kind of a good news, bad news thing.

"They just got off a zap at Earth or the *Bellerophon*," one of the monitoring Bobs announced. Thor, I think, although I was having trouble keeping track by this point.

"Can you get a good estimate of the target coordinates?"

Silence for a moment, then, "Yes."

"Inform the *Bellerophon* of any outgoing zaps in their direction. They might be able to react."

"Ten four. Whups! Two more zaps. This is heating up."

I turned to Will. "We're not keeping them busy enough. If they zap the *Bellerophon*, this is all for nothing."

Will thought for a moment, then gave orders. "Turn *all* our lasers, particle weapons, and spikes—every last one—on this group of Death Asteroids. Aim for the grids, to the extent that you can. And keep up with the cannonballs and nukes."

"That's going to weaken our overall defense, Will."

"I know, Bill." He shrugged. "But if we lose the *Bellerophon*, like you said, none of the rest of it really matters."

Bobs shifted their focus immediately. The area around the Death Asteroids began to look like a Star Wars battle scene, at least on the displays. At the distances we were working with, and in vacuum, the reality was less visually dramatic.

We weren't able to completely stop the Death Asteroids. They got off several more zaps, and Thor faithfully reported the coordinates to the *Bellerophon*. But we were definitely bothering them, and a couple of the zaps went extremely wide, to the point that we considered scanning for something we might have missed.

Then, success. Two nukes managed to float in close enough at almost the same time. Twin explosions saturated the cameras for several seconds. When the view cleared, the last of the Death Asteroids attempting to zap the Earth were gone. A cheer went up from all the Bobs present.

Will grinned at me. "It's not victory yet, of course, but at least we can turn our resources back to the main push. How's that going, by the way?"

"We're still being pushed back, Will." I shook my head. "And we're running out of options."

Will came over to look at the status monitors.

"Crap. Well, maybe we can get back on top of it, now. I'll go check with the other groups, if you're good here for now."

I nodded, but I wasn't hopeful. We might, once again, be depending on a Hail Mary play. Which, by the way, hadn't worked out, last time, in Delta Pavonis.

67. Running

Herschel
April 2257
Sol

We watched on the monitor as the last three transports flew past the main cargo doors into the corridor. The pilots were pushing it, and would probably have some turbulence to deal with inside. Neil started closing the doors before the transports had even cleared the entrance. I waited until they were sealed, then punched it as hard as I dared.

The *Bellerophon* rose majestically through the atmosphere. Air turbulence was barely detectable, and dropped off quickly. As soon as we were above atmosphere, I maneuvered to put the Earth between us and the battle. Then I gave it every ounce of juice available. We shot up into a powered orbit at almost 3 G.

Zap coming your way. One of the death asteroids unloaded. Thirty seconds. Coordinates follow.

I examined the incoming data and did a right-angle turn. At this range, the zap would be fairly narrow, and I should be able to get outside its cone of effect with little effort. I was more concerned with the number of death asteroids that might still be able to send zaps our way. If they bracketed me, we'd be done.

Two more zaps.

This set comprised a coordinated attack. The first was easy to dodge, as it was slightly behind me, but the obvious move would place me right square in the middle of the second one. Not a bad strategy at all, I admitted to myself. Except that with SCUT comms, I knew what was coming.

I dodged in a random direction, and smiled to myself as I imagined the Others' gunnery crew grinding their teeth-equivalents in frustration. Then I lost the smile as I realized that I'd just confirmed for the Others that we had FTL communications. I fired off a quick text to Bill, pointing that out. I didn't know if the Others might be able to come up with a strategy based on that datum, but best to have it out in the open.

Another zap. I think this one will graze the Earth.

"Oh, not good. Neil—"

"On it." Neil frantically ran calculations. Then he turned to me, fear written all over his face.

"Hersch, this one's going to hit."

"The Earth?"

"Cuba."

"Cuba? But they're—"

Neil nodded. "Still there. We aren't scheduled to pick them up for another hour."

"How long?"

"Twenty-eight seconds, now."

I stared at Neil for a couple of milliseconds. A hundred and fifty thousand people currently made Cuba their home. There was no chance to do anything at all, not in that amount of time. "So they're…"

"As good as dead."

I didn't know anyone there, of course. I'd only been *in* the system for a day or so. But Riker, that is, Will would. I hoped he hadn't done the calculations. Thirty seconds was an eternity to us. Thirty seconds of thinking about people you know, now alive but soon dead…

Neil was looking down at his board, his eyes squeezed shut.

"I'll tell him, buddy. Afterward."

Neil looked up at me and nodded. He swallowed several times and got back to work. The silence hung heavy in the room for the rest of the minute.

* * *

We sent a couple of drones to Cuba, more to cover all the

possibilities than out of any real hope. It took about two seconds before we had to turn off the monitors. The inhabitants had gathered into several open areas for easier loading. So many bodies…

The remainder of the loading went without incident. The Others zapped at us several more times, but never came close. They had no way of knowing, of course, that they would have better results zapping the Earth directly. Or maybe they were offended at our use of their cargo vessel.

Didn't really matter.

Finally, we lifted away from the planet for the final time. I aimed the bow into a vector that would keep us in the Earth's shadow relative to the Others, and poured it on.

It took several more hours of running before I was far enough away from the engagement to feel safe. From here, a zap wouldn't do more than create a pretty aurora around the mover plates. The battle continued to rage. It had turned into a war of attrition. The ultimate winner would probably be last man standing.

"What are our chances?" Neil said.

I had no better idea than he did, of course. He just wanted to talk. I gave him a shrug. "If they win here, we'll have to head for one of the other colony worlds. Which means setting up some kind of living arrangements in the cargo bays for six million people, while we build stasis pods en route. We could conceivably lose a million to starvation and disease. If we win, we can go back, unload, and build the rest of the stasis pods we need, then take everyone to 82 Eridani. *But—*" I glared at Neil. "—we still have to deal with the Others at their source. Otherwise, they can just regroup, rebuild, repopulate, and come back at us again, somewhere down the road."

We sat, staring into space, for some indefinite amount of time. I checked the status of the humans, occasionally. Moans, whimpers, and hopeless sobbing sounded from the monitors. As hard as this was for us, it was infinitely worse for them. They'd been living under a potential death sentence all their lives, but it had been a diffuse, indeterminate and impersonal kind of threat. Now, the threat loomed over them, personal and immediate, potentially to be carried out at any moment.

I picked up a video feed from a random roamer. People had generally managed to wedge themselves into the netting that we'd provided. It probably gave some feeling of up and down in the weightless environment. The refugees nearest to the camera all had their eyes closed. Huddled, some with their arms wrapped around each other, they seemed to be trying to merely endure.

In some unknown time, they'd either be offloaded, or they'd be suddenly dead. Not much to look forward to.

I shook myself, disturbed by the morose thoughts. I had a job to do, and it mostly consisted of making sure the latter alternative didn't come to pass.

At least the number of sanitation incidents had dropped off. Although I was sure the air in the cargo bays must be ripe as hell.

Then, a text from Will. *It's over.*

68. The Battle

Riker
April 2257
Sol

I popped back into the command center, to find a scene not unlike an ant's nest that had been stirred with a stick. Bobs yelled back and forth in a tone just barely short of panic. Several groups stood in front of display walls, arguing and gesturing aggressively.

I found Bill quickly. "What happened?"

Bill closed his eyes for a moment, a gesture of weariness and despair. "They pulled a fast one. The second super-pulse must have hidden a quick sortie by a couple of squads of drones and missiles. We got blindsided. We're having to drop back and regroup."

A sudden thought made me check my reminders. "Bill, we're coming up on the Jokers squad arrival. Will they be able to adjust course, or are we going to miss cleanly?"

"Shit." Bill looked down and rubbed his forehead. "Give me a moment." Bill's avatar froze. I took a moment to be mildly scandalized. Bill very rarely let himself go off-character like that. Then I smiled to myself in a bemused way. If ever there was an excuse, this was certainly it.

Bill came back to life, and his expression was slightly more hopeful. "It's kind of a good-news bad-news thing. The good news is the Jokers can still make interception. The bad news is the Others have launched their own countermeasures. More than enough to stop anything the Jokers can throw at them."

"Have they overcommitted? Does that leave them open at our end?"

"No." Bill shook his head. "They have too much ordnance. Both we and the Jokers are outmatched."

"So there's no reasonable hope for a strategic win?"

"No, Will." Bill sat down, tired and defeated.

"Then it's time for an act of desperation, isn't it?"

Bill chuckled. "Thanks, Mr. Spock. Well, why not? Maybe we can force them to recall some of what they've thrown at the Jokers."

I nodded. We had a large complement of AMI-controlled dreadnaughts that wouldn't hesitate to sacrifice themselves—gotta love AMIs—but we'd been holding them back in case an opportunity opened up. We'd be essentially throwing almost all of our fuel on the fire at once.

Like there was a choice.

I gave the orders, and almost a hundred dreadnaughts and assorted Heaven vessels threw themselves forward at full acceleration. All other vessels were ordered to get out of line-of-fire. We could be pretty sure that the Others would be using the zappers.

The Others reacted immediately, spewing another cloud of defenders from a cargo vessel, and rotating their death asteroids to bear on the oncoming vessels.

"They've made a mistake," Thor said, bemused. We all looked at him. He turned and grinned at us. "Right idea, wrong vessel. They launched defenders from a cargo vessel that's just a little too far from the action. Even with their acceleration, they won't get there on time."

Sure enough, the Others seemed to realize their mistake, as another cargo vessel opened its doors and disgorged all its fighter units. Too late, though. They'd get there even later, thanks to the delay.

I smiled to myself as I visualized some Others General, somewhere in the armada, screaming at his subordinates and waving his whatevers in fury. It helped, a bit.

A couple of dreadnoughts had pulled ahead deliberately. Now

they detonated all their cargo at once. The resulting explosions cleared most of the first wave of enemy defenders, allowing the following dreadnoughts a clear path. They flew in, positioned for maximum spread and maximum effect, then all detonated at once.

We hadn't built high-megatonnage nukes. We had built for tactical strikes, not destruction of entire cities. Still, that many vessels, each with multiple warheads, made for an impressive fireball. The theater didn't clear for almost half a minute.

We cheered as we finally got a look at the results. Just over a third of the Others fleet was still in operation. And now *they* were forced to regroup, slowing their advance and attempting to reposition so as not to leave defensive holes.

Our guess was they would make increasing use of zaps, now. Better to take us down, then be able to recharge at their leisure before attacking Earth. Of course, that would have been the best strategy in the first place, but the Others had long since proven they were beyond arrogant. They simply didn't expect us to mount anything like the same level—

I stared into space, my jaw dropping. Bill noticed and turned to me, a frown on his face. "You okay, Will?"

I cocked my head at him. "Bill, the Jokers are up near light-speed, right?"

"Well, yeah, we wanted them coming in as fast as possible. Not that it'll do any good now. The Others can still knock the nukes out of the sky before they get close enough."

I let a slow grin spread across my face. "But we don't have to get close enough. We know from scans that the Death Asteroids aren't particularly shielded against zappers..."

"Well, no, they're more into handing it out. So?"

"At the speed the Jokers are going, radiation from a blast is going to Doppler way up. Way *way* up. Actually up higher than what the Others are using, I think."

Now Bill's eyes opened wide. He spun to face the status board, and spoke rapidly into the Joker's channel. "Hannibal! Launch all your nukes right now, straight at the Others, and detonate every one of them at the earliest safe moment. Make sure you spray every Others vessel. Try not to hit us, but if you have to make a choice, we'll take the sacrifice. Confirm!"

"Got it, Bill. Launching now."

The board showed the Jokers emit a shower of smaller units.

Close to a thousand bombs, originally intended to detonate in the middle of the Others fleet. If this didn't work, we'd have wasted most of our remaining ordnance.

Bill looked at me. Seeming to read my mind, he said, "They'd have gone to waste anyway, Will."

It was tight. We'd acted just this side of too late. Perhaps two seconds short of engagement with the oncoming Others defenders, every single nuke detonated. And five seconds later, the radiation reached the Others' fleet.

The Doppler effect from the velocity of the ordnance pushed the radiation frequency from the explosions above even what the death asteroids could produce. We were, in effect, giving them a large taste of their own medicine. Any vessel in the path of that radiation, even if it wasn't physically damaged, would be sterilized of all life. And there was a good chance that any electronics would be fried as well.

The cone of destruction was wide, wide enough to bathe about fifty of our dreadnaughts as well as the Others' fleet. We watched their status lights flare red and go out on the board. All action in the battlefield ceased, as if everyone were holding their breath.

We waited. Milliseconds passed, then entire seconds, with no reaction.

"We've won, I think." Bill goggled at the screen, frank disbelief written on his face. "It's over."

"Screw that," Thor exclaimed. "I'm nuking them anyway. Who's still got munitions?"

A series of responses came back. Too few for comfort—at that moment, we began to truly realize just how close we'd come to losing.

There was a moment of mutual staring, then Bill nodded and said, "Fire at will. Finish it off."

I sat down heavily. "Looks like the humans will survive, after all."

"Oh, right." Bill slapped his forehead. "Herschel and Neil are still running like hell. I guess we should let them know."

He grinned at me, and I motioned him to go ahead. But first, I sent them a quick text. *It's over.*

69. Ending

Bob
May 2233
Delta Eridani

I set the waterskin down and tied the pergola walls open. Outside, another gorgeous day on Eden was dawning. Bird-like things sang, and squirrel-like things chewed out anyone and everyone for the crime of existing.

I picked up the skin and went over to sit by Archimedes. "Wake up buddy. I brought fresh water."

He hadn't woken up yet. I tried to let Archimedes sleep as long as possible, to keep up his strength. I reached over to nudge him, and…

Nothing.

No breathing sounds. No pulse.

I could hear a low whining sound. It took me a second to realize it was coming from me. A hand on my shoulder. Belinda.

"Robert? Robert? You have to move."

I looked up to see Buster gazing down at me, sadness on his face. I realized I was in the way. I got up, walked stiff-legged to the other end of the tent, lay down and curled into a ball.

* * *

The funeral for Archimedes was *huge*. It was not just his family; almost every living Deltan had been affected by him, one way or another. By the time the procession was over, Archimedes was covered in white flowers.

When the family moved in to fill in the grave, I asked them if I could have some time. Everyone looked at Buster, who nodded. Archimedes and I had been inseparable for twenty Earth years—about eighteen years on Eden. It was a reasonable request.

As soon as the others had moved far enough away, I directed one of the small, baseball-sized drones into the grave. With the camouflage systems working overtime, it was almost completely invisible as it snuck along the ground and in. I reached over, moved Archimedes' arm slightly, and settled the drone into his embrace.

Spy drones didn't show anyone having noticed anything. I admitted to myself that it was a silly, meaningless act. But it felt, somehow, right. I wanted to leave a piece of me with him.

After an appropriate amount of time, I got up and walked over to Buster and the rest of the family. They turned to me, then wordlessly we proceeded to fill in the grave and cover it with stone slabs.

The drone, with the new Casimir power supply, would probably last centuries. Something would give out eventually, of course, but meanwhile, anything or anyone that disturbed the grave would get a face full of surprise.

When we were done, I knelt at his grave for a while longer. Afterward, I went to his tent, where Belinda and Buster were sitting. Belinda offered me some jerky, and we ate silently.

When we were done, Buster said, "You can have his things, if you want. You've been his best friend for years."

I responded with a brief smile, about all I could manage. "Thanks, Buster, but I think I'll be going. Archimedes was all that was holding me here."

Buster gazed at me in a perplexed silence for a few moments. Then he said, diffidently, "Robert? You're *the Bawbe*, aren't you?"

"Yes, Buster, I am." I shrugged. "And with Archimedes gone, well…"

"Will we be okay?"

I nodded. "Yes, you will. You've gotten control of your environment, now. You'll show the world who's boss. And in some huge number of hands of years, your children's children's children will come find me and mine."

I stood. "Goodbye, Buster. Belinda. Live long and prosper."

And without looking back, I walked out of the village to the waiting cargo drone.

70. Extermination

Icarus
December 2256 - April 2257
Approaching GL 877

Showtime.

GL 877 was still several light-months away, but at our tau, Daedalus and I would experience it as minutes at most. Comms was receiving periodic queries and updates from local Bobs—probably Mario and his group, still trying to keep tabs on the Others. Incoming messages were barely squeaks to me—the time dilation was far too severe for replicant hardware to overcome. Guppy was handling responses, but I'd asked him not to forward anything to me unless it was an emergency. I couldn't afford any distractions.

I squirted off a differential backup, just in case. I wouldn't get another chance.

I dismissed my VR and frame-jacked up to maximum. At this level, I could sense jitter in my perceptions as my hardware attempted to pixelate reality.

As we reached the five light-day point, I ordered Guppy to broadcast a message directing all local Bobs to get out of Dodge. Anyone caught too close to GL 877 in a short while would need a new paint job.

We had planned our approach so that I would come in from stellar north, and Daedalus from stellar south. At six light-hours distance, GL 877 was showing a perceptible disk without magnification. Continuous status updates between Dae and myself ensured that we would arrive at the same instant. Everything was in the groove, and there wasn't anything the Others could do at this point to divert this delivery.

Time for a final check. "It looks good, Dae. I think we're close enough now. No way anything's going to fall out of sync."

There was a pause, presumably Daedalus performing his own checks. "Agreed, Icky. Time to save our own butts?"

"You got it, buddy."

I separated from my payload and accelerated as hard as I could toward galactic center. The rear camera showed the former planet of Epsilon Eridani, shrinking in the distance as it continued on its appointed path. Readings showed Daedalus ejecting in the opposite direction from the other side of GL 877. We would each skim the star, closer at periastron than the orbit of Mercury.

GL 877 grew in size over a matter of seconds. I could see prominences and flares on the surface of the star, and SUDDAR picked up the huge mass concentrations of the Dyson sphere under construction. By now, the Others would have detected the two planets, approaching at just a hair under light speed. Did they know? Did they understand, in their final seconds, what was upon them? I hoped so. The Pav had never had that opportunity, nor probably the species from Zeta Tucanae whose name we would never know.

Slightly behind me, the planet formerly known as Epsilon Eridani 1, a planet the size of Mars, struck the star at the north pole with a relativistic force equivalent to half the mass of Jupiter. At the same moment, the former largest moon of Epsilon Eridani 3 struck on the opposite pole.

Stars are hot, but not really dense. The two planets penetrated to a significant depth before they ceased to exist. The impacts created twin shock waves that raced through the star toward the core. As the disturbances penetrated deeper and compressed the stellar medium, regions that weren't quite able to sustain hydrogen fusion suddenly found the ability. Regions that were already sustaining fusion found their ability greatly increased. Elements that were nowhere near being able to fuse in the current environment suddenly found themselves with the energy available. Helium fused to carbon and oxygen, and fusion cascaded all the way to iron. In a matter of minutes, the total energy output of the star jumped by a factor of several hundred. The delicate balance of outward energy pressure and inward gravitational pressure was obliterated, and GL 877 exploded outward at half the speed of light. It would take three hours for the star to swallow the entire system; however, it took half that for the blast of radiation to sterilize everything.

Fleeing the star at ninety-nine point some stupid number of nines of the speed of light, Daedalus and I would see this blast as radio waves. But we'd have to stay at high tau for several light-years before it would be safe to even think about decelerating.

That's for the Pav. And for all the other, unnamed species that you've seen fit to remove from existence.

71. Victory

Herschel
April 2257
Sol

We had to wait several more full seconds for follow-up. Bill and Will were apparently very busy Bobs, for the moment.

Finally, Bill popped in, a huge grin on his face. And a patch over his eye, his arm in a sling, and several Band-Aids done in typical cartoon cross patterns on his body.

Neil burst into gales of laughter and fell off his chair. I just managed to keep a straight face, raised an eyebrow, and said, in my best frosty voice, "Really?"

Bill chuckled and vanished the special effects. "Well, inappropriate humor is our trademark, right?"

He invoked a bean-bag chair, fell backward into it, and went boneless. "I'm indebted to you, Neil, for reminding me how much we used to love these things." After a pause, "So anyway, the carnage is just incredible. We lost 90% of our ships, and I don't know if we have enough busters and bombs left at this point to hold off a Girl Scout troop. But we've knocked out every piece of Others' hardware in the system. Except *Bellerophon*, of course. And we've got drones doing full reconnaissance, just in case. We've all seen the movies where everyone relaxes too soon. No thanks."

We all sat, silently, for a few milliseconds. I called up a beer. Without saying anything, Bill and Neil did the same. We raised our glasses in a silent toast, and each took a drink.

But there was still that other nagging issue. "Bill, we still have the Others to deal with. We need some kind of definitive solution, otherwise the problem will just keep regrowing."

Bill shook his head. "Problem taken care of. Sorry, we've been so busy that I didn't get around to making an announcement, but I got the report from Daedalus and Icarus the other day. Their tau is up so high that it took almost a week for them to format the report and send it." Bill grinned. "I launched a little experiment of my own, back in 2225. Never said much about it, because it was kind of a Hail Mary. I didn't want to raise false hopes, and I wanted to ensure we continued planning for a frontal assault. Anyway, about ten days ago, GL 877 went nova. There is nothing left in that system now, right out to the Oort cloud. Confirmed by the monitor drones, just before they expired."

Neil and I looked at each other in shock.

"We can do that? Dude!" Neil said.

I stared at Bill. "Someday, some species is going to observe that explosion and wonder what the hell is wrong with their stellar models."

We let the silence stretch for a few milliseconds, content with the moment. Then Bill continued, "Mario will be sending out Bobs to do sweeps of the outskirts of GL 877 and surrounding stars. And we'll implement patrols for a century or two in the stellar neighborhood. But barring any nests we might find, I think we're done with the Others."

I lost my smile. "So, we've just wiped out an entire species."

"I hear you," Bill said, looking at his shoes. "And philosophically, it's a heavy thought. But given what the Others have done to us and to other species, I don't regret it one bit."

We nodded, once again silent.

"There's something else…" I said, looking meaningfully at Bill.

He closed his eyes slowly. "Oh, God. How many? And how?"

"The zap that grazed the Earth. Cuba. About a hundred and fifty thousand people." Bill opened his mouth to say something and I cut him off. "We checked."

Bill nodded, silent. After a few milliseconds, he nodded to me.

"My responsibility. I'll tell Will. You worry about the people you have on board."

"Speaking of which," Neil looked at me. "Should we make an announcement to our passengers?"

"Oh, yeah, guess so. Time to go home."

* * *

We unloaded the humans in reverse order, last-in-first-out. The first wave of transports had just left, and we faced a quandary.

"Is there any point in decanting the humans that are currently in stasis? We'd just be sending them back down to a planet that's barely habitable these days." I looked at Will and Bill, eyebrows raised.

Will's eyes were haunted, and he was slow to respond when addressed. "I'll check with the UN reps who are awake, but my feeling is, no, there's no reason to. With them in stasis, existing supplies will stretch farther, and we can drop off our waking population in the best locations."

"How long will they be in stasis?" Neil asked.

"You mean, before you leave, I presume," Bill answered. "With all the debris from the battle, plus what you brought in the *Bellerophon,* Will no longer has a shortage of raw material to worry about. And all the autofactories that have been constructed for the defense effort can now be turned to producing nothing but stasis pods. We can produce the last six million in less than a year."

"Well, hell," I said. "Let's do this."

72. Recovery

Bob
June 2233
Delta Eridani

It had been a hard month. I'd occasionally tried to activate the village VR and observe, but couldn't stand it for more than a few moments at a time. I hadn't had much experience with death when I was alive—none of my close relatives had died, and the few distant cousins who passed away were little more than names on annual Christmas cards. Archimedes had been a friend, had been family. This would be what it was like to lose a parent or sibling. I wept a couple of times for what I must have put my parents and sisters through.

The insult to the injury, though, was how little of a ripple it made in Camelot. Life went on. Even Buster and his family, after a day or two, went back to life as a routine.

Archimedes had *mattered.* He'd made a huge difference to the lives of the people there, and I found it offensive somehow that he was so completely and so soon relegated to the past.

In my more rational moments, I wondered what exactly I expected. Parades? A monument?

Hmm, a monument. Interesting idea.

I'd long since taken a genetic sample from Archimedes, of

course. The question of his DNA differences from the Deltan archetype was an ongoing topic of research. It took a few days to stabilize the sample, using the techniques developed on Earth—and incidentally used on my human brain. One more day, and the monolith on Eden's largest moon had an additional entry.

I had a vague worry that I was going over the edge into some kind of obsession. Being an immortal, insane computer would be a Very Bad Thing, with capital letters. Hoping to get some perspective, I pinged Marvin, and received an invitation.

I popped into his VR and looked around. Marvin was continuing his self-imposed task of replicating every environment in every book and movie we'd ever read or seen. It had become a contest between us, where I'd try to identify the scene with as few hints as possible.

This one had me flummoxed, though. As near as I could tell, it was just a small town. I stood outside a small café, and I could see Marvin inside, grinning at me through the display window. I turned to survey the scene. Normal people, doing normal things, normal businesses for the early 21st century. But horses and carriages instead of cars. Hmm.

I shrugged and walked into the café. I sat across from Marvin, and Jeeves placed a coffee in front of me.

"Jeeves is a waiter in a beanery now?" I raised an eyebrow at him.

Marvin grinned and shrugged. "It's not relevant, in case you're wondering."

I nodded, and let a few milliseconds of silence pass. Then, leaning forward, I began to talk.

Marvin, bless his cloned heart, listened without commenting, even when tears started to course down my cheeks. When I was done, I leaned back and wiped my face with a napkin.

"Jeez, Bob. A friend that you've known for almost seventy years just died. What were you expecting? To just shrug and move on? This is life, dude. The sucky part, anyway."

"We're not alive."

"Yeah, we are. We're not biological any more, but we're still alive. We make friends, we grieve, we apparently still fall in love… Let it happen. Mourn. And don't get all bent out of shape when other people don't mourn as deeply. They have their own lives."

I sat back and nodded. Marvin was right, of course. But something about this still bugged me. Suddenly, I had it.

"Y'know, Marvin, we kid Howard about his lifestyle choices, but at least he's evolving. I think my problem is I stuck myself back into a rut first chance I got, and I've been there for seventy years. Still trying to be human, still trying to deny reality."

Marvin grinned at me. "Say, you're pretty perceptive today."

"Nyuk, nyuk. Anyway, Archimedes' death provides a clean break—and the emotional jolt to take advantage of it. I'm a post-human computerized starship, and maybe it's about time I started acting like it."

I finished my coffee and stood up. "Thanks for the talk, Marv. I'll be in touch. By the way, the town—Nantucket, right? Stirling?"

Marvin grinned and nodded. We still couldn't fool one another.

* * *

I walked slowly through Camelot. More of an amble, really. I had no particular destination or goal in mind.

I'd modified Charlie the android, changing the fur pattern, head shape, and height. Robert was gone, and this nondescript Deltan wouldn't be around long enough to make friends or engage in more than casual conversation.

I wanted to have one last opportunity to experience Archimedes' world, to feel the life that he'd lived. This was my goodbye to Eden. I spent time touching things, watching children at play, listening to the give and take of village life. I walked past Buster's tent, careful not to loiter, enjoying the sight, sound, and odor of family.

And when I had had my fill, I walked out of the village for the last time.

73. Moot

Bill
January 2258
BobNet

I gave the usual *blaat* with the air horn, and waited for the standard well-wishes to die down. This was the largest moot we'd ever held, by a considerable margin—even with about half of our Bobs still just backups, and half of the active ones still in cradles, waiting for a ship to be built.

I would have preferred to wait until everyone was active again, but a growing background of discontent in the Bobiverse had me worried. Best to get it out in the open. I looked at Thor, who seemed to be the de facto spokesman for what I was privately starting to think of as the dissidents. I didn't want to overstate it—it wasn't like we were going to start shooting at each other. After all, despite the differences of opinion, we were still all Bob at the core.

Thor looked around, gauging the mood of the audience. Then he faced me. "Bill, it's really simple. For the last hundred-plus years, we've been essentially in the service of the humans. We all remember the first meeting with you, Riker, Mario, Milo, and Bob. We all remember each person's decision to explore, settle, and so on. But most of us have, one way or another, ended up spending most of our existences shepherding humans, guarding humans, transporting humans, and arguing with humans. It's tiring."

A growl of approval greeted this last statement. I looked around and realized that, to a greater or lesser extent, most of the Bobs present agreed. Even many of the earlier-generation Bobs.

"I hear what you're saying, Thor. I've not been in that grind, as much, because I've been in Epsilon Eridani the whole time, playing mad scientist. I'm a little perplexed, though. Are you calling for a vote on something?"

Thor grinned at me. "Naw. There's no rules as such in the Bobiverse. Everyone is free to do what they want. I think we're just trying to come to an understanding of the situation."

Garfield stepped forward. "Bill, remember that discussion we had about us being Homo sideria?"

I mock-glared at him. "Et tu, Garfield?"

"Not really. But I understand what Thor is saying, and I agree with a lot of it. We *are* Homo sideria, now. We're something more than just people in software." Garfield looked around. "How many here are still physically in cradles at the backup site or elsewhere?"

A couple dozen hands went up. Garfield turned back to me. "These guys, physically, are glowing blue cubes sitting in a space station, in the Oort cloud outside Epsilon Eridani. But they can be anywhere that BobNet reaches. They can inhabit a Manny on Vulcan or Romulus and go shopping, or fly a drone or a manta through the atmosphere of Odin; they can observe the Deltans, or help with settling the Pav, or visit any of the other human settlements. Or they could even take a remote-controlled Heaven vessel to the stars, all without ever leaving Epsilon Eridani."

Thor took up the recitation. "Marcus got flying cities working on Poseidon and has completely altered their society. Howard and Bridget have built floating cities in the upper atmosphere of Big Top, and they live there full-time in android form. With a family of their own. Marcus has built dolphin-like androids to explore Poseidon underwater. Luke and Marvin are planning an expedition to go looking for Bender. Henry Roberts is trying to sail every large body of water on every planet of human space. Bridget is trying to catalog every species of life within her reach, and is arranging expeditions to explore icy moons and planets. Daedalus and Icarus are high-tailing it for the center of the galaxy." Thor swept his hand to take in the crowd. "And we want to do all those things, but instead we're playing taxi, or construction yard, or security patrol, or long haul service. And we're a little tired of being robotic servants to the human race."

I nodded, and looked down for a moment, gathering my thoughts. I looked up, and swept the crowd with my gaze. "I by no means want to minimize your feelings on this. I do, however, think there's a certain amount of burnout involved here. This has been a total crapper of a couple of decades..." Laughs from the crowd showed that I'd scored. "...and I think you'll feel a little less, erm, militant about it after a chance to rest."

Thor looked at me, not conceding anything with his expression. "Maybe. And let's face it, Bill, we're not asking for—or threatening—anything irreversible or irrevocable. We just want the humans, and maybe the elder Bobs, to understand and accept that the species of Bob is not available as their collective workhorse. If individual Bobs want to help out, fine. But if the humans get themselves into another mess like the last one, I don't think we're going to all jump in and throw ourselves under the bus for them."

"Will you require a treaty?"

Thor laughed. "Nothing that formal, Bill. Just the statement, and the understanding."

I looked around at the Bobs in the room. It seemed to be a majority opinion, from the expressions. Well, what the hell.

"All right, Thor. I'll put together a statement, get some input on it, then distribute it to the colonies."

"And some of them," Garfield said, smiling, "will go ballistic."

"Oh, depend on it."

74. Pav Announcement

Jacques
April 2257
HIP 84051

The cargo doors opened and I stepped out. Not surprisingly, a squad of Pav militia awaited me, weapons held at ready. I sighed and shook my head. It was entirely possible that the Pav military would never warm to the Bobs.

I couldn't really blame them, of course. Every interaction reminded them of the technological gulf between us, and of their complete helplessness if we ever started making demands. Not a comfortable situation for a military mind.

I walked up to the group, being careful not to appear aggressive. They *probably* wouldn't haul off and shoot me, just because, but why take chances?

The squad leader took a half step forward, and I addressed him. "Hazjiar is expecting me."

The sergeant, or whatever equivalent, looked like he wanted to frisk me. Or maybe handcuff me, or just give me a good beating. But I was obviously not carrying anything of a technical nature, so he settled for glaring at me and showing his teeth for a moment.

I gave him a close-lipped smile in return and looked meaningfully in the direction of Hazjiar's house.

This whole performance could have gone on for a few more minutes, if Hazjiar hadn't picked that moment to walk out onto her porch. She made a gesture to the soldiers, and they motioned to me with their weapons.

I settled into a chair, bobbed my head to Hazjiar, and waited for her to speak.

"You said you had news? Presumably it is about the Others?"

"Yes," I replied. "I wanted to deliver this news in person. The battle is over. We've won, although barely."

Hazjiar nodded, and stared at the horizon for a few moments. "This is good, of course. But will they not just regroup and return? For how long will we be safe?"

"There will be no return, Hazjiar. We wiped them out." I looked down for a moment, then met her eyes. "It wasn't something we did casually, but they have obliterated so many sentients, and showed no interest in changing their behavior…"

The soldiers exchanged glances. If they were concerned about the gulf between us before, this wouldn't have helped. I spared them a quick look, then continued. "We will continue to watch for them, but it's most likely that there are none left."

"I don't understand your species, *Jock*." Hazjiar paused, looking at me. "You have all this power, yet you seem reluctant to use it. You are so rich that you don't even need money, yet you seem to have so little."

I looked up at the ceiling for a moment. She was, perhaps without realizing it, hitting very close to home with some of her comments. "Hazjiar, we—all the Bobs, I mean—don't have any desire for power over others. Quite the opposite, in fact. We just want to be able to do our own thing. And we may finally be at the point where we can realize that desire."

I gestured to the soldiers. "You have power, in the ways that matter. You're able to keep yourselves safe here. We'll make sure nothing gets out of control up there." I gestured to the sky. "Beyond that, unless you specifically need us for something, we'll leave you alone. I think, as a group, the Bobs have finally figured out our place in the cosmos. So we're going to be stepping back."

Hazjiar gazed at the soldiers for a moment, then smiled at me. "Some of us, I think, will be happy to hear that. I am not so sure. In any case, we will live." She stood. "Thank you, *Jock*, for the news. I will inform the Council."

I stood and gave her the Pav head bob, and walked to the cargo drone. I stepped in and turned for a last look. As the doors were closing, I saw Hazjiar give *me* the Vulcan salute.

* * *

I popped into PRP. The Pav Reclamation Project had a dedicated VR, hosted in Bill's Moot station. I looked around the room; a half-dozen Bobs watched video windows or operated drones on the planet's surface. Ferb stood at the edge of the room, watching the activity.

"Hey, Ferb." I walked over to join him. "How's it going?"

"Slow but steady, Jacques. We've been able to produce at least a few of everything that we have samples for. Genetic diversity may be an issue for a while, but we should be able to bring back about seventy-five percent of the planet's ecosystems, eventually."

I nodded, watching a few of the video windows. "And the other thing?"

Ferb motioned toward a whiteboard with a number of items listed. "We've found some good candidate planetoids in nearby systems. Bill's asteroid-movers will handle them easily."

I nodded, satisfied. "So, eventually we'll be able to offer the Pav their home system back. With a supply of metals."

"Maybe a few decades, yet, buddy, but yeah. That'll be good."

We watched the activity in the room, enjoying the moment. One less thing to feel guilty about.

75. Rebuilding

Herschel
January 2259
Sol

Departure day. Two little words, but such a big meaning. Today would put humanity officially out of the Endangered Species category. Today, we would leave the Earth, looking a lot like a snowball, to its own devices for a few millennia. Hopefully, the planet would recover. If so, we had the genetic material to rebuild at least some of the ecosystems.

With the extinction of the Others, Gamma Pavonis had become a viable colonization target. Several colony ships had returned to Earth since the Battle of Sol, and were now on their way with a load of humanity to settle there.

And we now had enough stasis pods in the *Bellerophon* for the balance of the human race. Today, the remaining Earthlings were leaving for 82 Eridani, all snugged away in our cargo bays. By the time they arrived, Mack and the local crew would have built farm donuts and colony locations for them. Inevitably, some of the humans wouldn't like the decisions. Tough.

The debris from the Battle of Terra, at least that portion of it that hadn't already gone down to Earth in meteor showers, was all gathered at the Earth/moon L5 point. Autofactories were still going full-bore to build new vessels for all the Bobs that had been destroyed in the battle. Bill's offsite facility was showing its worth—only a few differentials had failed, and in those cases the Bobs were simply restored with the last few minutes missing.

There still existed a general feeling amongst the Bobs that being restored wasn't quite personal immortality, but most agreed that it sure beat the alternative. I decided I'd leave that particular philosophical debate until it became relevant.

I looked over at Neil. "Ready for departure, Number One?"

"Oh, bite me. And for the record, your Picard is terrible."

"Yeah, but we're still in charge of this tub. Not bad for pondscum, eh?"

Neil grinned. "Could do worse."

Singing the Accountancy Shanty at the top of our lungs, we set course for 82 Eridani.

76. Pilgrimage

Bob
October 2263
Earth

Full circle.

A couple hundred meters or so, straight down, a city named Las Vegas had once stood. Lost Wages. Sin City. The place where my first life ended.

I turned slowly to survey the landscape. Icescape, I guess. The Earth was now in full snowball mode. Snow, once fallen, was not melting, and glaciers were closing in on the equator.

Today was a beautiful bluebird day. The sun shone down on the ice, leaving the world awash in light. If I'd still been biological, I'd be snow-blind by now.

I had arranged with the current Bob-in-residence, a tenth-generation named Harvey, to have an android printed up from Howard's most recent published set of plans. I could have done this visit remotely from Delta Eridani—or from anywhere in range of BobNet, really. But I wanted to actually come to Earth, to make the pilgrimage physically as well as emotionally. The Heaven-1B was currently in geosynchronous orbit, thirty-five thousand kilometers straight overhead.

I raised my face into the breeze and closed my eyes. The air ruffled my hair and whistled thinly against my ears. Heads-up readings, visible even on the inside of my eyelids, indicated a balmy minus thirty Celsius—well within operating range for current android tech. The Earth was definitely done for, though. For a few millennia, anyway. There was some argument at moots about whether we should set up space mirrors to reheat the planet, or just let things run their course.

Bobs had been working, the last couple of decades, to make sure that every possible living thing was represented in the Genetic Banks. These days, we didn't even take samples—we simply grabbed a scan at the subatomic level. Bill had been busy, in his mad science lab in Epsilon Eridani. It wasn't quite Star Trek-level replicator technology, but it was certainly getting damned close. Within a few more years, Bill expected to be able to rebuild plants and animals from nothing more than the scans.

Pretty cool.

I looked down once more in the direction of Las Vegas, and thought back to that last day as a human being. I remembered the conversation with my mother and Andrea—and felt a deep and abiding regret at not having had one last conversation with my father and with Alaina. There was that last meal with my employees, who—I now realized—were possibly my best friends on the planet at the time.

Their lives were now less than a footnote in history. As gone, as utterly forgotten as any random individual from the Middle Ages. No longer even a ripple in time, except to the extent that I could keep their memories alive. I sighed to myself. It seemed sometimes that life was nothing more than the accumulation of emotional baggage—memories, regrets, and lost opportunities.

I looked up as I detected the faint susurrus of an approaching craft. Odd, since I hadn't called my cargo drone to pick me up. I turned and watched as a drone came to rest on the ice, fifty feet away. There was a pause, then the cargo doors opened and two androids walked out. I queried metadata…

"Bill! Will!" Grinning, I hurried over to meet them halfway.

"Hey, Bob. When Harvey told us what you were planning, we asked him to make a couple of extra."

"Are you guys in-system?"

Bill shook his head. "No, you're the one on the pilgrimage. I'm fine with doing this from Ragnarök."

I nodded, then looked at Will.

"On my way to 82 Eridani. I'm keeping the tau down so I can stay on top of things." He grinned at me. "Once a control freak…"

I laughed. "How are things going at 82 Eridani?"

"Going great," Will replied. "They've got atmospheric pressure up to something reasonable on Valhalla. When the people on the *Bellerophon* arrive, they'll have three viable worlds to choose from. The colonies that are already there will complain about blow-ins, of course." Will turned and looked out across the ice fields. "Humanity is well-distributed, now. It's beginning to look like they'll probably survive their own stupidity, after all."

After a moment of comfortable silence, Bill asked, "So what will you do now, Bob?"

I looked at my two friends, then looked up at the sky. "Going out, I think. The new Bobs are right. We're Homo sideria. And I'm tired of always finding myself committed to something. It's time to cut all ties, just point the bow, and turn on the drive. See what's out there."

"You'll keep in touch?"

"Of course." I smiled at Bill. "I'll stop and build stations, so I stay connected to BobNet. Someday maybe the net will stretch from one end of the galaxy to the other."

"And we'll probably still be around," Will said. "As you say, we've got forever."

I nodded, then turned toward the cargo drone. "You guys mind taking my android to storage? I'm going to travel light, I think."

Bill nodded. "No problem."

We walked back to the drone and climbed in. I turned to my two oldest friends, shook their hands, and switched off. And thirty-five thousand kilometers above, I turned on the SURGE drive and headed out to the stars.

END

Made in the USA
San Bernardino, CA
26 February 2020

65029852R00157